WHISPERS AND SHADOWS

WHISPERS AND SHADOWS

Edited by Jack Fisher

PRIME BOOKS

WHISPERS AND SHADOWS

Published in the United States by **prime**
P.O. Box 36503, Canton, OH 44735
www.primebooks.net

ISBN: 1-894815-21-1

CONTENTS

DEPRESSURISED GHOST STORY

by Rhys Hughes

My soul lives on a ledge. I have always been a climber: my first conquest was the north face of our family home in Colchester. Alarmed by the sight of her only child scrabbling among the ivy, my mother rushed out and held her apron to catch me. But I succeeded in gaining the highest chimney and remained there until starvation compelled me to descend to my punishment, which turned out to be more hunger—I was exiled to bed. Always prudent, my father nailed my window shut, but I spent an intrepid night clambering over the precipitous furniture.

Later, in Eton, I forsook lessons to begin a passionate relationship with the gables and turrets of the college buildings. At this time, I was introduced to the telling of ghost-tales, courtesy of our Provost. Though untroubled by his morbid fables and anecdotes, I never became a confirmed sceptic of the paranormal. My fellow pupils exchanged his tombic romances like farthings, but I was simply uninterested in anything which could not be scaled and it seemed unlikely a spectre would afford a grip for boots, even those fitted with crampons.

After my wholly inadequate schooling, I attended university to study engineering. I excelled at mathematics whenever a quantity had to rise up the gradient of a steep formula; the rest of the time my failures were as immense and unlikely as a glacier. My tutor chided me one afternoon: "You have the loftiest intentions, but they reside in your feet." Over my door I fixed an ice-axe, a symbol of reality cooler than any abstract logic. I was not alone; other acrophiliac students joined me in expeditions around the dour peaks and chalk cliffs.

I graduated with a poor degree and immediately started out on a life above the clouds. I wandered over the Alps, rolling down one peak only to ascend another, like a snowball which has gathered infinite momentum.[1] My allowance was soon cut, but I did not return to face my father. I applied for a job in East Africa as a technical consultant. I found time to climb a number of equatorial mountains, though I was mauled by a leopard on the summit of Kilimanjaro and forced to rest on a plantation. One of my close neighbours turned out to be an explorer by the name of Shipton. Within an hour of meeting we were planning an ambitious expedition to Central Asia, among the unknown G— N— Range.

We shared a philosophy of light travel. He was a more lyrical fellow than I, the sort of climber who writes up his adventures in books. I have an idea he did actually publish his memoirs in several volumes. I have no reason to suppose he remembers me; our collaboration was rather brief. We argued over the exact location of the forbidden Q— valley, mentioned in a Tibetan folktale, one of those translated by X.D. Laocoön. A scuffle broke out; we exchanged blows with a map of the area. He threw me off his premises. Now I was fired with a determination to reach the valley before he did. I staggered away, silently vowing: "You have beaten me to a pulp, but I shall beat you to fame . . . "[2]

I spent five years saving money for the mission, collecting climbers and equipment, getting myself in shape for the arduous task. Eventually I was fit and rich enough to feel reasonably confident. Crossing the horrid peaks of the G— N— Range would cost a fortune in leather soles: I hired a Polish cobbler to accompany me. Other hopefuls applied from England and continental Europe. We arranged to meet in Calcutta. Arriving there after a rough sea-voyage, I was pleasantly surprised to discover all but one of my recruits had turned up. The missing chap was our radio-operator. Later in the Hotel D—, fiddling with a short-wave wireless, we picked up his attenuated signals, drowning beneath the civilised accents and restrained static of the BBC World Service.

We set off on August 5th, 19—, after a hearty breakfast of rice and lentils, heading north on the 09:05 express. We had an entire carriage to ourselves, for since my disagreement with Shipton I intended to do all my exploring in the opposite way to him—if he planned to take little on an ascent, I was determined to carry up as much as possible. It chaffed with my real principles, of course, but my pride outweighs my sense. And while my story is rattling along the rails, let me introduce you to the prosaic souls who formed the core of my party. Because I am quite modest, I shall refrain from saying which of the following names belongs to me, though it has the sweetest ring to it: C. Bowman, J. Tolkien-Twigge, O. Eckenstein, R. Darktree, M.A. Zimara, C. Weasel, H. Melmoth, E.S. Abbott, A.G. Woden, B. Cadiz, D. Delves, I. Evans . . . (The remainder of the list has just been obscured by smoke from the train).

I can hardly see the paragraphs in this fog. The quality of our coal must have been very poor. Having studied Hindoo ceremonies, I made a joke which raised blisters but no smiles—the stoker had died at his post and his wife jumped into the furnace. I repeat it here because I know readers have a darker sense of humour than climbers. Actually you are a very good audience: I wish you had come with me instead of those miserable fellows. But you would have grumbled about the cold in S—, where we disembarked and hired ponies to take us over the B— Hills. Right to the borders of M— we rode. (I know you are trying to reconstruct my route. You are bored with the pace of my document and want to make a dash for the end. I do not advise this. The narrow passes of L— are infested with bandits. Please stay close to my prose).

Months of hardship and weak tea sapped the energies of my follow- ers. We stopped in the shadow of R— D— and bathed in the thermal springs. Some of my team, rather less educated than the others, had never heard of X.D. Laocoön and the forbidden valley of Q—, nor were they overeager to learn the mythology of this region. I taught them anyway. Every valley in Tibet is filled to the brim with ruined cities, sorcerous treasure and immortal lamas. Q— was the only empty one. It was remarkable because of the things it did *not* contain. I suppose you might say that the places of magic which surrounded it gave it a lustrous presence and outlined the mystery: like depicting a tree by painting the sky which lies between its branches. According to Laocoön, it was the only place on the planet never trampled by any kind of feet, not even when there was only one continent and all the mountains were flat.

I was not entirely convinced by this, for I knew there were areas of Colchester equally untrodden, though these were generally very small. Yet the allure of Q— was excessive. I reserved for myself the first step onto its soil. Ringed and supported by a circle of jagged mountains, like a bowl of soup guarded by a dozen grumpy waiters, the valley was surveyed many centuries ago by a levitating monk. That, at any rate, was the tale related by Laocoön. I was too suspicious to query the word of one who has been criticised by doubters. Closer to our objective we lurched, pressing our destination into a corner. We traversed the Y— R—Glacier, losing our supply of teapots down crevasses while I cut spiral steps in the ice. At the end of this stage it was apparent we needed to employ porters from local settlements. There were caves in the bottom of the Glacier: muffled troglodytes played dice with frozen tears. They shouldered our cases with a stoicism exhausting to behold.

The porters were fine chaps, but they were difficult to address. The leaders of our initial group were Tsongkhapa and Dromtönpa. We soon added Langdharama and Shantarikshita to the ranks. Entering a remote village on the Z— P— Plateau[3], I was extremely grateful to hire Bertie. He was old and frail, but the simplicity of his appellation was a crucial factor in our offer of employment. Besides, feeble porters totter most carefully and are ideal for carrying scientific equipment. After two or three weeks of his dedication, I asked him how he came by such a name. It emerged his father was a Scottish engineer working in Bengal who decided to construct a bamboo bicycle and pedal home. This eccentric resolution carried him no further than the Himalayas.

"What happened there?" I inquired.

"He lost his way after turning left at Lhasa," Bertie explained. "He wobbled into our village with a puncture and a fever. After we tended him and restored his health, he became a shamanic figure, devising all manner of apparatus for our convenience."

These, Bertie went on to expound, included attaching electric-motors to temple prayer-wheels to accelerate local devotion. The engineer had an idea that the efficacy of these devices corresponded to the rate of spin. There was a threshold of so many millions of revolutions per minute above which a prayer would actually work. Unfortunately his career was finished when his sporran was caught in an axle. He was pulled in and rotated to a pious demise, leaving unfinished his dream of converting the entire world into a prayer-wheel by rearranging the mountains to spell out a mantra. I insisted that a single rotation a day would scarcely be enough to satisfy the highest Heaven. Bertie agreed.

"I did not say he was sane, merely my father."

There is no time for more extracts from the conversations we enjoyed along the way. They were wholly of this quality. But I am already exactly 1669 words into my account and at this point it is good manners to reward my readers with some action (with this bracket the total has increased to 1708 words — dash it! I am overwriting. Better edit the next line.) As we approached the serrated peaks . . . lucky to be alive. I have never seen any sunset to compare with that one. The slopes shimmered like enormous fires put to bed in clean sheets but rolling around. I was overawed. One of the English climbers fell to his knees and started muttering that these peaks were impenetrable. I wanted to shoot him like a mad yak, but mastered the impulse before dusk. We set up camp.

Before retiring, I made a speech: "We have braved many dangers since leaving the luxuries of home. But the peace of mind afforded by good food and wine will shortly be eclipsed. For on the far side of these mountains the serenity of Q— is waiting."

Bertie came to my tent after midnight. "The men are frightened. They have no problem with serenity, but ghosts might also be waiting. There is no lonelier or remoter spot on the surface of the Earth. Where better for evil phantoms to take up residence?"

I laughed. "That is a common misconception of mountaineers. Actually the opposite is the case. This is probably the only valley in Tibet which is not crowded with the wispy dead."

"How can you be sure? No-one has been here before."

"Exactly! Ghosts tend to hover near the place where they originated. In lonely and remote areas, where there are few beings to expire, hardly any can exist. Here there are none."

Pointing out the relevant passage in Laocoön, I sent him away with a relieved smile on his weathered face. My Polish cobbler, I decided, would be able to use Bertie's skin as leather if anything happened to the tough old McSherpa. As I lay in the fresh dark, I thought about my own logic. A valley without people is a valley without spectres. It seemed too obvious for comfort. Something was wrong. Unable to sleep, I lit a lamp and tired myself anew by catching up with my diary. Wonders avoided Q— with an unnatural consistency. Its ordinariness was miraculous. This is a paradox also true, I am told, of charladies.

The following morning I was shattered, but I insisted on leading the final push up the sheer wall of soft snow and slippery rock. More ancient than a stupa, Bertie bulged with exertion. Halfway up, he admitted he was not a Buddhist but a follower of the original Tibetan religion, Bon, with special protection from one of its obscure demons. I was pleased with his confession, as it released me from a moral obligation to assist him. When a devil watches over you, a more spectacular descent is usually reserved. It may be of interest to record that I was first to the top, though I did not boast of my achievement aloud, contenting myself with a little dance. The consequences of this action were . . . (yes, an avalanche has swept away the rest of this paragraph. It has taken one of my readers with it. There he goes! Him with the beard).

I was also first to descend into the valley proper. The inner slopes were gentler than the outer. (While you dig your way out, let me reassure you that none of the team lost our balance in the accident. We were above the fracture, whereas readers tend to lurk at the base of a story. I pity you. But it is your own fault for coming this far. Next time you must try to be more careful.) I planted the flag of my nation in the frost and sat in the slash of its shadow, trying to ignite a portable stove. There were no teapots so I brewed coffee while my colleagues joined me. Bertie, last of all, delivered the precision instruments to my feet. I set up a number of regulation experiments with the barometer and manometer, measuring the pressure differentials. There was a roaring pain in my head and the edges of my vision were indistinct.

I ignored my ailments. "Well, this is it!" I announced. "The last of all solitudes; the hymen of the planet. Now we are here, the world really has lost its virginity. Look around. Apart from a floating sage, no human has ever seen this fastness."

"I feel a trifle dizzy," answered Bertie.

"Altitude sickness," I replied. "The pressure is quite low.[4] If the feeling persists you must open a vein. Now then, I suggest we rush around like lunatics, to trample most of the unblemished spots before tiffin. An expedition must be thorough in its desecration. Otherwise our claim to be first will be open to doubt."

I exempted Bertie from the task. He sprawled on the snow, reading my copy of Laocoön. The valley was roughly the same size as Colchester, flat and completely barren of animal or plant life.[5] I made a total circuit, in the opposite direction to my companions, which was a decision they had arrived at. I felt agitated, but there was a force inside me which bawled with delight, as if my subconscious was enjoying a holiday. For a strange reason, I was reminded of my old Provost at Eton. After a hearty stamp of the valley, the other climbers joined me for a light meal. I said nothing about my experience, though they were equally disturbed. We fidgeted away the majority of the afternoon.

In the evening, I watched the stars wheel in the sky. They had never been observed from this region and I waited to catch them doing something different. Disappointed, I crawled inside my tent. I fell asleep rapidly, as if prompted to do so. My dream was remarkably coherent but pedestrian. I saw myself stand and leave the tent. My comrades were also emerging; we seemed pleased just to stretch our arms at full length. Then we got up to all manner of silly games: prancing, skipping and waltzing. We felt as if we were prisoners released from long captivity, ecstatic simply to have a space in which to exercise. Suddenly I woke in a cold sweat. Somebody was clawing at my tent. I cried aloud: "Who is there? Bertie, is that you?" I fumbled for my ice-axe. There was a mocking laugh. I gripped the tool and thrust the spike upwards. It punctured the fabric but did not penetrate a fleshy body beyond. I frowned.

Crawling out, I was amazed to notice that the tents of my companions were also shaking. There had been a fresh snowfall, but no footprints led away from my site. Like an economical cactus, each tent poked out a spike from an ice-axe. Then the occupants emerged and stood in confusion, while exchanging terrified glances. Nightcap askew on his head, Bertie began to chant a mantra, calling on his patron demon to guard his life. I insisted he refrain from his diabolism.

"But we are being attacked by ghosts!" he wailed.

I raised a hand. "Nonsense! I have already explained that no wraiths exist in the valley. No-one has ever died in this location. Therefore our ordeal must be due to some natural phenomenon. A practical joker perhaps? I suspect our radio-operator has finally caught us up. His silly sense of humour was well documented."

"If that is the case, where is he now?"

I scanned the horizon. There were no hiding places in the chilly dip and the starlight reflecting from the shallow walls illuminated the scene cheaply and efficiently. "I do not care to argue with a Sherpa. As leader of this party I order everyone back to bed. I will have an answer to your insidious question by morning."

Reluctantly, the explorers returned to their tents. Bertie wanted to curl up with me for safety but I warned him that the men might talk. With ninety-six little shudders, he pulled his nightcap down over his eyes and left me alone. I pondered. Quite plainly, the radio-operator was not with us. His aerial would be visible even had he hidden under a snowdrift. The remaining explanations were a freak wind in the shape of a body or else a levitating monk come to take revenge for our violation of his territory. I gazed up, but the stars were all where they should be, no constellation blotted by a serene silhouette.

I said nothing about the matter over breakfast, though Bertie huffed and agitated to bring it up. My colleagues were keen to begin the journey home, but I was too curious to depart now. I stalled them with scientific blather about the need to conduct a week's worth of experiments. Furious haggling was set in motion and we settled on a stay of three days. Bertie moaned at this news and retired to study Laocoön's anti-phantom remedies. Unfortunately, this section, at the back of the volume, had been eaten by a goat on the train to S—.

That night my dream came back, with a changed choreography. I danced a tango rather than a waltz. Each time I passed my berth, I heard fretful snoring coming from within. The others strutted with me, icicles clenched between their teeth. I woke to a staccato tapping of heels on the side of my tent. I sat up and placed my eye to the hole I had jabbed the previous night. There was nobody outside, but I saw the pale irises of my comrades peering from their own gashes.

Bertie was inconsolable. He gibbered in an embarrassing fashion from the security of his sleeping-bag. I crawled out and shook him free. To my extreme dismay, he repeated our dance, stark naked. He whipped up snow in a swirl which seemed momentarily to congeal into the shape of my Provost. Wagging a glacial finger, the illusion crumbled with a horrid jollity and I brushed academic flakes from my shoulders. Bertie fell to his knees and clutched at my swollen ankles.

"You promised an answer! Tell it to me!"

"Get a grip on yourself. Perhaps we are all suffering from delusions occasioned by extreme altitude. Or maybe we should stop cooking with yeti dung. The problem is medical."

Bertie shook his head. "It was a ghost."

I snubbed his hysteria and returned to bed, sleeping soundly until a beam of early sunlight poked through the rent, buying my brow with a coin of light. The climbers were in mutinous mood, refusing to cook breakfast. They lazed and shared Laocoön, alternately chuckling and yawning over his syntax. I persisted with my measuring and classifying, though there was a severe lack of things to which these processes might be applied. I worked without a break, eventually filling my notebooks with observations before packing away my instruments for the descent. I watched the moon pour over the horizon, licking my toasted face with its butter tongue. I decided to spend my last night in the open.

I perched on a folding stool and did my best to remain awake. But my bones were too heavy, knocking against each other beneath my skin. At the same time my spirit broke free from the rigging of my nerves, like a sail fleeing a mast in a storm. I was standing in front of myself, roaring and giggling, waving my arms in triumph. Soon I was joined by my comrades and we held an impromptu party. Bertie was present, looking less worried than in the daytime. I kicked and jabbed at my body, seated on its stool. Then there was a cry and another Bertie rose up from his sleeping-bag, shaking a fist as he raced past us in his slippers. He continued towards the edge of the valley, vanishing over the rim. Obviously his body was leaving his spirit behind. We did our best to console the soul, which seemed a trifle glum, like a yolk without a shell.

Once more harassing my sleeping torso, I was startled when it jerked and I was sucked back inside. I opened my eyes to see the others emerging from their tents. They demanded: "Were you making that noise?"

They began to accuse me of being the joker responsible for disturbing their sleep on the previous nights, but I protested vehemently. It was better to seal my lips about what I had witnessed—I did not want them thinking I was mad. I merely related the barest facts. "Bertie has deserted us. The barometer will have to be abandoned. He fled in his nightcap and pyjamas."

There was nothing we could do. Had he been British... As it was, the sensible course of action was to forget about him. At first light we left the Q— valley forever, heading back towards the Z— P— Plateau. A week later we reached the Y— R— Glacier. It was faster going down. We dropped off Shantarikshita, Langdharama, Dromtönpa and Tsongkhapa, useful workers but taxing on the grammar. We failed to rescue our teapots from a crevasse but brewed tea in the thermal springs near R— D—. Somewhere beyond M—, after crossing the L— passes into the B— Hills, we were astonished to notice a ragged figure coming closer. It was Bertie, a man so broken his decrepitude had turned full circle back to health. Only his toothless smile betrayed his identity. He screamed: "Out of my way! I must get back to Q— at once!"

I gripped his arm. "What happened, Bertie?"

His eyes were blank. "I ran all the way to S—, where I milked the local goats, hoping to bottle Laocoön's missing pages. I soon trapped the one who had devoured his anti-phantom advice. I drank the milk and became aware of my true predicament."

"Are you returning to collect your spirit?"

He nodded, struggling out of my clutch. "Laocoön knew the dangers of the valley all along. This is why the levitating monk did not attempt to land there. The human race has been around for a long time, and before us there were demons and ogres with souls. The surface of the planet must be crowded with ghosts. Trillions of spooks all competing for the same piece of land. Think how uncomfortable it must be! Layers of wraiths struggling for space, like ashes in an oven. Even in the polar regions there will be troll spectres crowding the icebergs!"

Plainly he had lost his sanity, but I decided to humour him. "Ghosts everywhere except in Q—? Without population it also lacks revenants. Doubtless a paradise for apparitions?"

"Absolutely. Land is now at a premium for phantasms. When we entered the valley, our souls were overjoyed to see so much open space. They were determined to stay there, rather than return to the crowded outside. They formulated a plot to ensure we remained. Every night they came out of our bodies and attempted to frighten us to death. Spectres must linger in the vicinity of their passing away."

"Come now, Bertie, this is claptrap. Spirits cannot depart bodies at will. They are strapped to the bones."

Leaning forward, the Sherpa tapped his nose. "That is normally true. But the low pressure caused our souls to expand and the ectoplasmic knots worked loose. Unfortunately our ghosts were not terrible enough to induce heart-attacks in our bodies. Every time we awoke, they had to take refuge back in the mortal shell. But on the third night, I ran away in my sleep. My soul was unable to stop me and I have been a hollow man ever since. It is essential I reclaim my spook!"

I shuddered. "What will happen otherwise?"

"Without a spirit I am a zombie. I can decay but not die. My phantom will thus never be registered as legitimate. This means suspension of all afterlife privileges. No free chains or walking through solids. I know it wants to leave the valley to look for me but it has no idea where I might be. I hope it has enough sense to stay put until I return. Now I must go. I am unravelling at the navel."

The climbers chortled as Bertie trotted off. They did not credit his story and maintained that even if it was true they would rather socialise with other ghosts when they expired, rather than occupy a valley alone. I was less confident and felt a peculiar need to follow the Sherpa. Instead I contented myself with calling:

"How will you reabsorb your soul, Bertie?"

He turned briefly and replied: "My religion has a ritual for such an event. I will devour the ghost."

"Bon appetit!" I watched him recede in the distance, a torn particle in a cosmos of unblemished snow.

Still joking over this encounter, my colleagues reached S— before me. I dragged my feet, resentful of their company. The shadow of a flying sage passed over the ground . . . I looked up at a rogue cloud . . . Everything I do ends in disappointment. I rejoined my expedition in the station. Its members were playing football with my Laocoön. Pages were strewn over the track. We boarded the 05:09 express to Calcutta, but I sat on the roof. I booked a passage back to East Africa when we reached the city. The others retired to the Hotel D—, a prime location for picking up the BBC World Service.[6] I had nothing to say to them; they did not even wave me off as my ship left port. Cold rascals.

Arriving at my plantation, I was dismayed to find it had been burned down. Witnesses claimed to have seen a man throwing burning maps onto the crops. I wondered who he might be. There was nothing for it but to visit my parents in Colchester, where I had left them so many years previously. I stopped in the Pyrenees on my way, but climbing had lost its savour. In a decayed cathedral town, I happened to bump into my old Provost, who was searching for rare books. He might have bought my Laocoön had it remained intact. I was desperately short of money. As it was, he asked me to share a bottle of wine (Vin de Limoux, not to be recommended . . . Dash it! I have spilled some over the next sentence.) We fell into conversation . . . but he insisted that when I set my experiences down on paper I should avoid dots as much as possible . . . He had no love for them. My confession was a purge and I left him feeling stronger.

When I reached my childhood home, I found it empty and boarded up. A neighbour peeped at me through her curtains and came out to relate a glum story: my father was dead and my mother had been locked in a madhouse. It seems they never gave up waiting for me to return. One night they heard a noise on the stairs. Rushing out to embrace me, they were shocked to find a pale Scotsman mounted on a bicycle. He required directions to Aberdeen. My father collapsed and his own ghost jumped onto the contraption: with a most ungentlemanly yell, the pair pedalled off into the aether. My mother grew depressed; she knocked on the door of the local asylum and asked to be admitted. Fortunately my father made a will before his demise, leaving the estate to me. I was thus ensured a reasonable degree of luxury in my troubles. It was a great help . . .

Now I sit in my room, planning a return expedition to Tibet. But the difficulties are insurmountable; I have lost my nerve. Besides, I hear on the radio that Shipton is already there, mapping the region with accuracy and panache. I search the bookshops and market stalls for another copy of Laocoön[7] but there are none to be had. I decide to make use of my skill as an engineer. I will knock down the house and rebuild it in the form of a mantra, a global prayer-wheel which may bring me even more solace. Only my Provost can really help me understand my predicament, but I am wary of him. I must stay away from Eton.

There is something on my roof again. Every night this happens. It is driving me to distraction: the tiles are scraped by unseen feet. At first I thought it was a levitating monk. Then I believed it was the wraith of my dead reader, the one crushed in the avalanche. But yesterday I levered open my window, thrust out my head and saw my own ghost scuttling behind the highest chimney. It is puncturing the eaves with intangible crampons. How did it get there? I have a theory. In the low pressure of the valley it swelled too big to fit in my body properly and was detached on the way to Colchester. Yes, my soul lives on a ledge. But the rest of me prefers the comforts of a furnished room.

NOTES:

¹ This is untrue. Had I really gathered infinite momentum, my mass would also have been infinite. The immense gravitational field set up around my body in such circumstances would have made me the centre of the universe. Obviously this did not happen.

² Then I returned to his villa and shouted the words through his window. He attacked me with a globe. At this point, I discovered that small-scale maps inflict more painful bruises.

³ For anyone who mistrusts my geography or believes I am being coy about cartographical detail, let me add that the Z— P— Plateau lies between the R— and J— Rivers. It is —miles long and —miles broad and contains the villages of B— and O—. In the latter village lives a chap named A— M— who distils a brandy from the W— plant. I suggest you try it some time, it may do you good.

⁴ I am disgusted with the way you always complain about the pressures of work. Try to remember what a lack of pressure entails: nausea, confusion, haemorrhaging. Reconsider before asking your boss for extra leave. Do you want to bleed from the ears and eyes?

⁵ This region is almost as devoid of life as the following 32 paragraphs are devoid of notes.

⁶ The BBC World Service had not even started at this time, but I hope to obtain employment with the organisation and am thus determined to make as many references to it as possible.

⁷ X.D. Laocoön's ethnographic books have largely been discredited, but a first-edition of his masterwork, *Fables From The World's Attic*, can fetch upwards of $1000 (enquiries to Gamma-Ray Russell, 5 Birch Terrace, Horam, East Sussex). Laocoön—"the translator without a conscience"—probably never ventured further than his own attic.

BEGGAR'S VELVET

by Scott Nicholson

Cynthia *knew* she should have left the light on.

Because now the noise came again, soft, like the purr of a rat or the settling of disturbed lint.

A layer of lint had gathered under her bed because she couldn't clean there. She was afraid of that dark, mysterious space that had never been explained to her satisfaction. She squeezed her eyes tightly shut and pictured the sea of dust, the fine powdered layers of accumulated motes. Beggar's velvet, she'd heard it called. But that thick gray fur didn't bother her. What bothered her was the *beggar*, the man that wore the dust, the creature that slept in the bright of day and made those terrible sounds at night.

The noise came again, a flutter or sigh. Louder tonight. The beggar must be more formed, closer to whole.

Cynthia had moved in three weeks ago, though the efficiency flat was a little beyond her means. She'd been attracted by the cleanliness, the wooden floors, the queen-sized four-poster in the bedroom. That, and the streetlights that burned outside the bedroom window. Best of all, the neighbors were within easy screaming distance.

Not that she would scream. If she screamed, the beggar would awaken, reach up with one monstrous hand and grab her around the ankle, tug her down twisted sheets and all, draw her into the deep, thick fog of the underthere. Better to bite her lip, close her eyes, and put the pillow around her head.

She shouldn't have moved so often. She should have stayed and faced him that first time, back when she had a roommate. So what if the roommate, a fellow college student, looked at Cynthia strangely when Cynthia crossed the room at a run and dived into the bed from several feet away? So what if the roommate poked fun because Cynthia always slept in socks? The roommate wasn't the one who had to worry about the beggar, because he only lived under *Cynthia's* bed.

Six months, and the roommate had forced Cynthia to leave. Cynthia's name wasn't on the lease, she was behind on her half of the bills, and she'd lost her job because she had to sleep during the day. Perhaps having to move out was for the best, though. Her roommate had started muttering strange languages in her sleep.

So Cynthia dropped out of college, worked the graveyard shift at the Hop'N Go, and took a cramped studio apartment downtown. That place lasted two months, and she'd ended up sleeping on the couch. Even with such a small space to work with, the beggar had still knitted himself into flesh, worked the lint into skin and flesh, formed arms and legs from the dust, shaped its terrible rasping mouth.

Though her new landlord said a professional cleaning crew had given the efficiency a white-glove treatment, the dust gathered fast, like clouds in a thunderstorm. The noises had started on the second night, so hushed that nobody would have heard them who didn't know what to listen for. Every night louder, every night another ounce of substance incorporated, every night a new muscle to be flexed.

But the beggar had never been as loud as he was tonight. Her night off from work, she should have known better. If only she had a friend to stay with, but she was a stranger in this city, locked out of the social circles by her odd hours. But here she was, in the dark, a silver swathe from the streetlight the only companion.

Except for her beggar.

Even with the pillow wrapped so tightly around her head that she could barely breath, the muted clatter reached her, chilled her, cut like a claw on bone. Maybe if she held her breath . . .

She did, her heart a distressed timpani, thudding in a merciless race to some vague coda.

But it worked. The rustling died, the velvet fell in upon itself, the dust settled back into its slumber. All was still in the underthere.

Cynthia couldn't hold her breath forever. Every time she exhaled, slowly, the air burning through her throat, the noises came again. With each new lungful of darkness, the beggar twitched. She should have slept with the light on. Not that the light made any difference.

But worse than the fear, the tension in her limbs and stomach from clenching in anticipation of his touch, would be actually seeing that hand rise above the edge of the mattress, claws glittering amid the matted gray fur, the beggar made flesh.

Better to imagine him, because she was sure her imagination could never paint as terrible a picture as reality could.

Better to hold her breath and swallow her whimpers and bathe in her own sweat than to peek out from under the blankets and see if tonight would be the night of the hand.

Better to lie here and never dream, eyes closed, better to wait for morning, morning, morning.

The next morning came as always, the sun strong and orange this time, not sulking behind clouds. It was the kind of morning where she could sleep, and no sounds rose from that strange land beneath the bed. She slept until early afternoon, then rose, still tired.

Cynthia always felt silly in the morning. She wasn't a child, after all. As Mom was so fond of reminding her.

With the sun so bright and the world busy outside, normal people on everyday errands, Cynthia almost had the courage to jump out of bed, go to the other side of the room, bend down on her hands and knees, and look at the empty space under the bed. Because everyone knew nothing was there. Just an old story to scare children with.

But she wouldn't dare look. Because *he* might look back, his eyes cold amongst the velvet, his hand reaching out, wanting to touch.

Cynthia shuddered, her bedclothes damp from perspiration. She kicked off the blankets and stretched her cramped body. She rolled off the side of the bed, looking between her legs. But he only stirred at night. The floor was safe.

She showered, brushed her teeth, adjusted the angle of the cabinet mirror so that she couldn't see the bed.

"Why don't you put the mattress on the floor?" her reflection asked. "That way, there would be no underthere."

"No," she said, a froth of toothpaste around her lips. "Then I'd *be* in the underthere. Lying right alongside him, or on top of him, or him on top of me, or something."

"It's only dust."

"From dust we come, to dust we go. Haven't you ever heard that?"

"Only crazy people talk to mirrors," her reflection said.

"You said it, I didn't."

Behind the mirror were drab vials with small pills. Pills could talk, if you let them. She couldn't trust pills, not with those strange runes scribbled across their faces. One therapist said they made you shrink, another said they made you grow tall. She wasn't that hungry.

The telephone rang. Cynthia went into the living room to answer it, standing so she could keep an eye under the bed. It was Mom.

"Hey, honey, how's school going?" Mom was five hundred miles away, but sounded twice as far.

"Great," Cynthia said, too loudly, too assuredly.

After a pause, Mom asked, "Have you had any more of your . . . problems?"

"They told me I was so much over it that I didn't need to come in for a while."

"I know we shouldn't talk about it—"

Yet they did. Every time they talked. As if this were all the two of them had in common. "I'm fine, Mom. Really."

"He wasn't like that when I married him. If only I had known—"

Here it came, the Capital-G Guilt Trip, as Mom shifted the blame from the one who deserved it onto Cynthia. That way, Mom wouldn't have any share of it. "I know I should have told you," Cynthia said. "But it's the kind of thing you just try to forget about. You lie to yourself about it, know what I mean?"

"Yes, honey, you're right. He's dead. Let's forget about him."

Forget *who*, Cynthia wanted to say. But lying to herself didn't do any good. "So, how's Aunt Reba?"

They talked about Aunt Reba, Mom's new car, and Cynthia's grades. Somehow Mom was never able to turn the conversation back to that sore spot she loved so much. Cynthia could never understand her mother's fixation with the past. Let the dead be dust.

"Got to go, Mom," Cynthia finally cut in. "Got class. Love you, bye."

Cynthia locked the apartment, left the beggar to his daydreams, and caught a bus downtown. A fat man with an anaconda face sat next to her.

"Afternoon for the pigeons," he said.

Cynthia stared straight ahead. She didn't want to hear him.

"At the airport, cannonball to the heart," he said, thumping his chest for emphasis.

He didn't exist. None of them did, not him, not the Puerto Rican woman with the scars on her cheeks, not the longhair with the busted boombox, not the old man asleep under his beret. These people were nothing but hollow flesh. Formed from dust, passing through on their way back to dust.

The bus stopped and she got off, even though she was two blocks from her destination. "Cigarette weather," the fat man shouted after her.

She bought a hot dog from a street vendor, after checking under his cart to make sure the beggar wasn't hiding there. She sat on a park bench, ate the hot dog, and threw the wrapper into the bushes. Pigeons pecked at the paper.

The bench was perfect for a late afternoon nap. The seat was made of evenly-spaced wooden slats, so she could occasionally open her eyes and make sure the beggar wasn't lying on the ground beneath her. He could have been hiding in the shadows of the tall oaks. But he was most likely in her bedroom, waiting.

Cynthia's back ached by the time she awoke near dusk. At least some of the weariness, built up over months of restless nights, had ebbed away. She hurried around the corner, ignoring the strange people on the sidewalk. Their faces were blank in the glow of shop windows.

The counter clerk at the Hop'N Go nodded when Cynthia walked in the door. They settled the register, Cynthia mumbling responses to the clerk's attempts at conversation. Her shift started at ten, and she rang up cigarettes, condoms, candy bars, corn chips, shiny products in shiny wrappers, taking the money without touching the hands of those giving it. At midnight, the other clerk left and the beer sales increased.

At around two in the morning, a young man in an army jacket came through the door. It was that point in the shift when the wild-eyed ones came in, those who smelled of danger and sweat. Cynthia wasn't afraid of being robbed, though. Compared to the beggar, even a loaded automatic was a laughable threat. But this customer had no gun.

He placed a can of insect spray on the counter. His fingers were dirty.

"Four-seventeen," she said after ringing up the purchase.

"You don't look like the type of person who works a night shift at a convenience store," he said. He put a five in her hand.

She tried to smile the way the manager had taught her, but her face felt like a brick. She glanced into the man's eyes. They were bright, warm, focused.

"How fresh is the coffee?" he asked when she gave him change.

"I made it an hour ago."

"Bet you drink a few cups to get through the night. Always thought it was weird, people who didn't sleep in a regular cycle."

There was a button under the counter which she could press and send an alarm to the police. If he kept being friendly . . .

"It's natural to sleep when it's dark," he continued. He smiled, his rows of teeth even between his lips. He looked to be two or three years older than Cynthia.

"Unless you have to work in the dark," she said.

"Throws your whole cycle off. Do you go to State?"

Another customer came in, this one the normal, shifty-eyed sort. The man in the army jacket poured a cup of coffee and sat in one of the corner booths near the refrigerated sandwiches. The shifty-eyed man bought a can of smokeless tobacco, glared at Army Jacket, then asked for a copy of Score from the rack behind Cynthia. The magazine was wrapped in plain brown paper, but Cynthia could imagine the lurid pose of the cover girl, airbrushed breasts thrust teasingly out.

The shifty-eyed man paid, rolled the magazine and tucked it under his arm, then headed out under the streetlights. Army Jacket brought his coffee to the counter.

"Pervert," Army Jacket said. "Bet you get a lot of weirdoes on this shift."

To Cynthia, the weirdest people were the ones who talked to her. But this guy didn't talk crazy. Even for a man whose mouth was a cavern filled with invisible snakes.

"It's okay," she said, feeling under the counter for the alarm button. "My job likes me."

He laughed, took a sip of his coffee, then poked his tongue out. "Ouch. That's hot."

She pointed to the sign that was taped to the coffee maker. "Caution! Coffee is hot," she read aloud.

Army Jacket laughed again for some reason. She read the name sewn in a patch above his breast pocket. Weams. He didn't look like a Weams, so she decided to still think of him as Army Jacket.

"My name's David," he said. "What's yours?"

"Alice Miller Jones," she said, making up a name from somewhere.

"Alice. That's a good, old-fashioned name. Most girls these days are named Maleena or Caitlin or something trendy like that."

"Ask Alice. Wasn't that in an old Sixties' song?"

Army Jacket, who might be a David as far as she could tell, shook his head and took another, smaller sip of his coffee. He reached in his pocket for change. "Guess I better pay for this."

"Ask Alice."

He smiled. "What do you do when you're not running a convenience store register, Alice?"

"Trying not to sleep."

His eyelids drooped slightly. "Sleep is the greatest waste of time ever invented. There are so many better ways to spend time. Even in bed."

She looked at him. His eyes were like Styrofoam picnic plates, bright and empty. "I have a strange bed," she said. "Would you like to see it?"

His hand shook, splashing a few drops of coffee on the floor. She took the change from him and the coins were covered in sweat.

"Sure," Army Jacket said, leaning stiffly against the counter in an attempt to look relaxed.

"How do you feel about dust?" she asked.

His eyebrows raised in a questioning expression. "I don't mind a little dust. Dust thou art, isn't that what the Bible says?"

"Only talking Bibles."

A couple of people came in the store, rummaged around near the candy rack, then came to the counter with a bottle of wine. Cynthia thought one of them had swiped a candy bar. He had a bulge in his front pocket. She decided to let him wait, so that the chocolate would melt and stain his underwear.

"I can't sell wine," she said. "It's illegal to sell alcohol after 2 AM."

The man with the bulge looked at his wristwatch, which was plated with fake gold. "Sister, it five o'clock. It already tomorrow, and I goin' by *tomorrow* time."

"Sorry," she said, folding her arms. "Cigarette weather."

"What the hell?" the man said.

His companion, a pasty-looking blonde, grabbed his arm. "Forget it, Jerry. I got some back at my place."

"This bitch tellin' me it ain't tomorrow yet," he said.

Army Jacket cleared his throat and straightened himself. "Sir, she's only doing her job," he said, looking down at the man from a four-inch height advantage.

"She's only doing her job," Cynthia said.

"Don't get smart with me, bitch." The man raised the wine bottle as if he were going to swing it. Army Jacket stepped forward and grabbed his wrist, taking the bottle with his other hand. The man grunted and the aroma of vomit and cheap booze wafted across the room. He struggled free and headed for the door, the blonde following.

At the door, the man paused and squeezed the bulge in his pants. "Got something for ya next time," he said. The blonde pulled him cussing toward the street.

Army Jacket placed his coffee cup on the counter.

"You get a lot of weirdoes on this shift," Cynthia said.

"I already said that. When do you get off work?"

They had breakfast in a little sidewalk cafe. Cynthia ordered coffee and butter croissants and scrambled eggs. Army Jacket was a vegetarian, but he said he could eat eggs. Cynthia thought that was strange, because eggs weren't vegetables.

They reached Cynthia's apartment just before noon. "So, where's this bed of yours?" Army Jacket asked.

Cynthia had a few boyfriends in high school. After the beggar had started sleeping under her bed, she'd quit dating. But now that Army Jacket was in her apartment, she decided that she'd been foolish to face the fear alone. She'd give Army Jacket what he wanted, and then she'd get what she wanted.

She led him to the tiny bedroom. She half-suspected that the beggar crawled from beneath the bed while she was gone, to sleep between cloth sheets and dream of being human. But the beggar belonged to dust, the dark, permanent shadow of underthere. The blankets were rumpled, just as she'd left them.

"You don't mess around, do you?" Army Jacket said.

"It's only dust," she said.

"I didn't mean *that* kind of mess," he said, looking at the dirty laundry scattered on the floor. He sat on the bed, Cynthia watching from across the room, waiting to see if the gray hand would clutch his ankle.

He patted the mattress beside him. "Come on over. Don't be shy."

She looked out the window. "Looks like cigarette weather."

Army Jacket took off his army jacket. Without the jacket, he was just a David. Not a protector. Not some big, brave hero who would slay the beggar.

"Come on," he said. "This isn't a spectator sport."

She crossed the room, crawled onto the bed beside him, mindful of her feet. They undressed in silence. David kissed her, then clumsily leaned her back against the pillows. Through it all, she listened for the breathing, the soft knitting of dust into flesh, the strange animations of the beggar.

David finished, rolled away. "Where are the cigarettes?"

"I don't smoke."

"What's this about 'cigarette weather,' then?"

"The man with the anaconda face said that."

"Huh?"

She put her arm across his chest, afraid he'd leave. She scolded herself for being so dumb. If David left, she'd be alone again when darkness fell. Alone with the beggar.

David kissed her on the forehead. "Ocean eyes like ice cream," he said.

She tensed beside him, sticky from the body contact. "Did you hear that?"

"What?"

"Under the bed. A noise."

"I don't hear anything." David made a show of checking the clock on her dresser.

The soft choking sound came again, the painful drawing of an inhuman breath. The beggar stirred, fingers creeping like thick worms across the floor. He was angry, jealous. Cynthia should not have brought another man to this bed. Cynthia belonged to the beggar, and always had.

"He's coming," she said.

David sat up and looked at the door. "Damn. Why didn't you tell me you had a boyfriend?"

"Only crazy people talk to mirrors."

David reached off the bed, grabbed his clothes, and began dressing.

"*You're* crazy, Alice."

"Who's Alice?"

David ignored her, teeth clenched in his rush to pull up his pants. "I hope to hell he doesn't carry a gun."

"Shhh. He'll hear you."

David slipped his arms into his jacket. Now he was Army Jacket again, just another one of *them*, a hollow man, a mound of dust surrounding a bag of air. None of them were real.

Except the man under the bed.

Army Jacket struggled into his shoes. Cynthia leaned forward and watched, wondering how far the beggar would let Army Jacket get before pulling him into the velvet.

"Green licorice. Frightened of storms?" Army Jacket asked, his breath shallow and rapid.

"No, only of *him*."

"Razor in the closet since yesterday." Army Jacket tiptoed out of the room, paused at the front door and listened.

"He doesn't use the door," Cynthia called out, giggling. The beggar would slide out from under the bed any moment now, shake of the accumulated dust of his long sleep, and make Army Jacket go away.

The phone rang. It had to be Mom. Seven rings before Mom gave up.

Army Jacket swallowed, twisted the knob, and yanked the door open, falling into a defensive crouch. The hallway was empty.

"Allergies," he yelled at her, then slipped out the doorway and disappeared.

Cynthia fell back on the pillows, sweat gathering on her brow. The beggar hadn't taken him. The beggar had not been jealous. The beggar was too confident, too patient, to be jealous.

She clutched the blankets as the afternoon sun sank and the shadows grew long on the bedroom wall. She should have fled while it was still light, but her limbs were limp as sacks of jelly. Fleeing was useless, anyway. He'd always had her.

Dusk came, dangling its gray rags, shaking lint over the world.

Under the bed, stirrings and scratches.

Under the bed, breathing.

Cynthia whimpered, curled into a fetal position, nude and burning and vulnerable. Waiting, like always.

The hand scrabbled along the side of the mattress. It clutched the blankets and began dragging the body that wore it from the vague ether. Cynthia closed her eyes, tight like she had as a small child, so tight the tears pressed out. She trembled, her sobs in rhythm with the horrible rasping of the beggar's breath.

She could feel it looming over her now, its legs formed, the transition from dust back to flesh complete. Cynthia held her breath, the last trick. Maybe if she could hold her breath forever . . .

The hand touched her gently. The skin was soft, soft as velvet.

Cynthia almost screamed. But she knew what would happen if she screamed. Because Mommy might hear and things like this are secret and it's okay to touch people who love you but some people wouldn't understand. Bad girls who scream have to be punished. They have to be sent into the dark place under the bed.

And they have to stay under the bed until Daddy says it's okay to come out.

So Cynthia didn't scream, even as the hand ran over her skin, leaving a trail of dust.

She didn't make a sound as the beggar climbed onto the bed. If she was a good little girl, then the beggar would go away after he finished, and wouldn't drag her into the underthere.

The dust settled over her, a smothering blanket of velvet.

If only she could hold her breath forever.

BASKING IN MYSTERY

by D. F. Lewis

It was a hot drizzly day as I entered the town.

I had suffered the exquisite agonies of blisters as they bloated out through the widening holes of my army surplus socks. I thought I was coming into Stromper, but this place was not at all like the photographs I had viewed at the previous stop-over.

The church tower seemed to lean somewhat from true, with a diamond-shaped clockface a third of the way down, showing that the time was later than what my ill-repaired wristwatch showed. Almost high time for tea.

The street lamps were most peculiar, tall thin poles of plaited green metal topped by squashed globes and, except for a few parked cars, no other sign of life.

I glanced back along the route upon which I had entered the town. The path led up into a clump of trees where the hill slopes had come to an abrupt halt. The town was quite unexpected in this valley. Stromper was some miles further on, I surmised. Still, I could stay the night here.

The architecture of the church showed that the place was not on its first legs. Its flush of youth was well behind it, as also evidenced by the seedy parade of shops, each with its independent roof—not shanties exactly, but the resemblance was sufficient for me to borrow shudders from my late mother: she had always cringed when faced with the second-rate. I was my mother's son, no mistake.

Those fleeting images were a composite first impression, as my poor aching feet trudged down the only metalled road that the town seemed to possess. I was trying to ignore vague ideas that the church tower was taking on an even steeper tilt as I approached it. The lamp standards, some mere stumps without lights, were not stationary, but following me to the door of a two star hotel that I had spotted on the other side of the market square—or so I imagined.

I was now on a dirt surface, which several other boots had scuffed up not long before, because the increasing drizzle had drenched some div-ots and not others. The glistening slate roof of the ramshackle hotel bore witness to things which I guessed must have basked in the earlier sun upon its slopes. My mind was indeed playing me tricks stranger than any I could credit it playing.

On entering the foyer of the hotel, I put from my mind all thoughts of being followed. The desk was tenantless. I rang the bell vigorously. Two women approached from the lounge area, with the undergrunts of a TV soap behind them. To my rain-blurred eyes, they were in identical uniforms, a cross between a chambermaid's and that of a Pris-oner-Of-War Camp commandant. One was decidedly winsome with a frivolous humour in the way she had to keep brushing her blonde fringe from in front of her large eyes. The other was older, less able to convince me of her humanity. Both were markedly more bodies than minds. Their hem-lines were a trifle too short for comfort.

"Yes?" said the spokesman, the older.

"I would like a room for the night. I'm too far from Stromper to make it before nightfall."

"Second best, eh?"

"Not at all . . . I just didn't know you were here."

"Few do . . . if THEY do."

"Shall I sign the Register?"

The younger one took a large ledger from under the reception coun-ter and opened it at the first page. I appeared to be the very first visitor, which I thought should surely not be the case.

"Don't you usually get guests to sign it?" I queried.

The younger spoke for the first time, her voice as smooth as wild honey: "You are the first to ask . . . "

If there is a mystery, I am usually the first to desire league with it, to be an ingredient as it were of its frustrating inscrutability. I even sup-posed that *I* might be the mystery and the town (with its strange hotel and leaning church) was ordinary and straightforward.

I entered the ledger with a signature that I had never used before, ending it with a flourish of lines and curls. Such an action was the very essence of self-delusion. I beamed with pride, as I rescrewed the top on my fountain pen.

The stairs were brightly lit by hurricane lamps, but the landing was left unaccountably dark, so I could not see how far the corridor stretched nor the approximate number of rooms.

My room, to which I was shown by the older woman with a cinema torch, was none too bad. Stromper would have been streets more comfortable with its speciality in four-posters and 24-hour non- discriminatory room service. However, this would suffice. The bed seemed lumpy but sleepable; the bathroom brown at the edges but doused with a cocktail of disinfectants; the ceiling stained with maps of archipelago worlds that I knew never existed and a trap door no doubt leading to that vast slated roof I had previously surveyed from below in the market square.

From my window, I could see the surrounding hills which had been the bane of my feet. The sun was at last just managing to peel back the dirty clouds, but too late for the weather's sake, since its huge red rim was dipping behind the trees almost too early for night. The square was still deserted, but the parked cars had gone.

I sat on the twanging bed and examined my feet inch by inch. I plumped them eventually into the wash basin which I had filled with tepid water. I could see from where I was now positioned that the odd standard lamps in the square were gradually seeping a yellowy glow, as the sun finally gave up its ghost to the moon.

It was quiet. Too quiet. They were evidently listening to me. Trying to fathom my mystery. So I spoke to myself to make it worth their while: "I expect those two women run this joint together, in between the TV programmes . . . they can't have much to do . . . they seem nice creatures enough . . . so affectionate, I imagine, with one another when the customers have been put to bed . . . "

I knew nothing about them. I simply surmised. I smiled, as I heard shuffling from above me in the bedroom ceiling.

"When I get to Stromper, I will tell of the two women . . . that it's nice to be looked after by such a couple, instead of by one of those plug ugly man-woman creatures which usually snoop around such hotels in the guise of managers. Two women's bodies are so nice as they lodge upon one another, with nothing poking in between them in the manner of a broken bed-spring . . . "

It was tantamount to reciting a speech that I had learned by heart as I rounded the hills. The drizzle had got my goat, but now I was safe and basking in the mystery which I conjured for myself and my auditors.

Then the trap door in the ceiling below the basking frame of the hotel's giant roof began to gape open inwards . . . but which direction was inward, which outward, I mused as I hummed mysteriously to myself? And memory itself is the mystery which saves me from the monster which instinct tells me must have squirmed through.

Morning came with a flourish, like my fictitious signature. The horizon was streaked with a sunrise of bloodhoney, picked out between the curlicues of impotent designer clouds. A solitary funnel betokened what I imagined to be a steamer on the horizon, leaning both ways in turn.

Lolling on the slate beach at Stromper-By-The-Sea, I almost craved for the return of the grey drizzly skies, so that I could again sense my mother shuddering. I would need her, of course, sooner or later, to absolve me from the mysterious guilt that sat upon my soul. But, in the meantime, I was most happy, as the baking sun-lamp beat down from the bluest sky imaginable, upheld against gravity by the vast twisted standard of my sheer belief.

SOILS OF THE WITCH GARDEN

by Michael Laimo

By the time we passed Richmond heading south on I-95, I'd begun to feel an unpleasurable tremor in my gut, an instinct that suggested something of bad ilk. When we got off the exit at Harper's Bane, I was damn near terrified to death.

In the southern half of the United States, Summer persists for an extended period of time, eating well into Autumn's tenure. Not unlike Long Island, the trees surrender their greens to more vibrant earth-tones, and the setting sun pulls its beams back around dinner-time. But the heat seems to find a way to stick around all the way into November, prolonging its welcome into a period of season where the Long Island children have to bundle themselves in parkas and knit beanie-caps before heading off to school.

The emergence of the warmer temperatures as we traveled south had Lisa and I feeling a bit giddy (she made a moot point of sticking her index finger out the window to measure the climate) and much looking forward to the well-deserved vacation in sunny Florida we really had no time to plan for. *I'm pregnant*, she'd revealed, her first offering of conversation as I walked through the door six nights ago after returning from work. *The party's over* I teased during a toast of orange juice and cinnamon buns, reflecting on the five years of wedded bliss and double-income/no-kid lifestyle we'd so naturally shared and enjoyed.

A romantic vacation was something far long overdue for us, and since a nasty case of the flu eliminated all the pleasures of our honeymoon five years prior, we realized that our very last opportunity to make up for lost memories would be right here and now, no delays, no hesitation. So we packed our bags, cashed in our vacation time and hit the road, Florida bound.

"I'm hungry, Brad."

"Please don't tell me you're craving pickles. Or ice cream."

She laughed. "No, not yet. A sandwich or something fast will be fine."

I switched to the right lane, slowed to the minimum and began looking ahead for signs of a rest area or town. There was nothing, and I tried to caution myself against impatience as the vividly-shaded trees and soft blue sky surrendered their colors to the dull-gray cast of dusk.

An eighteen wheel Mack and trailer roared past my car in the passing lane, a burly man in a blue denim jacket and mirror-lensed sunglasses eying me from the passenger's seat. The driver blasted the horn as they sped by, the truck leaving us in a spew of blue smoke. When the smoke cleared, the sign for Harper's Bane came into view. I thought it strange that I hadn't seen it before.

I slowed the car, signaled, and drove up the off-ramp.

Trees immediately surrounded the car, mostly pines bunched together and crowding against the sky like tall buildings, limiting my vision. If indeed there was a Harper's Bane, we couldn't see it from here. I grew uncomfortable when the off-ramp, instead of veining onto a main road, became a road itself, taking us away from the highway.

"Where are we?"

"Damned if I know." I sounded calm, but the looming trees and gathering darkness gripped me with claustrophobia, threatened to take my deeper breaths away.

"Brad—maybe we should turn around?"

I nodded and was about to voice my agreement when the trees fell away from the right side of the road a short distance ahead, revealing a small farm. I could see an unpaved road leading to queues of vegetable crops. It twisted left at the forefront of the field then pointed its way further ahead towards an adjacent house.

I pulled down the windows as we passed the house. The place was in shambles, an age-old wrap-around porch platforming shattered glass and rotting woodbeams. The immediate property was surrounded by a low fieldstone wall and wrought iron gates, witch grass growing tall and wild behind the wall and nearly obscuring the stone pathway leading to the porch. I could hear a million crickets chirping in unfluctuating ariettas.

I drove on, cotton-dry air seizing my mouth. There were a few more houses along the 'main road', and a bar called *Razzmatazz*. It looked closed, the windows dark, a rusted pick-up with a flat tire parked in the dirt lot outside.

"There's nothing here," Lisa offered. "No town *I* want to visit."

I couldn't have agreed more. "Next driveway, I'll turn around and head back toward the high—"

"*Brad!*"

My eyes had only wandered for a moment when Lisa screamed my name, and when I looked back at the road I saw something like a flash disappear below the front right bumper of the car. I struggled to find the brake pedal as a dreadful thump shook the car, first at the front tires, then the rear. The car skidded across the thin road onto a dirt shoulder, and Lisa put her hands against the dash to avoid colliding into it.

"Dear Jesus!" My heart was screaming.

Lisa fell into an immediate panic, her face drained of color. "An animal . . . it was an animal, right, Brad?"

Hands still glued to the wheel, I could only sit and stare at Lisa's trembling face, in denial of what I knew I saw.

I hit a child.

Lisa clawed the door handle, opened it and staggered from the car. I looked into the rearview mirror and saw her lumbering crookedly towards a twisting heap that resembled something like a beached sea creature. She looked pathetic at the moment, a woman stripped of all her elegance. Given the surreal predicament, I felt equally dazed.

I crawled out of the car and faltered back toward the scene. *I'm going to jail, a city boy in no-man's land where the law is a fat Sheriff named Earl just chomping at the bit for a little action in this otherwise ho-hum town.*

Lisa was kneeling next to the body, a hand over her mouth, sobbing. "Brad," she cried. "It's—it's a boy."

Driving down here I'd fantasized about her saying those exact words—but not for another eight months. Now, as her sobs turned to cries I commiserated over the cliche statement, my wife in near hysterics and unsure of what to do at the moment as her shadow bathed the body—the naked, bloody body—of a young boy no older than nine or ten years of age.

Clouds floated in like spaceships, masking the full moon. The scene went dark, the pool of blood tiding out from beneath the boy stripped of its luster. I noticed the emergence of mosquitoes. They were in droves and buzzing about the victim as if dispatching reports of discovered treasure.

"We have to get help," Lisa said.

"Is he alive?"

"How should I know? I'm not a damn nurse!" She pinned me with wild, accusatory eyes, features taut with panic. Her skin was as white as paper and she looked as if she might throw up.

I took a deep breath then kneeled down next to the body just as Lisa stood up. We both stared helplessly, unsure of what to do.

I gently nudged him.

No response.

"Close your eyes." I grasped the boy by the shoulder and turned him over.

Lisa screamed.

His dirty face stared back at us, eyes open and blinking, mouth gurgling blood.

"He's alive!" she yelled.

"Lisa, keep your voice down!"

"A-are you okay?" She kneeled back down next to him. Tears filled her eyes.

The boy didn't answer. Just stared, eyes glassed over, ruby lips trembling.

I stood up, took an indecisive step backwards, my rush of poise quickly escaping me. I felt suddenly hysterical, and I wanted to laugh, yell, cry, scream, take my heart, rip it free from my chest with my trembling fist and toss it into the nearby woods. Instead I forced myself to say, quite calmly, "He's in shock."

That's when I nearly collapsed. I felt the world spin around me, and as my body began to totter, Lisa stood up and wrapped her arms around me and squeezed me tight.

"Brad, please, we need to get a grip. *Both* of us. We'll be in a shitload of trouble if we don't." When the world came back into focus, she squeezed my face with both hands and said, "Let's find somebody to help."

I nodded. I wanted this nightmare to end.

"Can you go back to the car, get the blue beach blanket in the trunk?"

"Yeah," I answered, releasing a deep breath.

She squatted back down next to the boy. On weak legs I paced back to the car, satisfied for the moment that Lisa was taking control of the situation. I turned off the ignition then came around the side and opened the trunk. I retrieved the blanket and returned to Lisa, my eyes searching the night for someone who might be able to help us. It was at this time I realized that we hadn't seen a soul since taking the exit. Nobody had emerged from the nearby homes. None of the lights were on inside them.

I kneeled next to the boy and for the first time got a good look at him. White, brown hair and eyes (they still gazed blankly, moving back and forth between me and Lisa although never seeming to focus in), and fully naked. I heard him wheezing and concluded that he'd broken a rib, more than likely punctured a lung. I'd done an efficient job in running him over.

"Where are his clothes?" I wondered aloud, placing the blanket over his body up to the neck. I wedged my arms beneath him and scooped him up. His weight almost slipped through my grasp and I had to clutch him tighter as I plodded to the car.

Lisa opened the back door. I gently slid him in, feet first. "Don't worry, we'll find you some help," she promised.

Pulling the keys from my pocket, I got back into the car, started the engine. Lisa was crying. I ignored her, distracted from the ripe odor rising from the back seat. "The houses over there. Let's see if we can use someone's phone."

Another minute passed and we were in the dirt driveway of a simple cape-style home with a screened-in porch minus the screens. The lawn out front was in poor condition, the battle long lost against tramping footsteps. A littering of soda bottles and plastic dog bones were spread about like lost remnants.

We both got out of the car and walked up toward the house. I heard a yip behind us, and when I turned I saw a mutt pacing lazily about the street, head down and sniffing the road with blank disinterest. Must be the owner of the plastic bones, I thought. I knocked on the frame of the screen door. "Hello?"

No answer. I smelled something foul.

"T-they didn't hear you," Lisa stammered.

I knocked again. Nothing.

"Can't we drive further into town, go to a police station?"

"You want to spend the night in jail?"

She shook her head, biting a knuckle. "So then what in God's name are we going to do?" She walked across the front yard, examining the upstairs windows. "Hey you inside! We need some help out here! Please! There's been an accident!" Her yells echoed through the sparse neighborhood, nearly silencing the crickets. Me, I could only hang my head in denial of what was happening. I felt utterly defeated at the moment, and I wanted to laugh out loud, or cry, something. I couldn't figure it out. Maybe just toss the kid on the front lawn and hightail it back to I-95. My heart started pounding furiously, the dreadful silence spawning eerie feelings of being watched from all the shadowed points around us, from the black windows in the houses, from the copses between the trees in the woods. My mind was off exploring dark tangents. And I knew it too.

"C'mon!" Lisa called, her voice cracking. She marched around to the side of the house. "We need help out here!" No one came.

I turned and gazed at the house across the street. It was set back from the road about two hundred feet, the shrubs out front well overgrown. I thought I saw a staring face in one of the upstairs windows, but when I turned to get Lisa's attention, it was gone.

"Let's get back in the car, Brad. We'll find the town, a police station, drop him off. There's gotta be someone there who can help."

Someone who can help, I thought, realizing now that I'd be damned if something wasn't really wrong here in Harper's Bane, Virginia. *There's no one here except the naked boy in my back seat.* I peered again at the house across the street, then at Lisa. Her face was drawn, pale. She looked as if she suffered from mental illness, and it frightened me to think that she might be as helplessly scared as I was at the moment.

She screamed my name, pointing towards the car.

When I spun around I had a real tough time absorbing the scene. The dog—the same dog I'd seen sniffing the road not minutes ago—was in the car, its front half probing the back seat where I left the boy, its hairy-tailed rump and rear legs moving spryly about as they dangled from the open rear window. Muffled grows and hissing snarls issued, and the smell of something warm, something *organic*, assaulted my nose, making my gut go cold.

Somehow I found the strength and fortitude to stage an attack. I grabbed a large plastic bone from the assortment on the lawn. A deaf man could have heard me scream as I ran over and brought the makeshift weapon down upon the hindquarters of the dog, a total of six fast whacks just above the tail. Before I managed a seventh, the dog fell from the window in a drop-dead heap.

Even if my assault had caused some damage, it hadn't been the make of its ruin. Its throat was gone, ripped out and gushing. The dog twisted about on the ground, paws scraping the soil, its barks reduced to gurgles. Blood poured down the car door like spilled paint. A hot coppery stench hung thick in the air.

"Brad . . . " Lisa was crying again, her voice breaking up. "The boy, the boy . . . "

I bit my fist, staring at the dog. Its stomach undulated like a balloon, the shredded throat tossing blood in spurts. Its body rotated crookedly on the ground as it tried to right itself.

I pulled my eyes away, peering at the surrounding houses, wondering why nobody was coming to help. I started to tremble. "I-I can't."

"Come," she said unconvincingly, pulling me by the arm. "We'll go together."

I tried to resist her lead, but had no control, a slave to circumstance. We baby-stepped past the dog to the car and from a two-foot distance, peered into the back seat.

The boy was gone. My eyes explored the plush interior seating, once brown, now blackened and saturated with blood. In the middle of the back seat, like a strange growth, lay the dog's throat—a hairy hunk of flesh—wet, jagged, and matted. Lisa put her hands to her neck. "Brad, I'm so scared." She buried her face in my chest, tears dousing my shirt.

"We've got to get out of here."

"What about the boy?"

I clenched my fists, was about to yell, *You go look for him, I'm going home*, when a voice broke the silence surrounding us.

"They . . . won't . . . let . . . you . . . leave."

The tone ran low and raspy, like the voice of a man who'd smoked a lifetime supply of Marlboros. I looked up and saw a terrible face emerging from the backdrop of darkness in the upstairs window of the house, the skin old and withered, overcome with wrinkles. His eyes were black, staring in my direction.

Lisa—brave Lisa—stepped forward and started yelling, arms spread in question. "We needed help down here! You must've heard us knocking!"

The man looked at Lisa, then back at me again. "We don't ever come outside. The . . . the children. They bring us food from the farm." He started sobbing. "That one'll go back and tell the rest of them about you two. They'll never let you leave."

"The rest of who?" I asked. I felt a sharp lump form in my throat, hot and painful.

"The children. *Her* children."

"Whose children?" My heart slammed against my ribcage.

"Barlidas. The witch of Harper's Bane. Lives on the farm you passed. She makes the children there."

A wicked scream sounded, a howl nearly animalistic in nature, yet clearly defined and frightfully produced by human lungs.

"They're coming! They're coming! Barlidas' children!" The man's eyes searched the distance, spittle flying from his lips. He ducked down, disappearing into the darkness of his home.

"Damn him!" I screamed, charging the house. "He's got to help us!" I pulled the door open and hurtled into the porch. A foul odor met my nose and I saw a rotting head of cabbage on the floor by the window. The door inside was boarded over. I slammed my hands against the wood barricade, yelling, lost in a bout of temper.

I heard the scream again, closer, and that was when Lisa's own cries shredded the night's silence in an hysterical plea for help. I ran from the porch and bounded outside. I saw Lisa sitting straight up in the driver's seat, both hands on the wheel, her head rocking back and forth, from me to the right and back again.

"Brad! Hurry! *Please!*"

Then I saw them. They were racing into the yard, a mob of what the man in the window had called Barlidas' children. They were all very young, I guessed no older than twelve, some wearing jeans and tees and sneakers that looked as if they'd been through generations of hand-me-downs, some completely naked. They all possessed shrewd weapons, pipes, knives, baseball bats, and were upon the car like piranha in a goldfish tank. I fell into a panic, paralyzed as the crazed children swarmed the car, their weapons falling upon it in a symphonic cacophony. A pipe found the driver's sideview mirror, baseball bats dented the hood. Axes punctured holes into the doors, deflated the tires. I couldn't see Lisa anymore as the thirty or more children crawled atop the car like maggots on meat.

Glass shattered, the rear windshield caving in. The car tipped and swayed. The horn blew once, interrupting Lisa's unremitting cries of dread. I saw filthy greedy hands reach in, grab her by the shirt. I saw her fists, striking against them. Then I saw the passenger door swing open, three boys no older than ten years old dragging her out onto the dirt. One of them was the boy I'd run over. His mouth and chin was slathered with black hair and blood.

I finally broke my inaction and stormed toward the car, picking up a 2-liter plastic soda bottle along the way. It wasn't much of a weapon but I knew it would hurt pretty badly if I connected. I encountered a naked girl seven or eight years old with gold locks spilling across her shoulders in a flow of grease and dirt. She turned and caught my approach, mouth scowling, brow downcast, arms animated in preparation to claw me. I swung the bottle and smashed it into her jaw.

Her lips split open, a gush of blood bursting in a red spray. It splattered my arm. The girl cried out and fell to the ground, clawing her face. The mob went silent. They turned and gaped increduously at me as the girl howled in pain. I stood there like a fool, soda bottle in hand, challenging them. Their filthy faces contemplated me, displaying fiendish smiles and angry brows.

Damn, I thought, *there's not a soul here in their teens.*

A few kids in the front of the mob started giggling, as if amused by my predicament. Many more quickly followed, revealing yellowed teeth and grinning eyes.

Slowly, they walked toward me. Some of them were oddly deformed, their limbs and facial features contorted.

As if they'd been run over at some point . . .

I stepped back. "Where's my wife?" I demanded.

Someone screamed *get him!* and they ran at me, weapons raised.

I followed my instincts, turned and ran as fast as my legs could take me, resigning myself to the fact that Lisa, my dear pregnant wife, had been ruthlessly killed, or taken prisoner. I darted across the street then back up the road from where we came, my sneakers pounding the road, my breath escaping me much faster than I could catch it. I could hear them behind me, little feet and high wailing shrieks. I ran past the place in the road where I first ran over the boy, past the bar with the pickup and a few more dark homes whose occupants, I was positive, would not be willing to let me in. I glanced sideways at one house and saw two ghostly faces—a man and a woman—peering out from the bottom of one window.

Gaining some ground on the ten or so children still pursuing me, I darted back across the road onto the dirt driveway leading towards the farm.

I bypassed the house and headed into the crops area, my aching legs taking me further and further in, over cabbages, potato plants, stalks of wheat. Once camouflaged in the height of the wheat, I collapsed to my knees, heaving for air, my wife a mile or more away.

I wondered if I would ever see her again.

I could hear my heart pounding in my ears. I listened to the night air, but only the songs of crickets loomed.

The children. Where are they? How come they didn't pursue me here?

For twenty minutes I waited in agony, my mind immersed with visions of Lisa pleading for my help. I couldn't come to grips with what I'd done, how I left my wife to fend for herself against . . . against *them*. But was it fair for me to blame selfishness or cowardice for my decision, given the dire circumstances? Could I *really* have jumped in the shark pool to save her? No. I'd be dead too. Yet life without her, it seemed utterly impossible to face the reality of the matter, that I'd sacrificed her—and our child—to save myself.

Perhaps I still have a chance . . .

I dug my way back through the seven foot stalks, all the while attempting to make sense of the shocking scenario in Harper's Bane: the children, seemingly abducted or willingly surrendered from their homes to this so-called 'witch', the townsfolk stricken with grave terror at her very existence and fully succumbing to her perverse demands. Now, the children, raised in an unfavorable environment of wicked practice, wholly reduced to carry out this lunatic's dark expectations.

I pressed on. The wheat surrounded me on all sides, much like the trees had to my car upon first exiting the interstate. My feet crackled against the dry earth as I tunneled through the tall whispering growths, my hands and arms bleeding from their harsh contact. In the dark, my sense of direction melted away. I could do nothing but walk straight ahead assuming to eventually reach the outskirts of the farm.

Suddenly, in the darkness, came a whisper. A child's whisper?

Then, a whimper. No, not that of a child, but of a . . . *baby.*

I forged ahead, slowly pursuing the soft innocent whine. The moon's beams revealed the edge of the wheat field, exposing the presence of another crop area.

The whimpering grew louder. I could hear more than one infant, perhaps three, four, even more now as I located the edge of the wheat. I parted the stalks, looked out, and beheld an outlandish sight.

Four human babies lay fidgeting in the muddy earth. They were six feet apart, squared off within barbed wire corrals. Each was ensconced in a translucent casing, their tiny appendages writhing and sliding beneath the milky surface, trying to break free. One had already managed to partially release itself, its tiny head wriggling like a salted slug, shaking off strings of film. It opened its eyes. They were fully black, fringed with white. It looked *angry.*

She makes the children there . . .

Coerced by terror, I backpedaled, the sharp barb from another corral tearing into my leg. I spun, dazed, saw dozens of the small square yields. Each one contained a squirming ovum in turn which held its very own baby. Some of the fetuses looked fully developed, others seemed no further matured beyond the early embryonic stage. Each possessed a thick green umbilical cord that emerged from the navel. It slithered beyond the perimeter of the corral where it branched off into smaller arteries and disappeared into the ground.

Like roots . . .

I heard a woman scream.

Lisa.

I tried to run but a pressure had my ankle. When I looked down I saw a grotesque thing that was a newborn baby, now free from its placenta, one of its tiny bloody hands grasping my pant leg. Its oil-black eyes shot a horrible glance at me. It hissed like an angry cat and I could see four baby teeth in its dirty mouth. I shook my leg, kicked it away. It let out a pig-like squeal, a sentiment echoed by some of its near-born siblings. I darted away against the outskirts of the wheat, towards the direction of Lisa's scream.

Towards the house.

My feet trampled crops as I ran. I could hear airy laughs riding the distant night air.

The children. Barlidas' children.

I reached the rear of the house. A cold wind blew across my face, all thoughts of friendly southern warmth long diminished. The children were laughing inside. A cowbell tolled against the eave above the door as if signaling the start of a wicked act.

Lisa screamed again, loud and piercing as if she suffered great pain. There was desperation in her voice, pure terror.

"Lisa! Hold on for God's sake. I'm coming!"

At the sound of my voice, silence reigned. Lisa's screams were gone. The insane giggles, gone. I held my breath and walked to the house, opened the back door and went inside.

I found myself in a small kitchen. There was an age-old oven and stove, long stripped and rusted. Useless. Heaps of rotting vegetables covered the floor. In the center of the room sat a large black vat, filled with a thick brown liquid. It smelled awful.

I stepped forward, sneakers squashing the vegetables. I whispered, "Lisa?"

And then from beyond the kitchen walls she answered, her voice light and gay like tinkling bells. My heart froze into ice.

"Brad, is that you? I'm in here . . . "

I followed her voice, suddenly mesmerized. I exited the kitchen and entered into a large room. The children were all here, perhaps fifty or sixty of them. They circled the room, joined together by the arms or legs and sitting against the four walls at odd angles, as if modeling for weird sculpture. A number of torches burned at the center of the room. In the flickering light I could see their injuries, twisted marrings on their limbs, torsos, and faces.

These children weren't born with these scars. They suffered them in accidents . . .

A small group of children congregated at the center of the room, by the torches. "Lisa?" I whispered. "Are you here?"

The grouping in the center of the room dispersed and I saw a woman there. She was drifting a foot above the ground like a ghost. "*Hello Brad*" she said in Lisa's voice. She was *beautiful*, fully naked, her body untouched and unblemished, dark hair floating all around as if caught in the embrace of tranquil waters. I took a step forward, desiring her at that moment with her alabaster skin and chestnut hair floating down upon the smooth curve of her shoulders. She was an exotic siren in a tale of mythological lore.

I *wanted* her . . .

And then I heard Lisa scream. It broke my trance, and perhaps the spell of *her*. The floating woman grinned, and when she did I felt all my wants and desires ebb into fear—into a horror more icy than that of a crypt, more pale and hushed than the bones hidden within its walls. She raised her withered hands and cackled, her eyes now black and morose like those of her children, the exposed teeth horribly gnarled, rows and rows of blackened stumps grinding out the wickedest of sounds. Clusters of warts mottled her face, the smooth whiteness of her skin long lost to the blackest of rashes.

Behind her Lisa appeared, fettered by the arms of a half dozen boys. She'd been stripped of her clothing, her skin aghast-white, as if coated in snow. She screamed again and I reached for her. A number of children ran forward and seized me, wrestled me to the floor, crawled all over me and held me down. I could do nothing but watch as the evil woman laughed like a child waved her wicked hands in the air.

She held them out to Lisa.

The witch's hands clasped Lisa's breasts, her crusted fingers moving across her torso, leaving dark lines of filth trailing down. She opened her mouth into an impossible gaping hole that went from ear to ear. Something bright and silvery dripped out. It pooled onto Lisa's stomach then trickled down to her vagina. A strange-smelling puff of black smoke rose up, then a glow of blue light that was gone an instant later.

The floating hag fell to the ground, her laughs replaced by hisses, her face twisted into a mask of toil.

Lisa had passed out, her head turned to one side. Two children came over, grabbed her by the feet, spread her legs open. The witch started an odd chant and I saw rivulets of blood pouring out from between Lisa's legs. Her vagina sputtered, and then from within her tremoring canal emerged a twisting knot of gore no larger than a walnut. The witch crawled over, still chanting, smiling joyously. The throbbing knot slithered from Lisa into the evil woman's waiting hands. She placed it against her crumpled breast, where it settled at the nipple.

Our child. But no longer *ours*.

Now, a child of Barlidas.

Barlidas . . .

Moments later the witch plucked the squirming embryo from her breast. One of the children, a brown-haired girl of maybe ten, came to retrieve it. She carefully cupped it in her hands, turned trance-like, and stepped away. A dozen or more of her siblings joined her as she left the room. They passed through the kitchen and then out the back door towards the farm.

I knew what would happen next. The children. They would gather together in the farm and collectively plant my child in the soils of the witch garden, where it would complete its term and come into this world as one of them.

Barlidas . . .

Something about her name . . .

"Brad?" I turned. Lisa had come around, eyes blinking, seeking my assistance. She looked down at her naked body, at the blood between her legs. She screamed my name, but I couldn't help, for it was at that terrifying moment I figured out the true meaning of the witch's name.

Barlidas. It was a perfect anagram for our names, Brad and Lisa.

I passed out.

***

I heard a sound. Voices? I woke Lisa and she accompanied me to the window. We both peered outside. *Perhaps the children had come with food from the crops?*

A car was parked in front of our house—this house the children had given us. We woke up here just as they were taking away the bodies of the people who stayed here before us.

A man stepped from the car, looking about. Then a woman.

She was pregnant. Of course.

"Hello?" the man called. "We need help."

It's been a familiar story over the years. In the back seat of their car lay one of the witch's children, badly injured from an 'accident'.

It might even be *my* child.

Her name came into my mind, *Neseku*, and in a few short seconds I knew the names of these doomed people who were silently summoned from the interstate by the witch of Harper's Bane.

Neseku. A perfect anagram for Ken and Sue.
I stuck my head out the window. And warned them.
"They'll . . . never . . . let . . . you . . . leave . . . "
But I knew, it would do them no good.

NATIVE, WITH ICICLE ORCHIDS

by Charlee Jacob

Arctic Prologue:

Paul Zervas was eight-years-old again, in that magical way that memories have of transporting people back to the stage of events. The knowledge stored of years later vanishes and the mind is as it was. He could see the green and blue boat that his parents used when it was summer, painted in those colors to remind them of the Aegean Sea near their birthplaces in Greece.

They lived so far north now because they were both researchers of glaciation in The Ombre Strait, scientists of past and future Ice Ages.

Mellina and Speros waved to him from deck. He stood on the shore, wishing he could have been with them. But he always got seasick. The best he could do was observe from the beach, as the green and blue boat rode the waves where later—in another season—the water would be choked with ice cakes and floes until boating became very unsafe. The sea surface itself might even freeze solid enough to walk a short distance out on. That he could do, and did, when winter came.

He wished he had a camera. To take a picture of this so he could send it to brother Themi. Sixteen years older than Paul, Themi was in college. The boat was new. He'd never seen it.

Suddenly the engine sputtered, yowled like a mechanical timber wolf, and then there was an explosion. The green and blue boat was on fire, red and yellow flames quickly engulfing the small craft. His parents were screaming, sound carrying in the crystal air, filling his head with terror. The boy could feel the heat rolling across the water toward him, billows of it blasting from the first explosion . . . and from the second.

Mr. Suinot, who managed the lighthouse a couple miles away in Fantomatique, saw it. He found Paul curled up on the shore, arms clasped around little knees, eyes shut tight. The boy was whimpering, "Too much noise, too much color."

***

Back to himself, twenty years later. He was hiding behind crates of EnviroChem and bleach. But he couldn't curl up. The ballooning of the pressurized space suit wouldn't permit it.

"Dr. Zervas?" the voice (belonging to the veterinary pathologist, Dr. Kent) sounded anxious, peeved. "Where are you? We need your help."

Dr. Devore, a botanical pathologist, was shouting, "We don't have time for this. We've got patients to look after."

Of course, their voices were elevated. To be heard at all through the suits, one had to yell. It added to the confusion rattling about in Paul's skull.

"As long as he doesn't actually get in the way, we'll just have to work around it," Devore said.

A third voice, that of team leader Dr. Armstrong, said, "Man's having a breakdown. Too bad we can't airlift him out. But this area is quarantined. No one comes in or leaves until we know more of what we're dealing with here. Shame, but we can't risk this virus getting back home."

Too much noise. The leaves cleft their green palates, lisping whistles into the wind. Monkeys and parrots screamed from the trees, as down below them every predator in the jungle roared or howled in terror and fury. Formerly droning insect hums ratcheted, rose and fell unevenly, without music, chitinous with deadly cough. The indigenous people shrieked and moaned, calling out to God, praying and cursing equally in echo.

Paul shuddered. Instead of muffling it, the outside sound was somehow amplified by the blower in his suit which supplied him air.

The doctors went away. He contemplated ducking into a nearby hut, to find pain medication to subdue the headache begun days ago by the constant cacophony. He knew the pills should be saved for the sick but he decided it would be a pointless exercise anyway, since he didn't dare breach the suit to obtain a drug.

There weren't enough to go around. Everyone and everything was contaminated, the virus having reached extreme amplification.

Only those who'd come down to help the island in the rain forest—dressed in orange Racal space suits and thus protected from direct contact with the hot agent—were still healthy. But it was taking an emotional toll, especially on Paul. The clamor of the whole area was slowly driving him mad. Those who'd first spiked fever quickly began to suffer vicious cramps and headaches. They screamed until the soft tissues in their throats deteriorated, and then they gurgled.

Paul was drenched clean through the scrubs he wore closest to his skin. He was currently cursing himself for choosing to be an epidemiologist, an occupation certain to take one into the world's torrid areas. Why couldn't he have followed in his parents' footsteps, as brother Themi had? He would be back up north, home, cool. His breath would plume phantoms of architectured snow wreaths, instead of fogging the suit's headgear, making the clear plastic slimy with it.

He wished he could remove the suit, at least the bubble helmet. But that would be suicide if it turned out the virus was airborne. It was so hot within the Racal. Sweat had matted his hair, dripping from his eyelashes and the end of his nose. Perspiration actually squished in the protective boots and gloves.

He shouldn't be able to clearly hear the outside like this, not trussed up in biocontainment garb. Yet he did, piercingly, poignantly, a tumult to loosen the moorings of a man's mind . . . As surely as this new plague slipped the brain away from the skull in a lake of blood. As surely as it dissolved the connective tissues until skin hung upon the bones. It made the tropics seem exponentially hotter, positively radioactive, until even the already garish jungle colors blazed and blinded.

Too much color. Greens, blues, reds, yellows: the shades of livid bruises, blood, and jaundice swam before Paul's eyes, causing him to be dangerously nauseous every other second. He choked back bile, desperate not to vomit into his helmet, for there would be no way to separate himself from the curds or stench.

He stumbled past a pile of monkey bodies waiting to be burned, some alive and still twitching in final throes. The team had run out of euthenasia drugs a few hours before, yet the animals still had to be disposed of. Their infected hides radiated ghastly spectrums of boiling color. Those not past the point of death screeched and burbled. Paul was amazed that they could possess the strength to make so much racket. He stifled his own sob, wishing the monkeys would die and be silent.

The village of La Desconocida sprawled at the base of a mildly active volcano which was smoking faintly. The volcano sat in the middle of a still lake, moted into an island. Paul was trying not to be seen by the doctors and military personnel bustling around. He dodged behind one building and then another.

He finally sought refuge in a hut, walls peeling paint in the equatorial heat. The roof was covered in bloody-milk hued volcanic ash. It was a short distance away from other huts where the bodies of dead people had been temporarily stored, stacked like piles of sleeping bags in an army surplus store. It was at the opposite end of the road from the one being used as the necropsy house, where space suited doctors cut open the ravaged corpses of both humans and animals to try to understand what was happening—and if it was possible to stop the disease.

How does one stop such riot and tumult? You don't! They run their course and fall down . . . or you do.

He tried to block out the sound but the hut's walls didn't help. He heard a cry of discordant chimes, as of cathedral bells tolling even as they were melted in acid. Paul turned to look through the doorway. He saw the beautiful native woman who hadn't been sick when the team arrived. She'd acted as liason between the group and the rest of the village, so they would offer up blood samples without fear of the needles.

Now this woman was gravely ill, had been since yesterday.

She was on her knees, swaying, obviously third spacing—the stage of the virus when the victim hemorrhages between the layers of skin and flesh. At that point the skin swells, departing from the flesh, protruding yet sagging like a half-filled balloon.

She'd brought her head up and was looking at him, eyes going flat as the eyes of all others did. But not so expressionless that Paul couldn't see the pleading inside her: for him to save her, to do something besides hiding. But he couldn't go to her, hearing her cries mingled with the tantarara of the rest, like hypodermics being inserted into the canals of his ears. He couldn't take another step as blood clots and black vomit tided out of each of her orifices, disgusting him as he'd never been before.

The plastic in his helmet furrowed and rimpled, distorting his view until she became even more grotesque, as if reflected back in funhouse glass. And the condensation inside the plastic headgear had become so thick that—in the dim light within the hut—the helmet appeared to be covered in a layer of ice (those snow wreaths after all). Close to the face, it was as it might appear to someone who'd fallen into a frozen river and was trying hopelessly to find the hole through which to climb back out again.

For God's sake, go to her . . .

This was Paul's first field case outside of a lab. Some of the other doctors had been to Central and South America, to Africa, to India. They were seasoned pros at seeing other living beings crash and bleed out, trapped within the viral reservoir.

Not he. He'd truly believed he could handle it. But he'd never counted on the stew of the jungle, the extreme devastation bodies could undergo that no textbook prepared you for . . . the noise generated by so much unimaginable torment.

The woman slipped from her knees, twitching on the ground, convulsions unleashing tarry fluid from her pores. The native soon seemed to be floundering in a sea of slime. Paul closed his eyes, telling himself he'd not been drawn to that, hadn't been aroused a few days previously by the mass of her blue-black hair and the shape of her mouth. He sternly commanded himself to snap out of it, to go help her, to hold her hand as she died, something. His feet would not move, his eyes wouldn't open. His muscles cramped, cringing as the death throes of the rain forest shrilled, the virus having spread everywhere on the isle like a kind of wildfire.

Paul sobbed, crazed by the sound, his skull throbbing, helpless to make it stop. He began to beat his head against the central post-support for the hut. He heard the helmet plastic split. This both terrified and consoled him. Perhaps it would be over for him soon.

But then he woke up. He'd been removed from his suit. He was lying on a cot, and a plane was landing.

"You all right, Dr. Zervas?" asked Dr. Armstrong.

Armstrong was also no longer wearing the Racal space suit.

No one Paul could see was wearing the protective biocontainment gear.

Paul felt sluggish. He knew he'd been tranquillized. He managed to nod.

"Well, you've had a tough time, son," said the older epidemiologist. "Lucky you didn't try that stunt earlier—before the virus suddenly stopped. We still don't know why. It infected the village and everything that had been alive on the mountain. Then that was it. Quite a change from how green the place was when we arrived, huh? It was quite a paradise."

Armstrong gestured broadly, indicating the massive gray defoliation, the sterile moonscape of what had been a thriving rain forest community. The chempit where the bodies of the villagers had been destroyed still misted, slightly blue, more color than Paul could see anywhere else.

He knew that viruses could, for no reason, swell up, then virtually disappear. Ebola had done that in 1976 and 1995. If the team was now out of protective biocontainment suits, it was because the virus had consumed every host available and had nothing new to jump into. Perhaps it had been unable to spread into the lake, some special nutrient or fungus in the water prohibiting it. When everything else died (except the team in the Racal suits), it died, too. The odd thing was that it was able to make the jump from one unrelated species to another, plants included. No other known virus did that.

Paul remembered. It was a virus completely unlike any ever seen before. The team had arrived when there was only the index case, the first victim a lumber man who'd stumbled into La Desconocida while one of Armstrong's colleagues just happened to be there to study the volcano. There had been a dramatic drop in blood pressure, pulse, and temperature. The white blood count zoomed atsronomically as the red count almost vanished. Then water began to erupt from every opening, more liquid than it seemed possible there could be. But, truthfully, bodies were mostly made up of water, and the virus brought organs and flesh down to this basic component. It drenched, then calcified until the stiffening victim appeared to be freezing solid, as if encased within a cocoon of ice.

Paul had later watched the beautiful native, her eyeballs grown rigid and cracked like fried marbles. The movements of her limbs were those of a fly encased in sticky spider's web, fumbling only slightly as the shroud which imprisoned her smothered more rigorous attempts. She was as a sleepy swimmer, fighting and yet not really fighting. There didn't seem to be much pain as her golden skin and black hair paled out in the strange fossilization process. The monkeys and parrots lolled, petrifying whitely in the trees, as leaves and orchids withered into chalk. Jaguars and pythons curled up in hollows to pass into the vitrifying dream. Everything went white. Especially, everything became silent.

But he'd seen sickening color, the spectrum of feverish jungle necrotics. He'd seen vistas of blood and black hemorrhage like he'd read about as regarded cases of Marburg and Ebola. He'd heard the din of screams until he was nearly deafened by it.

Before he realized, he opened his mouth. He said this to Dr. Armstrong, about the hideous colors and the noise.

The team leader shook his head and peered at Paul through wire rim glasses. "What you saw never happened. It was white, son. Nothing like it before, pray to God nothing like it again. And silent as a tomb. The only one screaming was you."

***

It was determined—by that canon of luminaries who were apparently experts at such things as mental exhaustion—that Paul Zervas needed a long rest. He was ordered on sabbatical, the place to be of his own choosing. Themi Zervas had recently died, having never married and without children to receive his legacy. He conveniently willed the family house in the far north to his younger brother.

It was good to be back in The Ombre Strait, on a cliff overlooking the gray-green sea, two miles from the nearest neighbor. Mr. Suinot still ran the lighthouse down the coast at Fantomatique. He was an old man now, near seventy, but strong enough to mount the long steps and control the lights.

Home was the diametrical opposite of the jungle in every way possible. Except in late spring and summer, it was bitterly cold, a combination of periglacier and tundra. Paul hadn't visited here in ten years, not since he'd gone away to university and then, after graduation, had joined Dr. Armstrong's team.

He continued to suffer nightmares about the malarial rain forest, of sweating half-breathless, claustrophobic in the space suit. He still shook in the dogwatch hours, night terrors of scorching Biosafety Level 4 diseases, filoviruses consuming everything in feverbright colors. He still found himself, risen to sleepwalk, to sleeprun, in the perilous process of striking his head against bedroom walls, trying to block out the sounds of horror.

There was no relief in the fact that it replaced totally the nightmares he'd always had about his parents' end, the green and blue ship exploding into flames, their screams as they burned to death. Yet there persisted the one similarity. It was still dreadful smears of color, surreal with monstrous stridor.

The irony didn't escape him. Paul had realized that the plague their team had investigated actually bleached its victims, making them seem frozen inside calcimine shells. He'd understood that he'd journeyed back to a place of natural ice sculpture, permafrosted in cirque basins, moraines glittering in polished platinum streaks and swirls sometimes too shining to look at. And there was virtually no noise here, except for the roar of distant avalanches and the sometime sibilance of the wind.

It was silent as La Desconocida had become, mute because there was nothing alive anywhere. He'd only hallucinated the lakes of blood and gangrenous meat, the shrieks of agony. He'd been seriously overcome by the oppressive heat of the jungle.

That could certainly not happen at Ombre. Here he was never overwarm, did not break a sweat walking down the beach, didn't feel the air sucked out of him by swelter. He got up in the morning, gazed out the window, and was calmed by an unreadable prose of whites. There was nothing in sight which reminded him of his research, no insights into suffering and its elusive redemption.

No one called—but he didn't have a phone. None tried to reach him. For the word had gone out in the scientific community that Paul Zervas was officially in retreat.

It was at least a few weeks before he began to feel restless. He found himself pacing rooms, moving furniture, oversleeping, then suffering insomnia where he'd listen for some natural shifting in the walls or floor. He played the radio too loud, just for the comfort of voices, then shut it off in panic as the caterwauling brought his headaches back.

"Perhaps if I simply talk to myself, whisper things," he said outloud, half-chuckling.

But then Paul discovered he had nothing to say that he particularly wanted to hear. The breaking of the frozen hush seemed blasphemous anyway, like a piggish squeal in a church.

He spent four days standing before the bay windows which looked out across the sea. The first two days he was rock-solid, military in his posture, as if guarding a castle. The third day he'd begun to tremble. Believing he was just cold, Paul put a coat on and resumed his vigil. On the fourth day, he burst into tears twice.

Then he saw the spot on the water.

A ship? No. Over time it didn't change its position.

Paul rumaged a bit and found Themi's binoculars. He peered through. It was an island, about a mile from shore.

He'd never noticed there was an island out on the sea. There never had been one when he'd lived at Ombre as a child. He pored over a recent map of the coast but could find no isle indicated on it.

Perhaps it was a glacier berg, an iceberg calved from a large glacier's margin. It might have drifted in during the night. He adjusted the glasses and was certain he could see something moving there.

Paul bundled up and hiked out to the beach with the binoculars. The temperature had dropped severely, sky and water gone to lead. The sea's surface looked greasy, as if a tanker had broken nearby and loosed oil everywhere. Wispy tendrils of frost smoke steamed from this, and he could have sworn the ocean was solidifying before his eyes. Frazil ice was forming.

He put his eyes to the lenses and stared. Perhaps the spots he'd seen were a herd of caribou that had become isolated on a floe, exiled from the mainland. Perhaps he should summon help. He thought about having to get to the lighthouse down the coast and actually speak to someone. He was dismayed to discover the idea seemed very hard, an impossibility. Even if it was just old Mr. Suinot. Paul was in retreat; he shouldn't even be trying to communicate with anyone. He was virtually a monkish hermit in a solitary rocky cloister. It was as if he'd taken a temporary vow of personal sequestering: the better to pray, to dive into his soul for cleansing.

He thought, that is the truly white and silent place.

The surface of the island swam into view. It wasn't an iceberg. Creeper vines like clear plastic tubing overran the ground. Moss shimmered in rime. Crystalline shapes mocking rubber and gum trees rose, spreading out forked quartz branches. Through these vitreous arms ran silvery monkeys and perched frost-riven parrots.

Astonished, Paul jerked away from the binoculars.

"Impossible," he murmured. He tried to force himself to smile. "I must have cabin fever."

But the grin only felt rictal in the bitter air. His teeth chattered. Again he looked through the lenses. That couldn't be a jaguar he spied, fangs sparkling with permafrost. It must be a seal. There were spotted varieties. And that couldn't be a tree sloth lumbering through the frozen brush. It had to be a polar bear.

And there were flowers everywhere. Well, if he'd look down, he'd see ice rosettes on the beach where he stood. They were a common northern structure, created out of salt and frozen water. They were made as pack ice first began to form, right after the sea has started to freeze. Delicate things, beautiful, they were the origami of Arctic wasteland.

Then Paul saw the native. She was walking slowly under the frigid trees. The woman was as white as if she'd been carved from alabaster, or frozen out of salt and tears. Behind it he waited to hear screams—even as far away as he was on shore. But there was no sound.

"God!" He cried out, icy air stabbing down his throat.

Paul grew suddenly dizzy until bright specks of color invaded his vision. He tucked the binoculars into his coat and hastily abandoned the beach.

Back at the house, he built a very large fire in the hearth. But the heat terrified him as it scorched across his face and hands, so he put it out again. He took some of the medication the doctors had given him, soothing stuff, the opium (derivitive) of manic comforts. When he built up the nerve to peek from the window, Paul couldn't see the island. Not that he expected to. The things on it were from a more tropical zone, nothing that could be this far north. Even if they had been visibly iceshockled and hoary.

During the night, he hugged the silence. He treasured it, because noise had been a part of his breakdown, whether it had been a real function of his trials in the rain forest or not. It had definitely been a part of the hideous tableau of an eight-year-old Paul watching his parents die. An evident overlay.

That he'd hallucinated the island and the native was obvious. He didn't understand why he didn't rant the whole thing in infectious technicolor.

In the morning he saw the island from the windows again, only about three quarters of a mile out this time. He looked through the binoculars. A cloud of white bats flapped over the treetops. A white python curled around an ophite branch hanging with pearly, sleetslick mangoes. There were people sitting on the ground, or perched on boulders bleak as giant hailstones, swinging their feet, their formerly brown complexions matte with glaciation.

The beautiful native was dancing. She shook the white mane of her hair, adorned with icicle orchids. She seductively undulated the ice-sharp bones of her pelvis, promising a promiscuity as devastating as any hot agent. And she was facing the sea, the beach, his house. Paul was positive she was looking right at him, through the eyepiece. Not so different from the way—as an intern—he'd sometimes gotten the eerie sensation that a virus he was studying under a microscope was staring back at him.

"What does she want?" he asked in a strangled gasp.

Nothing. What could she want when she was dead? What could any of them want? He did realize that every human and animal he could see was also facing him, every numbing-pale eye fixed and following him like the gaze in some portraits.

Paul fastened the shutters, closed the heavy drapes, took more medicine, cried himself to sleep. Maybe he shouldn't stay there any longer.

But where was he to go? He couldn't stand any of the hot places. They suffocated and nauseated him, made him feel the swell of every microbe, the calenture of a billion lethal strains of corruption. And if he now couldn't bear the cold . . . Why? Because the island of La Desconocida had somehow pursued him there? What had he done? He wasn't able to make them well but it wasn't his fault they'd gotten sick. It wasn't his fault they'd died.

Except he'd hidden instead of helping. He'd resolutely refused to accept the circumstances of their deaths. Maybe this hurt those who perished under such extreme conditions. Perhaps the fact that he took their suffering—changing into something so utterly different from what it had been—forged a link between them and him. Maybe they couldn't rest until they convinced him of the truth.

It was so quiet. Like a world packed in thick white styrofoam, soundproofed against dread. The surrounding cliffs of ice swallowed up all noise. A man might believe he'd gone deaf. There didn't even seem to be any wind.

Suddenly Paul wished he had someone to talk to. That the house had a phone after all. It was the isolation causing him to imagine things. Making him dwell on the outbreak and its aftermath, instead of being able to escape it. Or even to simply face up to the grim realities of the jungle island. His nightmares were still febrile with toxic color, ringing with the screams of the dying. He knew he'd taken the genuine incidence of his parents' terrible deaths and given the rain forest over to it. Green and blue, red and yellow.

***

Arctic Epilogue:

When Paul got out of bed again, he opened one shutter and looked out. It was night but he could see the island under the moonlight. It was now only about half a mile from the beach. He hadn't noticed before that it was volcanic, steaming like the frost smoke which rose from the solidifying sea. Although why shouldn't it be a volcano? The island where La Desconocida had been was a volcano.

And, well, there were many volcanos far north. Iceland, for example, had approximately 200 of them. But they didn't float freely like that. They didn't pursue people.

"It will be here soon," Paul muttered, then bit his lip until it bled.

He tasted the blood, savoring the sour-salt. What does blood which has been contaminated in the hot zone of a dream taste like?

He knew he must get away from the house. Even if the island wasn't really coming for him, he realized he needed human contact to ground him back to sanity. There was no reason he couldn't make it to his nearest neighbor at the lighthouse. Maybe Mr. Suinot would have a phone Paul could use to call for a way out.

He might be better off in a hospital for a while, where there were doctors, other patients, some noise but not too much. And where there were controlled temperatures.

Paul donned his heaviest gear, a fur-lined parka framing his face from several inches in front of it. He felt claustrophobic in weighty boots and thick gloves, as if he was again in a biohazard space suit. He left the house.

If he'd gone up by the road, he'd have seen less ice and more wet tundra, boggy polygons and stone circles which marked the descent into lowland archipelago. But that route was less direct than the beach—even if better ordered—and it turned a two mile trip to the lighthouse into seven.

Paul climbed down to the beach and began the trek to the lighthouse by following the shore. He would not look out to sea, refusing to spot the island if it had reappeared.

He accepted that he was deeply troubled. He didn't need sight of it to confirm this. Any more than a man with a misplaced guilt complex needed to see ghosts to know he was haunted. (No, he reminded himself. It wasn't because he was guilty of anything that they were showing themselves to him. It was because he still hadn't claimed as truth how they'd died. It was somehow too frightening, even more so than the effects of Ebola which visibly dismantled its host by bloody degrees.)

Paul tried not to see any of the area around him. Why had he come here? Its peacefulness was deceptive. The ice encased and trapped, slowing you down with numbness until you lost volition, making you cease to care that you'd stopped feeling. Like heat, it could burn and steam, but only ice indicted the world of its apathy.

He glanced up and saw a snowy owl sail over him, seeking food. Its beating wings made a hollow in the air, a negative of sound. Paul violently shook his head, trying to throw from it any suggestion of coldly creeping anesthetization.

"The victims of the plague didn't really freeze!" he shouted (to what, the owl?). "It was some weird process of dehydration and calcification we don't yet understand! Fauna secreted what would become their own carapaces! Flora became chalky!"

But the island loomed in his peripheral vision. He turned, only by millimeters, and saw it there. He'd brought the binoculars. He almost didn't need them. The island had floated closer, was no more than a quarter of a mile from shore.

Still—for details—he gazed through the eyepiece. Without the amplification, he wouldn't be able to see the native's face, wouldn't be able to count the icicle orchids in her hair.

She was there, dancing, hips swaying, delicate ice flower hands beckoning. There were many animals and other humans in evidence. But she was the only one moving, summoning him. Amid the gum and rubber trees were snow-glazed cedars, spines on branches glistening like millions of hypodermic needles. Behind the isle, the moon was rising over the sea, farther out where the ice was chunked instead of flat. Slivers of silver glow cascaded every which way, as if the moon was a stone thrown through a mirror. The native's movements were slow, similar to those of a victim of the virus as the excretions from the body gradually calcified—yet graceful. As if she was still in the village street, struggling in languor against the numbing shell overtaking her . . . even as she reached out to Paul, begging voicelessly for him to help.

Paul found he was crying. Tears froze on his cheeks, were sharp in his eyes. He was terrified but knew he must cross to her this time. The sea was solid enough it should support him that far out. He heard the snow scattered across the ice crunch as he stepped from the shore. Before him the island called, hushed, a tropical illusion rendered in hard milk.

He looked down at his boots moving across the frozen sea's surface. He could see things underneath, swimming like pale spirits in ether. There were monkeys, spotted jungle cats, a flotilla of bats like a school of fish, people. Spectral, tranquil as those who have fallen through holes in the ice seem to be after their desperate struggles have ceased . . . and their minds and limbs have numbed.

No, there were only two. Mellina, Speros. The green and blue boat had disappeared. The time hadn't been summer but a late autumn storm. The temperature had plunged severely and the surface of the sea had first smoked, then frozen before they could get back to shore. The boat had become trapped, sinking, taking the couple down with it.

Their eight-year-old son had come to the beach looking for them. He'd walked out a short distance onto the frozen water and seen them passing slowly beneath his feet, faces still, pale as if they'd been scrimshawed from walrus tusk. Whiter. No longer fighting to find a way out. Solid and dreaming. Very silent.

That was why Paul hadn't been able to accept what he'd seen at La Desconocida. The white, the hard sleep, the soundless passing into pale disaster. He had no conscious memory of his parents dying—not screaming on a flaming boat, but frozen before they could even drown. Yet the memory had been there anyway until he'd developed a horror of white and silence. It rendered him useless, unable to reach out and help anyone, as he'd been when he couldn't reach Mellina and Speros under the ice.

There had been no explosion for Mr. Suinot to see from the lighthouse. No one came to find the boy curled up on the shore. In a trance, he managed to get back to the house and then just sat there. Several days passed in which he became very weak, just sitting in front of a window which looked out across the cliff at the sea. If Themi hadn't come home, Paul would surely have starved to death.

"Paul! What's happened?" Themi had cried, looking for some spark in his little brother's frozen, empty eyes.

"Too much noise, too much color," the child replied hoarsely.

He'd then spent one year on a children's mental ward, drawing pictures on white paper with white crayon.

Now Paul remembered and his shoulders slumped. The villagers and the animals had still died in a terrible way. A countless number of them, when you added together the toll in humans and wildlife. His mother and father had felt nothing at the end, rendered insensible by the ice's anesthesia. Not such a dreadful death after all, compared to others.

He blinked, frozen crusts on his lashes clacking together. The two bodies beneath his feet had vanished. There was only moonlight there, shimmering in the whorls and striations of the arctic ice pack. Looking up, he saw the island, too, was gone.

The quiet was stolen by a loud crack. Paul saw the fissure beginning to split beneath his boots. But he didn't turn back.

OTHER PEOPLE

by Don Webb

It was a matter of architecture. The angles of Jack Williamson High School just happened to correspond with the figures of the ancient Litany of Ool Athag. Bill Crowder figured this out one day at lunch. It was not without interest to me.

No one ate lunch with Bill. There were two reasons for this. One, no one wanted to eat with Bill, and two, Bill didn't want to eat with anyone.

Bill was a toad, no perhaps a ghoul. Ghouls have very white skin from avoiding daylight, and a tendency to run to blubber because of overeating things of a not very wholesome nature. Bill's main passion was knowing very strange things.

It was because of his brother Randolph. Randolph was fourteen years older than Bill. You see, Bill's parents had come to the conclusion that the baby-avoiding procedures weren't needed anymore, and Bill showed up not long before Randolph was to head off for college. Randolph always brought his books home in the summer, and Bill read them.

Randolph had taken a course on the Occult in Literature, and that had been his brother's downfall. Bill's overly white nose had been drawn into the fearsome crevices of the eldritch and the forbidden like a mouse after a rather smelly cheese. So Bill, with the aid of Interlibrary Loan had tracked down everything he could find. If it were weird enough, Bill loved it, and the weirdest volume of occult lore, as any sorcerer worth his black candles knows, is the Typhonian Tablet, a wonder book oblate antiquity that had been translated by Wallis Budge in the late nineteenth century (and had been the root of a lot of strange goings on about that time). The book went through a couple of popular editions, (one of them winding up in the hands of a Whipple Phillips, whose grandson Mr. H.P. Lovecraft modeled his famous *Necromoncion* on it, but I digress),because of the book's vile reputation, it was suppressed, and almost forgotten until Bill Crowder happen not only to find out about it, but order a copy. It arrived in Albuquerque, from Doublesign, Texas and Bill quickly made a Xerox of this most horrid of horrid books. The book was almost a hundred years old, so it was bound to be powerful.

It was, Bill thought, quite cool. It was 1978, and while Bill's peers were watching Happy Days, or whatever it was that they did, Bill was trying out the spells and procedures.

Part of the book claimed to be quiet ancient, prehuman in fact. The later parts were stories collected long after the fall of Egypt to the Roman Empire with examples of successful magic use. One of the stories told how a magician named Harnuphis had been able to conjure a storm for Marcus Aurelius by invoking Thoth-Shou. The invocation was given.

Bill tried it out one cloudy afternoon and within an hour, one of the worst gully washers to ever grace Albuquerque rattled the windows and flooded the crossings.

Of course, most people would have thought that storms often come after clouds, but Bill was not most people, as I mentioned above.

The book lacked any spells to get laid, win the lottery, or cure acne. It had spells for getting dreams, stopping chariots, knowing the outcomes of battles, contacting gods of other dimensions, and a spell that could move entire buildings into other planes of existence.

Most of the spells required things like camel dung, or the dust of seven mummies and so forth, so Bill was somewhat limited as even the finest stores in Albuquerque lacked these items.

However, the spell to know the outcome of a battle only needed water and olive oil. You poured a little oil on the water and watched the patterns while facing east and commanding Re to provide you with a vision of the battle.

Bill purchased a bottle of extra-virgin olive oil and kept in his locker. He felt a great kinship with the oil as he had never even kissed a girl and it was his senior year.

Ralph McKenna gave him a chance to check it out.

Ralph had been beating up on the two Vietnamese boys, Nugen-something-or-other. They were little guys, good in math and French, barely spoke above a whisper. Most of the jocks gave them hell, but Ralph in particular seemed to hate them. He would push them into the girl's rest-room, or slam their head down if they had been foolish enough to use the drinking fountain. They usually just slunk away. But on the way to a pep rally, Ralph had tripped one of them and the guy had had his bells rung when he crashed into the wall. The other one had gone ape-shit and told Ralph that he was going to kill him. This of course was music to Ralph's ears, and he had arranged to meet the guy after-school behind the gym to "teach the little gook a lesson."

This is great, thought Bill. During lunch he slipped off to the A/V room with a saucer, a test-tube full of H_2O, and the oil. He invoked mighty Re in his barque, and looked at the oil.

At first it looked like oil on water. Was he supposed to kind of guess what was going on here?

But suddenly the patterns resolved into Ralph and the Vietnamese guy.

The Vietnamese guy was whipping the shit out of Ralph with some kind of kung fu! This was great. Ralph had beat Bill up through Junior High, and had there been a death spell in the Typhonian Tablet, it would have been Bill's first incantation.

It was too good to be true. Maybe it was literally too good to be true, maybe Bill was just fooling himself, projecting a daydream on the shifting patterns.

He poured out the oil and water and rejoined his fellows in the cafeteria.

Someone was talking about they wish they could bet on Ralph. They would bet a hundred dollars.

"Do you have a hundred dollars?" asked Bill.

"Well no. I've got sixty." Mark Swansen said.

"I'll bet you twenty against your sixty that Nugen wins," said Bill.

The bet was accepted and a girl was given the job of holding the money. Ralph passed Bill in the hall and told him that he had heard that Bill had bet against him. Ralph promised to smash Bill's face after the gook.

The battle was short and intense.

Ralph took a swing.

The little guy dodged under him, and then gave Ralph a roundhouse kick to Ralph's right flank. Ralph bellowed in pain, and then the little guy was all over him raining blows on his face and chest. He knocked Ralph to his knees, and a group of guys pulled the little one off of Ralph.

Some people cheered. Most were stunned. A lot of them would be seen apologizing to the two brothers in the weeks that followed.

The girl gave Bill the money.

Bill went by Ralph, who was lying on the ground moaning, and said, "Good thing I taught him how to fight."

This was Bill's proudest hour.

***

One of the shortest spells in the book was one that moved buildings from one dimension to another.

The spell was short, the only tough part was having abiding with certain internal angles that made it easy to slip from reality to another.

The irregular octagon that served as the dance hall, pep rally staging area, and main meeting place in the school just happened to have the required form.

All that would be needed were to have certain strips of papyri hung at certain corners and the matter would be easily taken care of.

Bill had been wanting to go to another dimension for quite some time. It was probably in the seventh grade when he had decided that was a good idea, that was certainly when he retreated into Science Fiction. Even if the world he went to was populated by three-eyed wombats with green leather skin, Bill felt that he would fit in better.

So he began to study the Litany of Ool Athag.

***

In the furthest of the reaches of the dream lands that surround and support Earth, as the Nile does support a ship, is the city of Ool Athag, and in that city was a theater called the Heart's Desire, and there was performed a comedy every fourteen years that showed the crowd their heart's desire. So wonderful were the images of this play, that audiences would never be seen to leave the theater, and the power of its dreams was said to be so great that eventually the kings rose up and burned the theater to the ground. Others say the human kings burnt the theatre because of the sensibility of Sothis-Ka, the mad playwright, but that such actions have little effect on such as he. But the plays of Sothis-Ka were so powerful, that they continue to be performed on other worlds, as foolish creatures rebuild the theatre again and again. Because of resonance such buildings (if hung with the aphorisms of Sothis-Ka and having the right words said in them) can be made to slip into a space where the heart's desire will be seen. Find a building that has been shaped after the theater of OolAthag, write the aphorisms and say the words of transport. These are the words of transport, "R'lnytha naratarr k'n'ynthaningg Ool Athag naatar."

These are the aphorism of Sothis-Ka:

What is a lie, but a mistimed event?
What is truth, but a falsehood incompletely understood?
What is time, that she purrs when she is unfed?
Who dreams of yesterdays' dreamer dreaming of tomorrow without dreaming of being himself dreamed?

***

Bill's first attempt to move the school consisted of writing these gnomic utterances on strips of adding machine paper and breaking into the school on night. The "break in" aspect of the job was easy, the doors were unlocked so the custodian could to his job.

The custodian also busted Bill. Bill talked him into believing that Bill was decorating for an upcoming event, some University Interscholastic Thing-ma-jig.

Custodian Bob said that the approval to hang banners must come form the principal.

The next week a committee was formed to decorate forth Senior Prom. Everyone was surprised when Bill volunteered for it.

He hated the planning for this thing. He hated the debates about themes, kings and queens, refreshments, chaperons, the door policy. But he really wanted to be the one that hung the crepe paper from corner to corner of the room.

It was tougher than he thought it would be. All he knew about the clique system of high school was that he wasn't a part. He was unprepared for the intense political rivalry that prom themes brought out.

Fortunately he did have the divination spell of Re-in-his-barque, so he knew which side would win the battles and was correctly aligned.

But each miserable day of listening to them whine on and on, made his desire to get to another world stronger and stronger. He was tired of Suzy's idea for a Fifties night, Mark's hope for a Pajama party, Gerald's suggestion of a parish priest as chaperon. There was a heated debate over Angle Dust, the band that Sarah knew, versus Morag Fairchild, the DJ who was related to Mark.

All of them were idiots.

The Fifties Night won. As he had foreseen.

It was about this time that he realized that he would have to go to the prom.

Now this had not been his original idea. He was either going to have a few minutes alone with the decorations so that he could utter the spell, before the prom started, or a few minutes alone afterward.

Afterward wouldn't work, because some members of the committee had to start taking the decorations down as soon as the prom was over.

Before wouldn't work either, as there would be people coming and going and putting things up and taking them down almost till the moment of the dance. He didn't want to think about what might happen if the spell were said, and the chamber not correctly decorated.

So he rented a tuxedo. The only tuxedo in town for a chubby little fellow like him was a powder blue number with a dark blue trim.

He thought about asking some girl, but he couldn't think of anyone as pathetic as he was, so he announced that he was "going stag."

A few girls expressed sympathy for him, but the idea of going with him caused most of them shudders of a terrible sort.

He realized that when he uttered the spell, all the school and all the idiots would go along with him to the other dimension, but he figured that was their problem. Let them cope with a world they weren't meant for. He had done so for eighteen years, and it was high time that they have the goddamn chance to see what it was all about.

Every day as all the little indignities of High School life added up, from being thrown into his locker, to having to eat the miserable food at the cafeteria, to having to walk to school while most kids drove— Bill got more and more cheerful. They would pay. All of them. As they should.

The final afternoon Bill hung the green and gold crepe paper banners that had the aphorisms of Sothis-Ka written upon them in magic marker. He helped set up the DJ's area, he helped carry in the cutout cars and the Henry Winkler figure. He smiled and laughed and joked with the people he despised.

They thought he had finally come out of his shell.

He went home and put on the stiff and scratchy blue tuxedo, and his mom drove him to the school and he walked up the front door along with many couples that looked far better than he ever could. He looked at some of the girls in their décolleté, and decided that he might need a consort in the dreamlands, someone who would value his knowledge of the appropriate cantrip to drive away a Kanree, or the way to find food in the Mountains Who Sing. He would not only have his vengeance, he would be king.

Someone had taken down one of the banners.

He ran across the room and taped it up again.

The principal tapped him on the shoulder.

"You've done so much work, Bill, I had no idea you had such school spirit."

Everyone looked at him. Even when you are about to be king of the world you don't want people to hear the school principal complementing you.

The principal was closing the doors of the school. They would stay locked until the end of the prom. There had been a problem the year before of students sneaking out and smoking dope during the prom.

Bill was going to walk to the center of the room and say the words, but he decided to wait, to luxuriate in his victory.

The DJ played the first few numbers, and Bill made his way with the other losers to the punch.

He scanned the room.

Yet another crepe paper strip had fallen.

Some people were playing with it. He ran across the room, knocking into several dancers, to get the crepe paper away from the guy who was tossing it in the air.

Everyone was looking at him.

Well, let them look. It would be over very soon.

He had to get a chair to tape the paper back up. He climbed up, stretched and taped the aphorism back in place. As he got off the chair, he ripped his pants.

Everyone was looking. Some people laughed.

He said the words, "R'lnytha naratarr k'n'yn thaningg Ool Athag naatar."

Nothing happened.

Suzy asked if he was feeling OK.

The DJ was announcing another song.

That was it.

Volume.

He pushed his way through the crowd, through the happy couples, smiling their idiot ecstasies, and went up to the DJ.

"What can I do you for, man?" asked the DJ.

Bill grabbed the mike, and as loud as he could said, "R'lnytha naratarr k'n'yn thaningg Ool Athag naatar."

The volume almost blew out the speakers. Everyone covered their ears and were yelling at Bill. Nothing had happened. It had all been a joke, some trick played on people a hundred years ago.

By the time Bill reached the foyer his face was covered in tears, and in the foyer he found two things that surprised him.

The first shouldn't. It was that the doors were locked.

The second was me. I looked fairly human.

Bill started to pummel me. "You. You're the one."

He then said some amusing things about my ancestry and mating habits while he cried. He cried for a long time, but no one came out to comfort him or confront me. They were enjoying the prom.

Bill was setting on the floor when he grew calm enough to talk.

"This is unfair. This is not what I tried to do," he said.

"I don't know about unfair. I've never read the book you used, I've never even been to the world you come from."

"The theater is supposed to show people their heart's desires," he said.

I said, "They all look happy to me. That's what the theater shows, it is our big draw."

"But what about me?"

"You are not the audience. You just build the sets, just as I write the plays." I said, "That was my crime, I wrote plays that made people perfectly happy. You could have asked each one of them what they wanted, and they would have told you, that they wanted this night to never end. They don't want to grow up, work, and struggle. So they have the play of Sothis-Ka. They will dance and romance forever, their little world is sealed. Look out the windows."

Bill did so, and realized that indeed the school was on a different world.

He ran back into the prom and tried to get people to look out the windows, but they just laughed at him, so he tried to point out that it was five minutes to eight and that it had been five minutes to eight for a long time. They laughed at him. Some made fun of torn pants, some wanted to know what that weird shit was he yelled into the microphone. But mainly they wanted to dance, to hold their dates close, to laugh and drink punch and listen to the music. They wanted the night to never end.

After awhile Bill came back and asked me if the show ever ends.

"None of my plays end, Bill. That's why they burned the theater to the ground."

"Did you write this, with me and everything?"

"No, not exactly with you. I don't write with ink. I write with longing and hatred and pettiness. I mainly write with wishes and wants. That's what moves people to where they want to be."

"But I don't want to be here."

"That's what makes it a comedy, Bill. In your world do you not have the notions of heaven and hell? Well here it will always be five minutes to eight, you will always be wearing torn pants in a cheap rented suit, you will be surrounded by people that pay no attention to you. But the audience is happy, Bill, look at them. They are happy. They are in heaven. I have created another hit."

"You and I are just going to stand here and watch them dance for all of time?" asked Bill.

"No, I am going to start work on my next comedy. My own unhappiness, my own hell if you will, is that I never have a moment like them. You'll remain and watch. You were the one who wanted to be in another dimension. Well you've got your wish."

"What did you call this play?" asked Bill.

"I called it Hell is Other People. Your plight will provide me a great deal of amusement."

I turned from Bill and walked into a direction that he could not see, being as he was wholly human.

And without paper, nor pen nor anything man would understand as a writing instrument, I began writing my next play for the Theater of Ool Athag.

VEGGIE MOUNTAIN

by Thomas S. Roche

On the outskirts of the mid-sized city of San Esteban at the intersection of Northern California's Napa and Sonoma Valleys lie the Southernmost estates of the Monteverdi family. Certainly these estates are only the physical manifestation of a much greater empire, for any dedicated wine drinker from Berkeley to Beijing would instantly recognize the name Monteverdi.

It should perhaps be no coincidence that at the edge of that famous empire lie the grounds of the Monteverdi Institute, a series of research and treatment facilities for the mentally ill, and that on the Southern border of the Monteverdi Institute grounds is the Monteverdi Institute Lockdown Facility—known more colloquially as Mount Murder, for the Facility was established to incarcerate and study only the most violent cases of mental illness. Despite its somewhat gloomy location— the Lockdown Facility overlooks the Monteverdi Cemetery, the largest final resting place in Northern California—the Facility is today considered the premier institution for postdoctoral fellows doing work on the violently insane, and a place where those dangerous inmates can receive the best possible care.

But it *is* coincidence that it was the eldest Monteverdi who founded the Institute—pure coincidence—for the Facility was opened *prior* to the scandal that all but ruined the Monteverdi family. That Old Man Monteverdi, only three years after opening the Facility, saw his own brother and, later, his son, incarcerated there before taking his own life—that is a matter of consternation to tourists, certainly, but a mere footnote in California history, and of only passing amusement to those who use the Monteverdi Institute Lockdown Facility today, both as inmates and employees. Fate has its way of playing tricks on us.

The hall lights in the Monteverdi Facility are on. They're always on.

Martin Warren makes his rounds, peering through the tiny, reinforced window in each steel-plated door, noting each room found occupied on a clipboard he carries with him. Warren's institutional whites are cleaner than they look—the dirt and stains are but the intractable detritus of his two years at the Institute. He's not much of a housekeeper; he skimps on bleach and washes his whites on cold to save on the gas bill.

Warren performs his rounds without much interest. He's eager to get back to the poker game in the staff room, and not once in his two years at Monteverdi has there been a serious attempt at escape from the Lockdown Facility. Warren yawns as he makes notes on his clipboard.

He pauses outside cell 915, reading the name on the clipboard several times over. Can it be? No, it's impossible.

Warren puts his face right up against the reinforced window, tries to glimpse the face of the inmate. But Charles Quinn is sound asleep, his face buried in his pillow.

Warren goes downstairs.

"We almost started the hand without you, slowpoke," jabs Trev Altman as Warren enters the staff room.

"One buck ante too rich for your blood?" asks Ramon Gutierrez, shuffling the cards.

"Hey, anything's too rich for Marty's blood," says Stevens, riffling through a stack of crisp $1 bills he's brought especially for tonight. "But you'll cough up, won't you? Martyboy can't bear to be left out of a poker game."

Marty Warren takes his place at the poker table. His plastic chair's still warm.

"That new loonie up on nine," says Warren. "Charles Quinn."

"Oh, Marty wasn't here for the big show," laughs Trev Altman. "The big serial killer, comin' in all peaceful. Pretty yawnsville."

"That's *him*."

"Correctomundo." Trev picks his teeth as Gutierrez deals the cards. He was a blackjack dealer in Tahoe for ten years; each card sails effortlessly into position in front of the players.

"*The* Charles Quinn."

"Right."

"The fucking homo serial killer."

"What part of 'yes' don't you understand, motherfucker? Didn't you know he was being transferred here?"

Warren shakes his head.

Gutierrez: "And in case you didn't know, Marty, serial killers prefer to be called *gay*."

The table erupts in laughter.

"No, I didn't know he was coming here. That's fucking disturbing."

Trev: "We've got a guy on six who filleted his wife, Marty. Ate her with a side of mustard greens. A girl on four beat her mother to death with a plastic lightsaber. Why is it any more disturbing than either of those, or any of the other half a zillion fuckin' nut cases we got bending the bedsprings at this dive?"

"Because he's a fuckin' homo."

"Hey, Trevelian on seven's a homo. He sucked alien cock, at least he thinks he did."

More laughter around the table. "You got jacks or better, motherfucker, or has serial murder somehow become more important than a good game of poker?" Laughter.

Warren hasn't even looked at his cards. He picks them up, leafs through them. "No good."

"I've got 'em. Three bucks," says Stevens.

Everybody tosses their cash into the bedpan in the middle of the table.

"Besides," says Stevens. "The guy's not technically a serial murderer. I guess you'd call him a mass murderer, but he ain't very mass."

"What the fuck do you mean," snaps Warren, "he's *not* a mass murderer?"

"Hey, lighten up, motherfucker! He's just *not*."

"How is he not a mass murderer?"

"He only killed two people, dumbfuck. The ambulance driver and the EMT."

"Yeah, but he fuckin' ate them."

"Oh, come on, he barely ate them at all. Just their dicks and part of their faces."

"That sounds like a mass murderer to me."

Stevens snorts in disgust. Gutierrez and Altman laugh hysterically.

"I'm afraid our diminutive friend is correct," says Altman. Stevens shoots him a dirty look; he's incredibly sensitive to any comment about his height. "Charles Quinn does not qualify as a mass murderer. Two victims does not a slaughter make."

"Marty! Marty!" It's Gutierrez, screaming at the top of his lungs.

Warren jumps, looks at Gutierrez blankly.

"Do you want any fucking cards?" shouts Gutierrez.

"Oh," says Warren. "Fuck. You scared the fucking shit out of me. Don't shout like that."

Stevens: "Yeah, Ramon, don't you know you're not supposed to scream in an asylum unless you're tryin' to eat someone?"

"In more ways than one," chortles Altman, and makes a mock-felatio gesture with his hand around his mouth and his head bobbing up and down while his tongue jabbed his cheek.

"Hah! Now that you mention it, I am gettin' kinda hungry—hey Warren, you mind if I nibble on your earlobe a little?"

"Don't even fuckin' joke about that shit," snaps Warren. "That's fuckin' disgusting. I'll take four."

"Jesus, Marty, you just want me to deal you another hand?"

"Just give me the fucking cards."

A round of betting goes by in silence, dollars piling up in the bedpan. Marty stares at his cards, unseeing, and grinds his teeth.

"Why is he here? Shouldn't that bastard be at a prison facility? Full security, guards with real guns and shit?"

"Jesus, Warren, what's with you? The sonofabitch was found not guilty by reason of insanity. He hasn't committed a single bit of violence in five years. Takes his meds on time, goes to therapy and talks about his best friends the corpses who love him and want to have sex with him." Altman giggles. Gutierrez and Stevens just smile.

Warren fumes, his lips pursed tight. Warren's a big guy, well-suited for working in the Facility. Well over six feet, about two-fifty. Good with his hands.

"You've got to admit, it's a fucking disturbing case."

Altman, grinning: "I've got to admit that *you* think it's fucking disturbing for some reason." He's known Warren the longest. He's worked the night shift the entire two years that Warren has. He knows how to annoy him.

Warren stares at Altman accusingly. "And you don't, motherfucker?"

"Hey, I do, motherfucker. Some underaged prevert eats a couple of paramedics, swallows their dicks, eats their faces—yeah, okay, I'll be the first to admit that's a little disturbing. But you seem to be obsessing over it."

"You've got to fucking kidding me. I am not obsessing."

"Sure you are. You read every article published on the case when it happened."

Warren stares like a trapped rabbit; his face twists in anger. "So I'm fascinated by fucked-up shit. You telling me you're not?"

"Oh, I just think it gets old after five years of working at Monteverdi. Guys eating other guys genitals . . . blah blah blah. Give me some lesbian pro-wrestling serial killers—that'll get my motor going."

"You think it's all right what he did?"

"Hey! Hey! Hey!" Gutierrez. "Are you going to fucking bet, or are you just going to argue all night?"

"I'll call," says Warren. "Pair of kings."

Altman laughs hysterically.

"Full house, cocksucker. Read 'em and weep."

Warren looks like he's about to hit Altman in the face, but he just yells and smacks the table instead. The bedpan jumps as if at a gunshot, and dollar bills scatter everywhere. Altman, Gutierrez, and Stevens look at Warren and laugh. Warren just shakes his head slowly back and forth, his face the color of blood.

***

"Fucking disgusting, a guy like this," mutters Warren, staring through the tiny window at the sleeping Quinn. It's three hours later, the poker game long since ended with Warren forty-three dollars down. Altman's the big winner, a hundred-something ahead. Son of a bitch just has to be cheating, Warren knows it.

"Motherfucking faggot. Sucking dead dick," mutters Warren, staring. "How could someone do that? Absolutely fucking disgusting."

Five years ago: Charlie Quinn was nineteen or twenty years old, working as a night-shift security guard at the Guerneville morgue, taking delivery of stiffs, watching horror flicks on late-night TV. Easy job, right? Easy as pie. Well, it turns out this sick motherfucker was screwing the bodies—and not the chick corpses—that, Warren could understand. He wouldn't think it was OK, mind you, but if you gotta fuck a body Warren could sure understand wanting to do some chick, right? Especially a young one, kinda sexy. Anyway, this ambulance driver and this EMT—Sanders and Coltrane, their names were—seems they walked in on Charles Quinn doing his thing. Quinn went berserk. Little weasely kid, maybe 125 pounds, but he managed to kill both Sanders and Coltrane without sustaining any injuries to himself. He did it with his bare hands. Then—and here's were it got *really* disturbing—he started doing it. Warren shudders every time he thinks about that sicko's teeth digging in to dead flesh. What the hell could be a bigger perversion against God and man and everyfuckingbody?

But it didn't stop there. That was just where it got *really* weird. Seems when Charles Quinn had finished his meal—and things got a little hazy here, since Quinn was obviously either lying or hallucinating, probably both—he must have stumbled to the john and puked it up, flushed it. They couldn't find any human tissue when they pumped his stomach, so that was the only explanation anyone could figure out. Then after Quinn's done with his little purge, he pops open all the coolers, and starts dragging out bodies. Men, women—old, young. Buries himself, and the two ambulance jockeys, too. Just lays there with the chilled corpses getting room-temperature on top of him for the next three hours until the morning shift comes in. They found him sobbing, curled up naked with the half-eaten EMT underneath him and the ambulance driver on top.

And what did Charles Quinn claim happened?

"The bodies did it, your honor. They came alive, and . . . and . . . crawled out of the drawers . . . "

Warren unclips his keychain, turns the lock, opens the door to 915—slowly.

***

"Where's Marty?" Stevens has his feet up on the desk. He's reading *Hustler*.

"Three-o'clock rounds," says Altman, crashed out on the couch reading a Stephen King novel. Gutierrez is snoring loudly across the room. "He likes to take his time."

"Don't even joke about that shit," giggles Stevens. "That's disgusting."

Altman shrugs.

***

Warren hopes none of the others will notice he's killed the alarms; he figures even if they do, they'll cover for him. Besides, the alarm'll be back on in fifteen minutes, when Warren finishes what he's going to do to that sick little bastard.

The mammoth guard has serial killer Charles Quinn restrained to the bed by his wrists by the time the little fuck wakes up. He starts to yell, but Warren sits down on his legs and gets Quinn's ankles strapped in while Quinn demands, then begs to know what's going on.

"I haven't done anything, I haven't done anything," he keeps saying, his voice hoarse with sleep.

Warren stands up, whips the remaining covers off of Quinn's body, and looks down at him, one key jutting between his fingers like a short knife. He reaches into his back pocket, brings out his other hand. It holds a black plastic stun gun—250,000 volts.

Warren stares down at Quinn, his face twisted in disgust. Quinn looks up at him, quaking. Warren smiles—a gesture so wrong on his face that it makes him look like some kind of clown from a child's nightmare—from Charles Quinn's nightmare.

"Oh yes you have," growls Warren, his voice inhuman. "You sick faggot."

Charles Quinn takes a deep breath and screams at the top of his lungs.

***

"What's that noise?" asks Altman.

Stevens shrugs, his attention buried in a motor-oil-drenched full-color threesome. "Alarm didn't go off."

Altman puts down his book, gets up, walks into the other room. He comes back a minute later, shaking his head angrily.

"That son of a bitch," says Altman. "Warren turned off the alarm. He shouldn't be able to do that without all three keys."

Stevens doesn't look up from his porn mag. "Well, then, how'd he do it if you and Ramon still have yours?"

Altman feels in his pocket. "Oh, fuck," he says. "Son of a bitch must have taken them when I was in the can. Hey, Ramon!"

Gutierrez wakes up with a start, looks around nervously, closes his eyes again.

"You got your alarm key?"

"Huh?"

"I said, do you have your fucking alarm key?"

"It's hanging in my locker."

"You don't even *lock* your locker, Ramon. You're supposed to have the key on your person at all times."

"Who gives a fuck?" says Gutierrez, and goes back to sleep.

Altman goes into the locker room. Stevens can hear him cursing. Altman comes back in.

"All right, all right. I'll go up and get him. Son of a bitch is probably paying a visit to that Charles Quinn guy right now. I knew he was up to something. I'm going to get him for this. I'll be back in a minute."

"Yeah, whatever," says Stevens.

***

Charlie Quinn still hasn't stopped screaming. Warren's stun gun flashes again.

"You like dick, motherfucker? You like to suck dick? Suck this!"

Charlie Quinn gags, tries to scream, can't. Outside, somewhere, he can hear sobs. He starts to curse, deep inside.

"Yeah, you fuckin' cocksucker. You like this, don't you?"

Marty Warren laughs.

***

Stevens jumps like a jackrabbit when he hears the pounding on the steel-reinforced door. Gutierrez jerks once, sits up, then lays back down, closes his eyes.

"What the fuck was that?" asks Stevens, grabbing his Maglite and going over to the door.

The pounding comes again, and Stevens screams and jumps back, watching as cracks appear in the door jamb on either side of the door.

"That's fucking impossible," he says to himself. What was it Altman told him, once? *You could drive a Mack truck into that door at fifty miles an hour, and it'd hold.*

Stevens tells himself this can't be happening. He tells himself this can't be happening. He's still telling himself that when the door explodes off its hinges.

***

"Marty! What the fuck do you think you're doing?"

Warren laughs. "I'm teaching this little pervert something about the wrath of God, motherfucker. I will repay, sayeth the Lord. Ain't that right, Charlie?"

Charlie gurgles.

"Marty, don't do this to me! You know I'm technically night-shift supervisor! I could get up to my ears in shit for this, pal. Get out here!"

"Soon as I'm finished."

Altman stalks into the room, his face red with fury. "Don't pull this shit, Marty! You and me'll both be in a hell of a lot of trouble for this, you son of a bitch! Lay off!"

"What's the matter, you want a piece?"

Something in Altman cracks, and he starts for Warren, his fists balled. "Yeah, I want a piece, motherfucker!"

Charlie Quinn begins to sob as Warren's bulk lifts off of him. "No," he says. "Not again . . ."

***

Gutierrez is still waking up. He looks all around—figuring he's dreaming.

He feels the cold tile under his sock-clad feet. He feels the air-conditioned air. He's not dreaming.

He has to be dreaming.

Ten feet from him lies the shattered body of Stevens, the jellied limbs bent in ways they shouldn't be. The steel door has been lifted off his body; it's leaned up against the wall, on its front a distorted imprint of Stevens' body—in blood.

Three men in suits crowd around Stevens, their faces powdered with makeup, their ancient flesh drawn taut over bone. Their flesh crawls—no, *seethes*. Their jaws work as they crouch and crawl over Stevens' ruined corpse, one of them clawing at his face and taking a mouthful.

Other men and women are approaching Gutierrez—all of them well dressed, powdered with pancake makeup and blush. Many old, a few young. A dozen of them, two dozen. More crowding through the open doorway. Three dozen.

One of the men on Stevens gets a flap of the boy's cheek between his eagerly-working teeth. He bites, rips flesh. A spray of blood erupts over the old man's face. Stevens' body spasms in convulsion—and a pathetic moan escapes the boy's lips.

Gutierrez's eyes go wide. Stevens is still alive.

Another old man digs his teeth into Stevens' arm.

"Hail Mary," says Gutierrez as the walking corpses advance on him. "Full of grace . . . the Lord is with thee . . . "

Then he, too, screams, as he feels the teeth—and he goes down in a shudder of fear and agony.

***

Altman is not a small man, but Warren still has fifty pounds on the guy. Of course, Warren has his pants around his ankles, but that barely hinders him as he shoves his fist into Altman's groin, pushes the guy off of him, and dives on top of Altman.

He's got his hands locked around Altman's throat, and Altman's trying desperately to scream for him to stop. But he can't get air into his lungs. And to his dismay, Warren's laughing.

"You want to stick up for the little faggot, eh? You want to stick up for the faggot? Maybe you're a fuckin' faggot, too! All you goddamn queers stick together—"

Altman's vision goes dim, and he tells himself over and over again that this can't be happening, this has to be a bad dream. Warren can't have cracked, not like this—not tonight, not ever.

His ears ring, loud; all he can hear is the sound of Charles Quinn's weeping. "No, no, no, no," the kid moans. "Please God, don't let it happen again—"

Then the grip on Altman's throat disappears, and the weight of Warren on his body vanishes as someone hauls him off. Altman is too far gone to scream, but somebody does, and it's not Charlie Quinn.

Altman's not sure at what point he blacks out, but what he sees next simply has to be an anoxia-induced hallucination. It just has to be. It fucking has to be.

***

Trev Altman can see dawn through the barred window as he comes to his senses. His throat feels like its been cut. He massages it, takes a few experimental deep breaths, feels his lungs burning. It feels like there's sandpaper inside his body.

He sits up, looks around the wrecked room.

Charles Quinn is gone, the restraint rent—not as if by a knife, but as if ripped apart by brute force. And Marty Warren lies in the place once occupied by Charles Quinn. It takes a good five minutes of staring in disbelief at what has happened to the body of Marty Warren before Altman feels his stomach clenching, his midnight lunch coming up.

***

Altman stumbles numbly through the corridors, making his way to the elevator. He goes back down to the first floor, walks into the staff lounge, already knowing what he's going to find.

"Oh, Jesus, Jesus."

Gutierrez and Stevens sprawl ruined amid the wreckage—the smashed tables, the clawed-open sofa. And Charles Quinn is nowhere to be seen. The steel door to the outside world leans up against the wall, the blood-pressed imprint of a human face and body coagulated upon it.

There in the door stands Judy Breckenridge, the morning supervisor. Her face is white as a sheet.

"Trev . . . what the hell happened?"

Trev chooses that moment to faint, falling unceremoniously across Stevens' shattered body. Judy rushes to grab him.

***

Even if they didn't put him on administrative leave pending review of his actions on the night in question, Trev Altman never would be able to go back to the Facility. He will doubtless eventually end up as far away as San Esteban as he can possibly be, and will try—unsuccessfully, of course—to scourge the incident from his mind.

But for the first seven years, they'll keep him in Monteverdi North. Where Trev Altman sits, and stares. And occasionally screams.

***

On the outskirts of the mid-sized city of San Esteban at the intersection of Northern California's Napa and Sonoma Valley lie the estates of the Monteverdi family. On the edge of those estates is the Monteverdi Institute, that famous series of research and treatment facilities for the mentally ill founded by the patriarch of California's most famous wine-growing family. At the northernmost extension of the Monteverdi Institute's ground lies Monteverdi North, where only those most non-violent of patients are taken for long-term treatment, care, and study when they show not the slightest possibility of clinical recovery. The poor prognosis for residents of Monteverdi North has led that facility to be called, in the jocular slang of Institute employees, Vegetable Mountain. Or sometimes just "Veggie Mountain."

That there should be, incarcerated in deep in the bowels of Monteverdi North, a former attendant from the Monteverdi Institute's Lockdown Facility, where a famous mass murderer further solidified his legendary contribution to the annals of American violence by committing an atrocity so horrible as to render his previous crimes a mere prelude—and then vanishing without a trace—is perhaps the cruelest and grimmest of ironies. For if the keepers of the madhouses become, through their experiences, mad, then who is to draw the line between keeper and keepee?

Most of the time, Trev Altman stares blankly at the wall. He has to be fed, and changed. Sometimes doctors talk to him. Most of the time, they leave him be—since in the years since the incident at Mount Murder, he has not once uttered a single coherent sentence.

Sometimes he makes noise, though.

They turn out the lights sometimes at Monteverdi North. Trev Altman screams at the top of his lungs when they do that.

TOMORROW EYES

by Peter Crowther

One

I was down in Miami to persuade a saw-faced dentist from Iowa City that it did not do to take a vacation when you still owed seventeen grand to Cuddles Ken Calhoun, who is not in any way cuddlesome despite a considerable frame which tops the scales at almost 400 pounds.

According to a pimply hotel clerk with a cow-lick and a tendency to put a query at the end of every sentence, the dentist was currently away from his room. I tell the clerk I will wait and he suggests I wait in the bar. He will send the party to me when he returns, he says. I say I will do this and thank him for his time. He tells me I am welcome.

I tell the clerk his efficiency and matter-of-fact politeness are to be commended, and he thanks me. I tell *him* that *he* is welcome.

Walking through the lobby in the direction of the bar, I am feeling magnanimous. Everything is right with the world.

I have already spoken with the dentist on the telephone and he does not take too much convincing that a substantial part payment of his outstanding debt and a trip to New York City to make amends with Cuddles will be more advantageous to his long-term health prospects than the Florida sunshine. He agrees to give me a partial six thou when he sees me. Then he agrees he will board a train back to New York and I will spend the next couple of days doing nothing but watch the world drift by.

Now, I am not wanting that anyone should infer from this that I am in any way reluctant to return to NYC myself, but simply that it pays to take a rest now and again, whatever your line of work. And I am particularly tired and in need of rest.

I have spoken with Cuddles the previous evening by telephone, informing him that the dentist from Iowa City proposes to hand over six thou in folding, which stash I will commit to safety in a leather pouch about my midriff. Furthermore, I tell Cuddles, I will bring said folding with me in two or three days but, meanwhile, he can meet the dentist at Grand Central the following day. I have no doubt that the tooth-man will be true to his word because I outline the possible scenario resulting from his not delivering the merchandise. What I have *not* told him is that Cuddles has intimated anyways the possibility of his writing off both the outstanding debt *and* the dentist somewhere around South Carolina. Cuddles is by no means a happy man about the situation, he tells me, and he feels that continuing problems on the account are likely.

There comes a time in any business dealing when the expediency of cutting one's losses works wonders for indigestion, and Cuddles, whose propensity for both wind and acid are legendary, is now of a mind, he tells me, that he feels such time has more or less come for the dentist from Iowa City. Being as how it is everyone to his own, I decline Cuddles' indisputably generous offer to draw a permanent line under this particular account if it comes to it, and he tells me that this is fine enough and that, in such an event, he will offer the project to a gentleman from Jersey called, variously, Peppermint Sam and Sweet-Tooth Sam on account of how he enjoys sucking on mint candies. I have long ago ceased worrying about things the outcome of which I cannot influence.

"Am I assured that the six gees will be safe until such time as we meet again?" Cuddles Ken Calhoun's rasping voice asks me over the telephone.

"You are assured," I assure him.

But, of course, I have not made allowances for Arnold Schweison.

Two

The last time I saw Arnold Schweison was in a casino in Dallas, sitting at a green-baize-topped table flicking pasteboards to a group of Sunday would-be gamblers trying either to turn a dollar into five or to regain the dollar they had just lost. Although I, like any man, have an occasional dream wherein I have enough folding not to have to drive up and down the country persuading errant dentists from Iowa City to honor their commitments to the likes of Cuddles Ken Calhoun, I have never been tempted to gamble. Not even so much as a lottery ticket. I have seen what it can do to a man.

I have an open admiration, however, for those with a highly developed skill with the pasteboards, though it remains a source of singular confusion that the amateur cannot seem to equate that skill with the professional's subversive art of ensuring that he rarely loses. And *never* in the long term. But the world is divided into sheep and shepherds and, on the sidelines, predatory animals such as Cuddles Ken Calhoun. And, maybe, even people like me.

In Dallas, Arnold Schweison had been his usual self, if a little older than the previous time I had seen him, which was in Cedar Rapids maybe eight years earlier, his sideburns peppered with gray and his thick mustache almost white. Here, in a two-bit hotel bar in Miami, he looked like his own father or grandfather, hair unkempt and straggly, his black jacket stained and creased, and his neckerchief greasy-looking and limply tied.

He was sitting alone at a small side table, a bottle and a shot-glass to one side, staring at a pack of playing cards face down in front of him between his hands, which were spread-eagled on the ring-marked baize top. Nobody seemed to be paying him any notice and, even stranger, Arnold appeared to be making no attempt to entice anyone in the bar to join him in a hand or two, the means whereby he had always made his living, and a handsome one at that.

Thinking I was perhaps mistaken, I sidled over for a closer look, at which point Arnold—for it was indeed he—looked up from the neat pile of pasteboards and stared right at me, though at first he seemed not to recognize me. This is when I see the two tell-tale trickles of moisture on his cheeks.

"Arnold?" I say to him. "Arnold Schweison?"

The eyes focus, and he frowns for a moment, and then a look of hazy recognition flickers. "That you, Bones?" he asks me. "Is it really you?"

I assure him that it is me, pull out a chair across from him and plonk myself at the table. After a minute or two of saying nothing, during which time Arnold wipes his cheeks with a grease- and oil-stained handkerchief, I decide to get the conversation moving.

"You are clearly unwell, Arnold," I say. "Is it a sickness of some kind? Is it family troubles?" I ask him, though I do not recall ever hearing of any family to speak of.

Arnold shakes his head so emphatically that, for a second, I think he may dislocate his neck, but he does not provide an alternative explanation for his condition.

"Is it some kind of trouble, then, that you are in?" I ask him.

Another shake and this time he accompanies it with a sigh of such profound sadness and not inconsiderable volume that I look around and give a small smile of assurance to a group of men standing at the bar watching us. As I am about to explain to them the common courtesy of allowing people to converse without an unwelcome audience, Arnold says, "It's a long story, Bones." And then he proceeds to tell it to me.

Three

"It started in Frisco," Arnold begins. "I was out west for a while," he says, "playing the barrooms around the Bay. There were a lot of good pickings to be had there and business was good.

"I am planning to move up to Washington State, maybe even go over the border for a while, when this group of Chinamen comes into the drum I am working. They are loaded up with moolauw and earnestly seeking some action."

At this point, he lowers his head and shakes it slowly, and I can hear him muttering to himself something about Why? Why? Why? I wait a minute and he looks up at me, gives out a weak smile and pours himself a generous shot from the bottle beside him. I look around as he throws the shot back in one and then watch him shake a cigarette from a crumpled pack of Luckies he produces from his jacket pocket. He jams the cigarette in his mouth, lights it and, around a dense cloud of smoke, he continues.

"I see the opportunities as they present themselves," Arnold Schweison says, "and, hoping to accommodate their requirements before somebody else does, I ask the Chinamen if they are interested in a little poker.

"They jabber amongst themselves in Chinese and I wait politely. I cannot understand Chinese."

I shrug and shake my head to confirm that I am similarly disadvantaged.

"Anyways, the leader of these guys—there's a half-dozen of them, maybe seven, eight—he turns to me with a big toothy smile, introduces himself as Chin Li, and he says, 'Sure, why not,'" Arnold says. "And so we commence to playing.

"The leader, this Chin Li, he stands at the back of the table, looking around the room. At first, this distresses me but after a while I forget he is there. But even when I glance up at him, he is not looking down at the pasteboards on the table or even at those in the hands of his friends.

"Anyways, I get ahead of myself.

"At first I worry a little that maybe these guys don't know poker from Shinola, you know? Because this can be almost as troublesome as a mark who is on the make."

I nod to indicate that I follow this reasoning.

"But," Arnold continues, "I have no cause for concern because they play just fine, betting when it mostly makes sense to bet and folding when it makes sense to fold. Anyways, we play like this for a good while—maybe five, six hours, all of which time this Chin Li maintains his position at the rear of the table—and, eventually, pretty much all the greenbacks slowly find their way across onto my side. In fact," Arnold says, "we get to a point where only one of these guys has much moolauw left—the leader, this Chin Li fellow, the only one appears to speak English, who waves a fistful of folding and taps this other guy on the shoulder to take his seat.

"So, Chin Li sits down and I deal the boards. Betting is brisk and bold—too bold, I am now thinking to myself—with Chin Li looking very uncomfortable at the table. This I put down to some religious observance that he is maybe transcending."

I shrug. "It does take all kinds to make a world," I say.

Arnold Schweison smiles sadly. "Amen to that, Bones," he says before continuing with his story.

"So, we are at the point where we have had the change and we are now circulating the players to arrive at a final bet. This Chin Li fellow—who now looks to be in some kind of pain, like from an ulcer or an appendix?—takes one last look at his boards, and then he pushes his last bills along with a quantity of loose change into the middle of the table."

Arnold sits back at this point, shakes his head—like he is remembering it all over again—and takes a long pull on the Lucky. "I should of known," he moans around the smoke, "should of known right then and there that something is not right."

Thinking that the events in Arnold's story seemed to suggest that everything had been proceeding according to plan, I inquire as to what problem this action could have presented.

"There are laughing," Arnold says. "Giggling at each other and watching me. Everyone but Chin Li, who looks set to fall off of his chair and onto the floor."

I shrug. "Maybe they figure they are on a winning hand," I suggest.

"Yes, this is what I think also," Arnold says tiredly. "But none of the others seem to bother about looking at this Chin Li's boards.

"Then, looking like he is in a daze, the sweat trickling down his face in thick runnels, Chin Li reaches into his pocket and drops what looks like a couple of marbles on top of the greenbacks. 'I raise you,' he says."

"He must of had some hand," I presume aloud.

Arnold nods in agreement. "This, too, I think," he says. "And I look across at their faces, all happy and expectant, and I look down at the pile of lettuce with these two stones right smack in the middle, and I shake my head."

"You refuse the bet?"

"I have four joes," says Arnold. "Pair dealt and two more in the change. I know two of the other guys each has queen king, and one has a pair bullets plus a couple fours, fives . . . I forget which. Chin Li himself, he has been dealt by my reckoning—and I do not make mistakes with the boards, Bones, as I am sure you know—"

I nod. Arnold Schweison does not make mistakes with the boards.

"—he has been dealt three eights and maybe he pulls a fourth in the change. I cannot not be sure but, anyways, I know I cannot be beaten."

"You get *soft*?" I cannot keep the incredulity out of my voice.

Arnold shrugs at me and smiles, grinding the butt of his Lucky into the ashtray. "I do not want to take all of their money," he says to me. "And, most assuredly, I do not want to take some family heirloom. I tell them the money is enough and say I will show my boards.

"At this point, the Chinaman's hand shoots out like a whip and clamps itself around my wrist before I can flip my boards. 'No!' he says to me," says Arnold Schweison. "'I *raise* you!'"

He raises his shoulders and holds his hands out, palms up, and I notice suddenly how thin he has gotten. "Now," he says to me, "a man has got to retain his dignity and his professional reputation and, being as how there is a whole a bunch of folks standing around watching by this point, I was not about to display weakness. So, instead, I look down at the baubles and say to him, 'With what?' I say, 'With what are you raising me?'"

Again the bony shoulders reach for the ceiling.

"This Chin Li, he smiles at me—a smile that suddenly seems to look very crafty indeed . . . 'And where is this sick-looking man now, Arnold Schweison?' I ask myself, in my head—and the Chinaman leans back on his chair and says, 'Tomorrow eyes.'

"'Tomorrow eyes?' I say to him," says Arnold Schweison. "'What on God's green earth are tomorrow eyes?'"

I nod to show that I, too, am unacquainted with such a thing.

"Well," says Arnold, "the Chinaman mops his face with a piece of rag and picks the two baubles out of the stash. He rattles them in the palm of his hand a couple times and rolls them back against the greenbacks like craps. '*These* are Tomorrow eyes,' he says," says Arnold, his voice taking on a menacing kind of tone, and I wonder whether this is the Chinaman's voice coming through or whether it is Arnold's own voice, tinged with something about the baubles that he has since discovered.

"Anyways, I reach out for them, asking him what they do, these to-morrow eyes, but the Chinaman places his hand over them—and the stash, too—and he says to me, 'They tell you the future.'"

Arnold Schweison sighs and reaches for the bottle. As he pours him-self another shot, I see that his hands are steady as a rock. Somehow, this bothers me more than if they shake like jelly pudding. He drains the glass and thumps it back onto the table next to the pasteboards. Then he starts to speak again:

"We look at each other a minute or two, Chin Li the Chinaman and me, and then eventually I pull my hand back, lift up my boards and fan them out in front of me, holding my other hand around the back of them. The joes are still there and I don't need no fortune telling doodad to tell me the hand and the stash are both mine. So I ask him what I need to put in to take a look at his boards. He shrugs and smiles—and it was a cold smile, Bones . . . you know what I mean? A smile without warmth or humor?"

I have seen such a smile and I nod to Arnold.

"Anyways, 'One dorrar,' he says to me, just like that, without any ells. So, without any more thought, I throw the required amount of jingle onto the stash and I say to him, 'Okay, show me what you got.'

"Then Chin Li turns over his boards and I see he has a ten, an eight, tray of clubs, and two deuces. I frown at the cards. This means that the Chinaman folds two of the three eights on the change—maybe all of them—and I am not wrong about that, Bones," Arnold says.

I wave to him and give a long blink that says I appreciate what he is telling me.

"Which means," Arnold continues, "the Chinaman means to lose the hand all along."

"Why would he want to do that?" I say, to which Arnold says for me to let him tell the tale his own way.

"At this point," he says, "everyone just stands up, gives a short bow, and they leave the bar. Without so much as a by-your-leave, they just file out, even as I'm reaching for the stash. Everyone but Chin Li. He just sits there and watches me, this smile pulling at the sides of his mouth making him look for all the world like *he* was the one won the game and not me.

"I lift the baubles from the stash and roll them around in my hand for a closer look." Arnold holds his empty hand in front of him, cupped like it has something in it, and we both stare at the crooked, dirty fingers.

"They *do* look a little like eyes, I see then," he says, softly, resting the hand back on the table, "but a *lot* of eyes. You know what I mean?"

I shake my head.

"They have little circles all over them, each one overlapping another and that one overlapping still one more. And they feel clammy, like they really *are* eyes, warm but not *living*-warm. I figure that maybe this is from the heat of the place and maybe the fact that they have been in the Chinaman's pocket, and I toss them back onto the baize and pull in the stash. Truth is that I felt a little dizzy, things whirling around my head . . . which sensation I put down to the pressure of playing the hand. The Chinaman gets to his feet and nods to me. As he turns around, I ask him why he will not let me touch the baubles—the tomorrow eyes—when we were playing the hand. He smiles to me and sits down again.

"'Different futures,' he says. 'Different futures?' I say back to him.

"'If you do not possess Tomorrow eyes, you see *your* future, not future of other person,' he says. 'I not want you see that future.'"

"What did he mean?" I ask.

"I do not have any idea as to the meaning of such a statement," Arnold answers. "Anyways, after that, he leaves the drum."

"Just like that? He says nothing more to you?"

"Well, yes he does say one more thing. As he is leaving, he says for me to follow that simple rule. 'Do not,' he says to me, 'under any circumstances, allow—' —this he pronounces *'arroww'*— '—the tomorrow eyes to be touched by another while they are in your possession.' And this is the full extent of his closing remarks."

"*Then* he leaves?"

"Then he leaves."

"And then?"

"Then, I pick all the bills out, turn them the right way, counting as I go along, and scoop the loose change into my pocket. I make the tally to be around four hundred on the one pot, and I already have three thou plus safely in my pocket. Then, all that is left on the table is the boards and the marbles."

"The tomorrow eyes?" I say.

Arnold Schweison nods. "The tomorrow eyes."

Four

Arnold reaches for the bottle and then pushes it away. He looks at me and seems to consider going on. "You want to hear the rest?"

"Tell me it all," I say to him.

"Okay," he says. "I am walking down the street, outside the drum, and I dip into my pocket for a nickel for the newspaper dispenser. What do I find in there but the tomorrow eyes, tucked up amongst my loose change. And this despite the fact that I have left them on the table."

Maybe it is just me but, around this time, the air takes on a chill and I think maybe I am coming down with something. Then Arnold starts to speak again.

"And this is just the first time," he says. "I try everything I can think of to rid myself of the things but all to no avail," he says in a dispirited fashion.

"I leave them in my room and they are in my pocket minutes later on the street. I drop them into some guy's jacket or a dame's pocketbook and, fifty yards along, they are back with me again. I toss them out into the bay, next day there they are on my bureau top. Roll them out into the traffic, I get them back couple hours later." He stops for a deep breath and looks at me like a sick dog. "I cannot get rid of them, Bones."

I ask him why does he want to get rid of them so earnestly, and he laughs a short sharp snort.

"At first, I do not want to get rid of them, I confess," Arnold confesses, "though I do think it a touch strange that I leave the things on the baize and suddenly they are back secreted about my own person. But I figure to myself, 'Hey, Arnold Schweison, why do you worry so? You must have thought you had left them on the table when, in fact, you had dropped them into your very own jacket pocket . . . like a putz on a bender!'

"But then I start to get the visions," Arnold says, softly.

"Visions?" I say.

"Visions," says Arnold Schweison.

Five

"The first ones were in a game of stud with two drifters from Tennessee who would soon be on the lam for murdering a family of homesteaders, and a second-string card-sharp from Kansas City who was about to be persuaded to leave town by a small committee who had discovered his knack of dropping a board to the floor during gin games."

"They give you this information freely?" I ask in amazement.

Arnold shakes his head. "I see it in the cards. None of it has happened.

"With the two from Tennessee, I see the woman's face pleading for mercy as they slap her around. I see her clothes coming off, see the bruises . . . and I see what they do to her. But most of all, I see what they are planning to do to me, a little later, down an alleyway in an old part of town where they invite me to partake of a beer or two with them in order to celebrate my winnings—I see that, too. I see they plan to get their money back, fair means or foul does not matter to them."

"How?" I say to Arnold. "How do you see all this?"

"It all comes to me in a flood," Arnold Schweison says. "Like dreaming only with my eyes open . . . I cannot even blink away the images. The scenes are like the motion picture shows, only in color, and I see every movement and every expression. And I hear the voices in my head.

"At first, I look around at the other people—the drifters and the card-sharp were the first, as I say already—but they all look at me like I just jump from a train and maybe hurt my head in the process. 'You hear that?' I ask the one guy, one of the two from Tennessee, and he looks at me. 'Hear what?' he says, frowning, like he suspects I already spotted his tendency to deal from the bottom of the pack . . . which I have, of course, and have taken appropriate measures to make sure I still get the boards I *want* to get.

"Anyways, thinking I have maybe lost my mind, I stand up at the table and put all of the winnings back in the stash, empty my pockets—pulling out the linings . . . you know? Like an elephant's ears?—and I leave the drum. When I get home, the only things in my pockets are the tomorrow eyes. These, too, I left on the table—hence the elephant's ears?—but now they are with me again.

"Next day, same thing."

"You think maybe you should see a medical person, Arnold?" I suggest.

He shakes his head. "This I have thought of, but what would I say to this person?"

I shrug. He has a point.

"So, next day, I am sitting across the baize from an Okie name of Bill and I get to see the woman with whom he spends time while he is away from his wife. She is a little overly generous with her affections, this lady—as many are, I have found, who trade their soft voices for folding instead of for companionship—and I get to see him picking up a little something that does not go away with itching cream. I see what it does to him, one day down the line, and I pocket the folding—a little over twenty dollars—leave the change and make my apologies, even though he has shown me a roll of bills as thick as my own arm." Arnold holds out his arm as proof, and I whistle appreciatively. "This, I decide, is what I have to do.

"At first it is just the people I sit across the baize from, seeing them on the boards as I fan them out, watching their lives unfold right before my eyes . . . seeing everything that is in store for them, from now until whenever. And I only ever see the shadowy things that wait around the corners, never the pleasantries that occur for all of us, even though we may say we are down on our luck from time to time. This is one very one-sided doodad, and make no mistake."

Arnold pulls out the same battered pack of Luckies and shakes free another cigarette. I wait until a thick cloud of smoke is swirling about the two of us, and then I ask him what is it that he intends to do about the situation.

"I cannot play the tables any more, Bones," he confides in me, and I see the truth of what he says reflected in his own eyes, which I now notice are watery and hooded, and rounded beneath with colored bags of skin.

"Because you are afraid of what you might see?" I venture.

Arnold Schweison nods. "You are a perceptive man, Bones," he says softly. "Exactly that. I am not able to concentrate on the boards. I cannot recall what has gone before . . . and cannot decide whether the mark before me holds a straight or a nine high. This is not good in my profession, as I am sure I do not need to tell you. As to what I intend to do . . . " He lets his voice trail off before he says, softly, "I have to get rid of the tomorrow eyes."

His response does not surprise me, although the intensity with which he voices his intentions does. Although more an acquaintance than a friend of any close standing, we do work the same street . . . albeit different sides.

We all of us get to a point in our various endeavors where the consequences of those endeavors begin to take a toll. This realization affects different people in different ways. With Arnold Schweison, taking the Chinaman's baubles had laid on him a guilt trip the size of the San Andreas fault. I see this. And I see, too, he needs to lose the tomorrow eyes but, if he cannot play the boards with a mark, how can he effect this?

Now, don't ask me where these things come from, they just come.

This one comes to me right then, in a smoky barroom which smells of weak beer, cheap liquor and lost hope. I have never been what some might call 'close' to Arnold Schweison—any closer than I feel to *any* man—but I feel a sudden deep kinship. I reach out and place a hand on his bony arm. "How about you and me play a hand for the eyes?" I say to him.

Arnold Schweison looks across at me and his own eyes they light up like beacons. "You mean that, Bones?"

"Never have I been more serious," I tell him.

He does not need me to tell him twice. The bony hands dart out and grasp the pack of boards which he then proceeds to shuffle. The deck made, he offers me the cut. I tap the top card and he smiles at me, acknowledging my trust in his honesty.

He throws a card to me and one to himself, then another and so on. Presently, we are sitting with five boards face down before us on the table.

"What is the bet?" I ask him.

Arnold Schweison looks puzzled.

"I mean, apart from the baubles, " I say.

His face lightens and then clouds up again. "I have no money, Bones," he says. "Nothing to play with except . . . except the—"

"You have no folding whatsoever?"

He shakes his head.

"Not even car fare?"

He lays his boards on the table, carefully fanned out, and reaches a hand into his pants pocket. I hear a jingling noise. He removes the hand and glances down into it. "Sixty two . . . sixty four cents?" he says, looking up at me.

"This amount even I can cover," I say.

Arnold places the coins in the middle of the table and I pull two quarters, a dime and a nickel from my jacket. This wager I place with Arnold's change and I remove a single penny.

"Okay?" I say as I pick up my cards.

He nods to me and reaches for his own cards.

"What about the rest of the wager?" I say, fanning out the boards in front of me.

He frowns and then realizes what I am referring to. He slips the same hand into his jacket and brings it out clenched. He moves the hand above the stash and opens it. Two gaudily colored stones, perfectly circular, drop onto the change.

Without thinking, I reach out my free hand.

"Bones, no!" Arnold shouts, and I see two men turn around from the bar where they are drinking beers. But his call is too late. I have the tomorrow eyes in my hand and I am already bringing them back to get a closer look.

I hold the stones in front of my cards and look at them, feeling a dizziness come over me. And as I look, I see a movement on the faces of the cards. I focus my eyes onto the cards themselves and watch.

A strange thing happens.

I see a table, a table not unlike the table at which I am now sitting, and there is Arnold Schweison. He is getting to his feet and reaching inside his jacket . . . then he is producing a small pistol—a Derringer, perhaps . . . I cannot make it out—and he shoots it. Once. Twice. A figure slumps across the table in front of him, face down. There is a lot of blood on the table. The Arnold on the card steps back from the table, his head disappearing momentarily behind a figure 8—the card is the eight of clubs, I now see—and he slips another couple of slugs into the gun. He places the gun in his mouth and fires. As the scene fades, I look at the figure lying across the table. It is wearing my jacket. I suspect it is also bleeding my blood.

"Arnold?" I say, looking across at him, but he has folded his head into his hands. When I look back at the cards again, another scene is appearing.

This one is an alleyway. Another Arnold leaps from the alley and grabs a man passing by, pulls him down into the darkness. In the spare light from the street at the end of the alley, I see Arnold lift a long-bladed knife and bring it down into the body, twice. Then he lets the body slip from his grasp, bends his neck backwards and cuts deeply into his own throat. As he falls onto the body of the man he has stabbed, Arnold knocks the man's head so that it faces me. It is a face I have studied in many mirrors.

As the scene fades and another starts to form, I place the cards face down on the table.

"What . . . what is that?" I say.

"Possible futures," Arnold Schweison mumbles from his arm hideaway. He lifts his head and looks at me. "You saw things that might happen, Bones."

I am shaking my head, looking down at the boards. They look so innocent, so unthreatening. "That *might* happen?"

"Might happen if you do not possess the tomorrow eyes," he explains. Then he asks me, "What is it that you see in the boards?"

I look across at his fear-haunted face and realize that that is what he is now; haunted. If he is not successful in ridding himself of these baubles, he will take my life and then his own. As I look, I realize that he does not know this yet. He has no idea as to what I might of seen.

I shift my arm against my side to check the reassuring presence of my piece, and unbutton my jacket to allow easy access. "Let us play," I say.

Six

"Hello?" a voice says by my side. "Mister Bonnedusky?"

I look up from the tomorrow eyes lying in the palm of my hand and see a worried-looking face looking down at me. "This is me," I say.

"I'm Fred Bichwall." He waits for some recognition from me. "The dentist? The clerk told me you were here."

Suddenly I remember. I ask him to sit down with me.

"Here?" says Fred Bichwall. "Here at this table?"

"Certainly at this table," I say. "Or we can discuss the matter outside in the alleyway," I suggest.

He pulls a chair back and drops onto it. "Here will be fine," he says.

I place the baubles on the table between us.

"What are those?" he asks.

I shake my head. "Trinkets, nothing of value."

And in truth, they cannot be valuable, these tomorrow eyes. For, less than a half-hour earlier, did not Arnold Schweison and I do our level best to ensure that we did not win them in a simple game of draw poker?

I had been dealt two pairs, both of which I break on the change, leaving myself with an eight—the club eight on which a possible future Arnold Schweison had taken a gun to a possible future version of myself—plus the four of hearts and the two of diamonds. After the change, I am sitting with a pair of fours. But still I beat Arnold Shweison's nine high. The mark of a true professional is that he will not only win a hand he wants to win but also that he will lose one he wants to lose.

"Do you have the folding?" I inquire of the dentist from Iowa City.

He pats his jacket on the right hand side and nods.

"Good," I tell him. Then I say to him, "I have a proposition for you."

"Proposition?" He frowns at me and I see his eyes drop to the table and the pack of pasteboards which Arnold Schweison left. He looks up at me and shakes his head.

"You have not yet heard the proposition and already you are turning it *down*? And you are a *gambling* man, Fred Bichwall?"

"I'm not playing cards with you," he says emphatically, although his eyes and the first tell-tale bead of sweat on his hairline speak another way.

I hold up my hand. "Listen," I say to him. "We play a simple game of five-card draw. You win and you get to keep the six thou, which I will personally wipe off your outstanding debt. Then you go back to New York and make your piece with Mr. Calhoun?"

"Six thousand? On one hand?"

I nod my head. "Plus you get these baubles," I say, pushing forward the tomorrow eyes.

"And if I lose . . . what do *you* get?" He frowns at me and leans on the table. "What do *you* get?" he says again.

This is a good question. I intend to ensure that the dentist from Iowa City wins the hand, so the consequences of his losing have not occurred to me.

"If you lose, you give me a thou. How does this sound to you? One thou of your folding against the six thou in your pocket." I do a quick piece of math in my head. "This by my reckoning would mean the seventeen gees outstanding is immediately reduced to eleven—which detail I will relay to Mr. Calhoun by telephone this evening—and then it is *further* reduced by the six you hand over to Mr. Calhoun when you see him. This arrangement will make him exceedingly happy."

"Why?"

"Why will it make him happy?"

"No. Why are you doing this? Why give me such odds?"

I glance down at the tomorrow eyes. For a second I see Arnold Schweison standing up from this very same table a little while ago, looking ten years younger, as though a monkey has been removed from his bent back, saying to me, as I rattle my 'prizes' together in my hand, 'You are a good man, Bones.'

I sigh and wave an arm around me. "I do it because it is a good day," I tell him. "The sun is shining, I feel good and I want to give you a chance." The words taste sour in my mouth.

The dentists frowns and considers what I say.

"Okay," he says. "But I deal."

"You deal." I push the deck across to him and then push the tomorrow eyes further into the middle of the table.

I watch him shuffle the cards. His dealing does not bother me at all. If he cheats—which I do not expect him to do—then he will win. If he does not cheat, he will win anyway. I do not intend to keep anything worth keeping.

The dentist deals a card, then another. Soon I have five cards face down in front of me. The dentist places the deck on the table, alongside the tomorrow eyes, and picks up his own cards, fans them out in front of his eyes and looks.

I do the same.

Amidst the cards—a good hand, I see: two kings and two sevens plus the spade five—I see a scene unfolding. This scene shows the dentist from Iowa City standing in a train corridor. He is talking earnestly to two men in dark suits and snap-brimmed Fedoras. One of the men keeps glancing up and down the corridor and the other, holding something against the dentist's stomach, appears to be chewing something. I cannot hear the conversation, but I can guess it.

A few seconds later, the glancing man leans over and opens the carriage door. The chewing man—as he turns and pushes the dentist towards the open door, I see that it is Peppermint Sam—he smiles, reaches into the dentist's inside jacket pocket and removes an envelope. I know what it contains. Sam glances in the envelope, his smile growing wider, and then he shoots the dentist twice in the gut. The dentist grabs for his stomach, now red and wet, and stumbles backwards out of the train.

I close my eyes tight and suddenly hear the dentist talking.

"I said how many cards?"

When I open my eyes, the dentist from Iowa City is glaring at me impatiently, the thumb of his right hand caressing the top card on the deck he holds in his left.

I look back at the cards. The same scene has started again but now it's held in motion, the dentist staring concernedly at Peppermint Sam, his mouth open mid-way into a sentence, while Sam's sidekick is staring right out of the card at me, like he's waiting for me to make a decision. That is when I realize that this is exactly what he *is* doing. Right now, I have the power over the dentist from Iowa City's future.

If I change the three cards I intended to change up until a few seconds ago—breaking the pair of sevens and ditching the kings, so I have only a seven and a five in hand, and both different suits—the chances are that the dentist will win. It is not certain, but probable because, of course, the dentist will be trying to *improve* his own hand while I am trying to decimate mine. That way, he wins the hand and the baubles. And he goes off back to NYC, whereupon he meets Sam and his friend on a dimly-lit train corridor and ends up taking a walk out into the passing foliage of South Carolina with his stomach ventilated.

If, however, *I* win the hand . . .

But, no. It is not the winning of the hand that matters, I suddenly realize. It is what I say to the dentist.

"You must have one hell of a hand for it to take so long deciding," Fred Bichwall says to me.

I look at him, smile and shrug a small apology.

Looking back at my cards, I realize that there is a chance that he will win anyways. Even if I keep the kings and the sevens. Two pair is a three-legged horse against three of a kind. If he wins, I can still give him the advice he needs to avoid meeting Peppermint Sam but I cannot allow him to take the tomorrow eyes. I have plans for these, I now realize.

"I fold," I say to him, laying my cards on the table.

"You *fold*?"

"I fold. The game is finished. You win." I reach across and lift the baubles from the table. They still feel warm and clammy but now they feel better somehow. Less threatening.

"I win? Without even taking a change?"

"Without even taking a change. You keep the six thou. But I keep the baubles."

"Hey, wait a minute," Fred Bichwall says.

"In exchange for the baubles, I give you some advice." I drop the tomorrow eyes in my jacket pocket and lean towards him.

"Call it a change of heart. Call it getting old, getting soft, whatever. Listen to what I am going to tell you."

The dentist leans forward.

"Are you listening?"

"Yes, I'm listening."

"Do not take the train back to New York."

"Say again?"

I lift the cards I had laid on the table and fan them out in front of me.

Spread across the two kings, I see the dentist and a bright-faced woman running out of a house in a pleasant leafy suburb. Running in front of them is a child—a boy . . . maybe ten, eleven years old. They are running to a waiting cab and they are carrying valises and suitcases.

Most of all, while they look a little nervous, they are laughing excitedly.

Without looking up, I say, "Call home now—right here, in the hotel—and tell your wife to start packing. Take everything you need but nothing you do not need." I pause and watch the woman stepping into the cab. For a second or two, it seems she looks around off the cards and looks right at me, smiling.

"She is very pretty, your wife," I say.

"Hey, now, just wait a min—"

"And your son? How old is he? Ten?"

"How do you know about my son?"

"Do you love him?" I feel like the man in the magazine, the one with the big hat . . . only *I* say, *I know what* goodness *lurks in the hearts of men.* "Do you love your wife?" I ask him.

The dentist seems to roll back in his chair. "Sure I love her. I love them both. It's just that—"

"Then if you love them, look after them. Call her now. Tell her what I said for you to tell her. Then use some of the six thou to fly home. Do not take a train—too long—and do not delay. You need to move, to move on. Get a new life and a new name. Forget the gambling. If you do not do this, I fear you will soon be dead."

The dentist from Iowa City bites on his lip as I glance down and see the cab speeding away from the leafy suburb into bright sunshine. Then the scene fades and another starts to take its place. Without waiting to see what it shows, I fold the cards and return them to the deck in front of Fred Bichwall.

Without another word, he stands up. "Thanks," he says. "I don't know why you're doing this—why you're giving me this chance—but thanks. I won't let you down."

I shrug. "It is not me you will let down, Fred Bichwall," I say to him.

He nods and walks quickly away.

Seven

In the washroom I stare at my face in the mirror.

It is an easy face to change, I realize. To change so that Cuddles Ken Calhoun will never recognize me, however hard he looks. I dry my hands and walk out into the hotel bar.

Tomorrow, while Peppermint Sam is walking along a train corridor looking for the dentist from Iowa City, I will be removing all my modest savings from my bank account. And while the dentist and his wife and son are climbing into a cab in a leafy suburb of Iowa City, I will be taking a Greyhound to parts as yet unknown.

In one jacket pocket, I have the tomorrow eyes. In the other, I have a deck of cards. I am not a good card-player, but I am strong and healthy and I can take small jobs. And in these small jobs—pumping gas, picking fruit, delivering mail—I will meet people, people with uncertain futures who maybe face some difficult decisions. It may be that I will be able to help them.

I reach into my pocket and grasp the baubles, feel their distant warmth in my hand, and I feel a power I have never felt before. Not in all of my journeys to persuade errant debtors of the need to make amends.

The tomorrow eyes may be fortune *tellers*, but *I* am a fortune *maker*. As, indeed, we are all . . . in greater and lesser ways.

THE THIRD EYE OF THE WORLD

by Henrik Johnsson

Through the midnight alleys of a nameless city strolls a madman. His name is Jack Edmonds, and his madness defines his reality; he is the victim of an omnipotent entity which pervades all of creation, and which is inherently evil. Jack is certain that this supreme entity, this demonic world-soul, is out to get him.

His clothes are tattered and filthy; he has no money, since he can't get a job, instead living on welfare. A faded trench coat reaches down to his knees and gives him the appearance of a flasher.

His face is of an almost sickly pale hue, his features marked by too much alcohol; a grey stubble of beard covers his chin. His hair is unwashed and unkempt, and he's slightly bald. He's maybe forty, forty-five years old. His gaze is unfocused, and he keeps looking back over his shoulder, trying to spot some unknown assailant.

The street is almost deserted, except for a couple of hookers further down the street. A light fog clings to the ground, caresses the litter-strewn pavement. The surrounding houses are tall, imposing office buildings; some with ten or twelve floors, some with only three or four. The irregularity of their height creates the impression of a ruined castle; a few turrets have fallen down, while others have remained upright. Or else the broken skyline resembles the jagged teeth of a beast of prey; the city itself is a hunter, choosing the weakest of its inhabitants to gorge upon.

Most of the windows are unlit, dead; but from one or two there shines a pale, cold light, which provides some small measure of illumination, but neither comfort nor warmth. The clatter of a trashcan, perhaps disturbed by a stray cat, is heard. Jack sees a car coming down the street, slowing down, pulling over in front of the hookers; Jack strains to hear what is being said.

"Is that enough?" the man in the car asks.

"Yeah, that'll cover it," replies one of the hookers, and then turns to her friend. "Will you be alright?"

"I'll manage, Cindy. Be back within the hour," says the friend.

"I will," her friend says, and gets in the car. As the car drives off, the other hooker is left all alone, with no one to protect her against the ravages of the night.

Standing there in the shadows, watching her, Jack suddenly feels an excruciating pain in his head, and he knows that it is his mind's eye opening. The god itself occasionally shows him its ways through the third eye of his soul, and he is then forced to watch its dealings through his mind's eye. The image of a man slitting a woman's throat flits across Jack's mind, and he recognizes her to be the hooker who just drove off with her trick. Jack falls to his knees and grips his head in a vain effort to drive away the pain, which grows more intense as he is shown the struggle that led up to the final killing. The fear that grips the woman as her would-be trick takes out a knife from the glove compartment transplants itself into Jack's soul, slicing through his mind; and he sees how her fear is overshadowed, but not replaced, by surprise as the knife plunges into her neck, just above the collar bone, the blade burying itself in her flesh; and as though it were the crash of a boulder tumbling down a mountainside or the sudden eruption of a smouldering volcano, her scream as she comprehends what is happening to her resounds through Jack's mind, deafening all other sound.

As the murderer withdraws the knife, producing a cascade of blood that spatters onto the dashboard, the woman desperately tries to open the door of the car; and Jack, unable to do anything except to watch, keels over onto the pavement in pain. He clenches his teeth in an effort not to scream in concert with the woman as the murderer drives the knife into her arm, her back, and, as she finally manages to open the door, her leg; when she tumbles out into the deserted alley the car is parked in, a thin sliver of hope cuts through the pain in Jack's mind.

Lying on the street and panting with exertion, Jack watches as the woman somehow finds the strength to get up from the ground and start walking, limping from her wounds, holding her hand against her neck in an attempt to stem the flow of blood; she walks towards the other end of the alley, which opens onto an ordinarily well-lit and well-trafficked street, and which now appears to her as some sort of Paradise. Jack is relieved, glad, that she has managed to evade her would-be killer. But then he remembers the image of the woman's throat being slit, and when he sees the murderer getting out of the car, he knows that there is no salvation for the woman; because when the demon-god at the centre of the world decides to kill one of its creations, nothing can stop it from achieving its purpose.

At last the woman, whose name Jack recalls is Cindy—perhaps short for Cinderella, as though she were a princess of bygone days, whose knight in shining armour had turned out to be the big, bad wolf—makes it out onto the street, only to be met by absolute silence and emptiness; it is as deserted as the alley she has just escaped from. With blood dripping from her wounds like tiny rivulets of redness squirted from a pipette she limps out into the middle of the street, hoping thereby to attract someone's attention, or find some means of escaping her pursuer.

The killer approaches her; he's hurrying, occasionally running, so that his prey won't get away. As she turns round and sees him, Jack starts to cry; for he knows what is about to happen.

The killer grabs his victim by the hair, and forces her onto the ground. He puts the knife to the woman's throat, and is about to cut it, when suddenly he stops; a man is standing across the street, watching them. The woman sees him, and looks at him. Her eyes meet with his—silently imploring him to help her, to come to her rescue. To stop her from being butchered.

The man averts his eyes, and continues on his way.

Behind her, the killer smiles, and slits the woman's throat. A short choking sound, blood gushing from the wound, and then nothing more. His work is complete; he has done what he was ordered to do.

Jack has stopped crying. His mind's eye is closed; he's still lying in the alley, assailed by fear and revulsion at seeing the world-soul reveal its hideous might. A blackness seeps into his mind, and a buzzing as of a swarm of fat flies flows through his brain; it is the demon-god speaking to him:

"You see," it seems to say to him, "the common man is every bit as evil as the murderer; they are no different."

And Jack knows that this is true. He knows that everything in the world is a part of the malign world-soul; even its creations are a part of that ultimate evil, although it thrives on their suffering and deaths. All is evil, there is no good; thus was the gospel he had learnt from his ability to see the true face of reality. He had mounted the chariot of God and met the Lord in all His glory, and realized that He was mad.

Jack got up, and slowly walked out into the street, not caring if a car drove by and hit him; he walked past the remaining hooker, and kept on walking until he reached those streets which saw more activity during the night than the one he had left behind. Blinking neon lights replaced the unlit office windows, cinemas, bars, office buildings, drunken revellers, and the hookers. An ocean of noise engulfed him; and with nervous glances he watched the men and women around him, who by the looks of them seemed to belong to that part of the human race with whom he had never had anything in common—the healthy, sane people.

He wanted to be like them, but he knew that this would never happen. At an early age, some form of harm had been done to him; he could no longer remember what it was, for his mind had long since suppressed the memory of it; his life up until the age at which he had first begun to discern the existence of the world-soul was a blur to him. Whatever the case, he had become alienated from his family and friends, and had isolated himself from the outside world, instead spending his time constructing elaborate daydreams and fantasies in an effort to escape from a reality he had come to loathe. His hatred of the world, and the resulting fear of it, had with time developed into madness; he'd started killing small animals—the neighbourhood cats and dogs, and birds when he could catch them—until he was seized with an insatiable desire to slay a human being, which had erupted one night in a bar, when he'd drawn a knife and stabbed a man who'd been talking to a girl Jack himself was unsuccessfully trying to chat up.

The man had survived, and Jack had undergone psychiatric evaluation, during which his insanity had been revealed for all the world to see. He'd been shut up in an asylum until his youth had gone and he was the broken wreck of a human being that now stood watching the passersby on the street, loathing them and yet wanting to be accepted by them. Although officially cured of his disease, Jack was still forced to see a psychiatrist once a week; and, despite his hating to have to confront his madness on a regular basis, Jack felt a strange sort of comfort at knowing that there was at least one person in the world who cared, although only on a professional level, about his problems.

It was during the first year of his incarceration that the great secret had been divulged to him, and he'd realized that if indeed he was mad, it was only because the world was mad as well. When he asked himself why evil in all its forms seemed to be the sole force that governed the world, he could only come up with a single answer: the world itself was evil. How else could he explain his own pain? And how else explain the pain of others?

If the world wasn't evil, then mankind would have become nobler and less like savage beasts with the passing of time, but even a cursory glance at the history books showed him that this was not the case. If the world were inherently good, then murder and competition would not be such integral parts of both the animal and human realms.

And even if the world was amoral, and took no consideration of those who lived in it, then that still didn't explain how every action that Jack had ever taken seemed to result in an increase of his suffering.

This realization inevitably led to his next discovery—the existence of an animate world-soul which was actively hostile to humanity, its creations.

It all made perfect sense to him; the world could not be either good nor amoral by nature—it must be actively evil, or else there was no explanation to account for his pain—and he could not bear to contemplate the possibility that the suffering that had been with him since youth, like a second shadow clinging to his soul, could have no cause, but was simply there, for no discernible reason.

He had never been able to figure out why the demon-god had chosen to reveal itself to him; perhaps it derived some perverted pleasure from displaying its wickedness, like an artisan of evil proudly showing off his handiwork. But the fact remained that he was able to see clearly its influence stretching out into the world, corrupting and torturing its creations, until it tired of them and slew them. Old age was simply its way of saying that it had grown weary of inflicting harm on that particular individual. Premature death occurred either out of hate or a fit of rage on the part of the demon-god.

Jack contemplated the nature of the world as he watched the men and women walk past him on the street, busily engaging in the pleasures of ordinary people. A man with his arm around the waist of a large-bosomed blonde laughed and planted a wet kiss on her perfume-scented neck. A man sat on a bench by a bus stop, perhaps waiting for a friend. A woman came out of a cinema, apparently having gone to see a movie by herself; she cast a glance at the people around her, and went on her way.

But now Jack began to see the evil in the soul of humanity as his mind's eye opened once more. The people on the street became either murderers or victims. The man with the hot date would rape her when they went home to his apartment and she didn't put out. The man at the bus stop was going to sell drugs to his friend, which when taken would cause an overdose and make the provider one friend poorer. The woman who came out of the cinema was just as mad as Jack; something bad had happened to her too, and she tried to alleviate her own suffering by inflicting pain and death on others.

An onrush of images of hate and destruction flooded through Jack's mind, and he put his hands to his head in a vain effort to dispel them. He saw how the people around him looked at him with loathing; they despised him, and were glad to see their master, the world-soul whose obedient puppets they were, inflicting such beautiful pain on one who so richly deserved it. Doing his best to ignore their hateful stares, Jack began to make his way home.

Once inside his apartment, he turned on the lights in the hall, and went into the almost cupboard-sized space that served him as both diningroom and bedroom. Still panting from the exertion of running through block after block of deserted city streets, he removed his trench coat, lay down on the bed in his grime-covered clothes, and tried to block the flow of images in his mind. He'd tried to drown them out before with alcohol and drugs, but it never worked; instead he had to wait until the demon-god grew tired of harassing him and picked on another puppet to play with. Finally his mind's eye closed, and the woman's death struggle, which had been repeated to him as though he were watching a film that insisted on rewinding itself and showing the same scene over and over again, disappeared.

He resolved to call his doctor, a man by the name of Rostrand whom the government had decided Jack was to see once a week. They'd said it was to make sure he was cured and able to be reintegrated into society, but Jack knew it was only so he would never forget just how mad he was. Jack picked up the phone, and dialed the doctor's number.

***

The phone rang at Dr. Rostrand's apartment. The doctor's wife, Leila, picked it up.

"Hello, Rostrand residence," she said, still proud of her new status as Edward Rostrand's wife, which she had become in a ceremony four months ago, one month after she'd found out that she was pregnant.

"Hi, is Edward there?" asked a heavy, seemingly laboured voice on the other end. She didn't recognize it, and so said:

"Who's calling?"

"Jack Edmonds. I'm a patient of his," replied the voice.

Leila felt a sudden stab of fear. She knew her husband treated patients who had been released from institutions for the criminally insane, and it was easier for her to just ignore his line of work, and block it from her mind. One of her husband's patients suddenly calling her at home made her feel distinctly uncomfortable.

"Wait, I'll get him," she said, and laid down the receiver. "Ed?" she called.

"What?" her husband answered from the kitchen, apparently annoyed at being disturbed in whatever he was doing.

"Phone for you."

Dr. Edward Rostrand, an athletic, spectacled man with sandy-coloured hair and in his late thirties, came out of the kitchen and looked at his wife.

"Who is it?" he asked.

"One of your patients, he said his name was Jack Edmonds."

A look of puzzlement crossed the doctor's face, and he picked up the phone.

"Hi Jack," he said. "You can't call me at home, you know that. Respect my privacy and call me while I'm at the office."

"I know, doc, but something awful happened tonight. I saw a woman get murdered," replied Jack.

"Yes, it's always terrible when someone dies, but that's no reason for you to call me at home," the doctor said. As she heard this, Leila felt even more afraid.

"But I really need to speak to you!" Jack exclaimed.

"It can wait till tomorrow."

"No, it can't!"

"I'm not an emergency hotline, Jack. Call one of those instead," the doctor said, and then added with a wry smile: "I'm sure you have the number."

"I do, but I —"

"We'll talk about this tomorrow, Jack. Alright?"

Silence from the other end.

"Alright?" the doctor repeated.

"Alright," Jack said, sulkingly.

"Good. I'll see you then," said the doctor, and hung up.

He turned round to see his wife standing and looking at him, with an expression on her face resembling sheer panic.

"What?" he asked, unable to understand why she should be so upset.

"Who was it?" his wife asked, referring to the patient.

"Just one of my loonies, nothing to worry about."

"You sure?"

"Positive! Now, shouldn't you get to bed? Staying up late can't be good for the baby," the doctor said, eyeing the bump that had deformed her once beautiful figure.

"Yeah, I guess I'd better," his wife replied.

"That's the spirit. Now be a good girl and get off to bed."

"Will you join me?"

"In a minute," he said, not eager to lie beside her now that her inflated stomach prevented him from exercising his conjugal rights.

"Goodnight," Leila said, and started to ascend the stairs to the bedroom. When her husband didn't reply, she turned to look at him; he was still standing by the phone, watching her with a gaze that reminded her of a scientist staring at a specimen in a microscope.

"Goodnight," she said again.

"Yes, goodnight, sleep tight and don't let the loonies bite," her husband said, and flashed a sardonic smile.

Leila could think of nothing to say, and so continued up the stairs. Dr. Edward Rostrand remained below for a few moments, somewhat bemused by the sudden realization that he could probably drive his wife insane, if only he applied himself to the task. Smiling, he went back into the kitchen, to finish the game of chess he'd been playing against himself.

***

"It's after me, doc. I can feel it every waking moment. It's stretching out its tendrils, trying to enslave me. It hates me because I defy it, and dare to speak out against it," Jack said.

He was sitting in his customary seat on a couch in Dr. Rostrand's office. Besides the couch, the room was sparsely furnished; a large wooden desk behind which the doctor was seated, a filing cupboard where the doctor kept his notes, and a bookcase where he kept his journals and books on the maladies of the mind. Generic paintings of blue seas and cloudy skies, designed specifically so as not to disturb the patients, did their tacky best to enliven the walls of the room. A window behind the doctor's back had the shutters pulled down so he wouldn't appear to the lunatic being treated as a mere blackness sitting behind a desk and talking to him.

Dr. Rostrand regarded his patient over the rim of his spectacles. "And it came after you last night as well?" he asked.

"Yes, it showed me the pestilence at the earth's core, and in the hearts of men," Jack replied.

"Hmm ... You've explained your stance on misanthropy to me in the past, but has it ever occurred to you that you might hate other people simply because you want what they have? And that your feeling of rejection from your fellow men has caused a defensive reaction in you—if you hate them you have no cause to fear them?"

"No, no, no, that's not it at all. I'm not mad. I've seen the light; I know the truth. We're not going to make any progress until you agree with me on this."

"I'm sure we will, even if I don't subscribe to your theory of a universal conspiracy against your person. But please, can you tell me more about this supposed demonic world-soul?" the doctor asked. Almost all his patients had histories of violence, and some even made Jack look like a saint in comparison, but Jack was probably the one patient who most intrigued, and, in a way, entertained him. In a batch of white lab rats, he was the unique black one.

"I've told you about it a thousand times already."

"Please, Jack, one more time, if you don't mind," said the doctor, who found this to be the most amusing part of his patient's delusion.

"Very well, if I have to. It is what created the world; the prime mover, the One from which all emanations of matter come. Whatever you've heard about God or Satan or anyone else has been false—all those others are just parts of the world-soul's schemes, designed to prevent us humans from learning the truth. But I have seen the truth, and I am not duped!" Jack exclaimed.

He was looking straight ahead, into empty space, seemingly not aware of the doctor any more.

"Only the world-soul is real, the rest are illusions. You see, in the beginning there was only hate, and this hate was all-pervasive, and omnipotent; it was the all-in-all, the pre-existent, uncreated greatness. It is incorporeal, infinite, indivisible. All I can say is that it hates, and this is what causes it to be; it hates, therefore it is," said Jack, and snorted something that was a cross between a grunt and a laugh. "Out of this abyss of hatred arose a beam of pure white light, as of a shining pearl rising up out of a sea of darkness; this was the world which we inhabit. I can't say why this happened, why the material world came into existence, but I believe it is because the demon-god, with nothing to torture except shadows, willed the world into being so it could have something to expend its hatred upon. And so the world was created, and we along with it, so as to provide the demon-god at the heart of existence with a play-thing, a toy to be thrown around and mangled as the world-soul saw fit. For it thrives ever on the misery of its creations; and those it does not kill it assails, until they acknowledge defeat, and accept their fate as subjects of an insane, malign god."

Although he'd heard the story many times before, Dr. Rostrand was nonetheless intrigued at hearing Jack's version of how the world had come into being. Looking at the patient sitting upright on the couch, lost in the fantasy he had constructed to account for his own madness, the doctor felt some small measure of respect for the man: he must have spent endless hours figuring out this explanation for the hurt he'd felt all his life. Such an elaborate system was worth admiring.

"But the thing is," Jack continued, "that nothing can come out of nothing. Since the hatred has no soul, it can by necessity not provide its creations with souls; thus, we are all shadows, dreams if you will. We are simply congregations of matter with no animating spark, no immortal soul; we are but puppets, barely sentient. And yet, since we are the children of an evil god, we are all, by extension, evil as well."

Jack leaned forward in his couch, and looked the doctor square in the eyes. Fearing that Jack could somehow read his mind, Dr. Rostrand was struck by a sudden feeling of nervous panic. His calm reasserted itself as he saw that Jack had simply moved to light a cigarette.

"And ever since we were created, we've had nothing but pain. I mean, look at the basic conditions of human existence. We don't want to die, and yet we have to. We don't want to be alone, and yet we are born as a single person. We want to build and create things that will last forever, and yet the whole universe will implode in the end."

"Yes, you've mentioned that. But if the hatred has made everything, why would it let—" the doctor asked, but Jack interrupted him:

"Why would it let it all go to hell, you mean? Simple. Hatred can't create anything that lasts, so it has to recreate the universe once in a while. Everything dies, but is created anew in the end."

"Ah. That explains it," said the doctor.

"And so we live our lives, unaware of the one true god—this force of hatred, of unrelenting evil, which is present in every human being, in every atom, and which is incessantly striving to find new ways of tormenting its creations."

Jack leaned back in his couch. He had spoken such profound truths that the doctor was sure to believe him; now there could be no more doubt on the doctor's part. He would soon come to understand the true nature of things.

But Dr. Edward Rostrand was not in the habit of succumbing to the contrivances of his patients. He crossed his fingers and put them to his forehead in a gesture of contemplation, and spoke.

"How come you're the only one to have perceived this demonic demiurge?"

Jack experienced a fleeting moment of intense frustration and anger—the same feeling he'd had before stabbing the man in the bar—when he realized that the doctor didn't believe him. For a split second he toyed with the idea of strangling the doctor. As though he understood what he was thinking, the doctor looked up at him, and met his stare. Jack averted his eyes; Dr. Rostrand felt a surge of victory at this sign of submission.

"The world cannot hate you; but me it hateth, because I testify of it, that the works thereof are evil," Jack said in a subdued voice, as though he were whispering an incantation.

"Pardon?" the doctor said.

"Because I've angered it by speaking out against it. I became aware of it through my insanity—I admit, I was mad—and I think some madmen, but not all, have done the same. Madness is simply when you see the truth, unobscured. But through my madness I have learnt to see its ways; everything the monster at the centre of the world unleashes upon its creations, I see in my mind's eye. Everything that is evil and corrupted, I see here —" Jack said, and tapped a spiny finger to his temple.

"If you say so, Jack," was the doctor's reply. "We'll have to talk more about that next month, I'm afraid; our time is up," said the doctor. Jack looked at the watch on the wall, and saw that this was so. He turned to the doctor, to pose him a question, but all rational thought evaporated from his mind as he laid eyes upon the doctor: for no longer was he a man, but rather one of the demons sent to plague Jack.

The doctor's eyes were burning coals from which spouted flames, yellow, red; his skin was stretched tight across his skull and furrowed, like that of a man a hundred years old or more; his ears were become pointed like an animal's; his head was bald, all hair gone; and his lips were curled into a snarl, exposing sharp, pointed teeth eager to tear the monster's prey to pieces.

Jack gasped aloud in horror at the apparition. The demon looked at him with eyes that burned with fire and hatred, and spoke, in a voice that was like a rumbling emanating from some Stygian abyss:

"Hey Jack, I have a secret to share with you."

Jack didn't reply. He stared at the monster with a blend of awe, disgust and terror; for the first time, one of the demons had shown itself for what it really was.

"What's the matter, Jack? Don't you like my new face?" the demon said.

There is a strange sensation in Jack's chest as though he had already died and was waiting to be buried.

"You can be like this, too, as pretty as I am. You can if you only want to. Give up, Jack, just give up, and you'll be beautiful, like me," said the thing that had been Dr. Rostrand.

Jack started to cry. He knew he couldn't fight the creature in front of him. There was nothing left to do but surrender.

"Alright, I give up. I can't defeat the world. I'll accept my fate, I won't try to escape it anymore," he said.

"Good for you, Jack. But I'm still going to kill you!" the demon said, and laughed.

Jack gasped with fear, and jumped off the couch as the demon leapt over the desk and hurried towards him; Jack managed to open the office door and run out before the enemy could catch him. The doctor's secretary looked up as the two of them ran out into the reception, apparently unfazed by the demon pursuing Jack. In a split second Jack understood that this was, of course, because she knew about the doctor's true form. Running out into the street, Jack began to make his way to his apartment, which fortunately for him was located not far from the doctor's office, in the hope of reaching it before his would-be murderer caught up with him. Looking over his shoulder he saw the demon coming out of the building where the doctor's office was housed; spreading its bat-like wings, it flapped them a few times to gain momentum, and then launched into the air, all the while shouting at Jack:

"I see you! I see you!"

And Jack kept on running through the streets of the city, ignoring the puzzled looks of the men and women around him, who for some reason could not see the demon hovering above them, flying clumsily, as though it were not used to this mode of transportation, which made it look all the more grotesque. The world appeared to Jack to be overcast as though by a funeral pall, muting all sound and slowing down movement; he felt as if he were running through a quagmire or the waters of an ocean. But at last he reached his apartment, panting and covered in sweat; locking the door, he lay down on the floor, not even having the strength to make it to his bed.

Suddenly, something started banging on the door, and Jack got up from the floor. The voice of the demon boomed into the apartment: "Little pig, little pig, let me in!"

Letting out a scream of fear, Jack hurried into the toilet and locked the door. A crash was heard from outside as the door to the apartment was, presumably, broken down by the demon. Jack heard steps running up to the bathroom, and then:

"Come on, Jack, let me in, I really have to take a leak," the demon implored.

Jack had started to cry again; he had no idea how he could ever stand up against the demon. But in a flash of inspiration, he knew that he must at least attempt to defeat the beast, or else he would have given up without a fight, and this was not something Jack felt any desire to do! No, he would resist the evil that was now scratching on the bathroom door with its talons, imploring him to let it in so it could empty its bladder and perhaps have a bowel movement as well.

Yes, he would fight!

Jack flung open the door, hitting the demon and causing it to topple over.

"Mene mene tekel upharsin!" it screamed at him as he raced into the kitchen, there laying his hands on a knife; running back into the hall, he saw that the demon was now standing, watching him with a look of bewilderment.

"I can bend but I cannot fall! I can bend but I cannot fall!" Jack shouted, and plunged the blade into the demon's chest.

The knife entered deep into the fiend's body, causing black ichor to spurt from the wound.

"Ah, you pricked me, and I bleed!" the demon exclaimed, and fell down onto the ground, having been struck the deathblow; the knife had entered its heart.

Jack stood looking at it for a moment, but then, thinking he saw its eyes move, he knelt down beside the demon and started strangling it, to make sure that it was dead.

"Ha! That's what you get for messing with the wrong loonie!" Jack exclaimed, triumphant.

Suddenly, he saw that the demon's face had changed into the visage of Dr. Rostrand; and with puzzlement cutting through his rage, Jack regained his senses enough to see that he was back in the doctor's office. The doctor showed no trace of his demonic alter ego; he simply lay there on the floor, dead, apparently strangled by Jack, although Jack could not for the life of him recall having tried to murder the doctor in his human form.

Hmm . . . That was strange, Jack thought. But then he understood; it was not the demon's corporeal form that had chased him through the streets, it was the demon's soul that had been hunting his own! And when he had slain its soul, he had also slain its body! That was it!

That explained everything!

Jack stood up, and looked at his fallen adversary. For a single second, he was in a state of perfect bliss. No one could touch him now; he was immortal. He had achieved transcendence.

Deep inside his insane mind, he started to laugh; and the demonic world-soul, the epiphany of evil which resided in the centre of all, laughed with him.

***

Through the midnight alleys of a nameless city runs a madman. He is exultant, for he has won a great victory; and he feels, for the first time in his life, that he actually stands a chance of winning the war he is waging against the demon-god at the earth's core.

But he knew that it would only be a matter of time before the god's agents caught his scent and tracked him down, and so he ran on, in search of a safe place to hide until the hunt died down.

As he ran, it seemed to him that the shadows cast by the dim lights of the street-lamps lengthened and came alive, as though they were tendrils stretching out to trap him and engulf him in their web of revulsion. Everywhere he looked the shadows stretched out their lightless fingers towards him; and he knew them to be the physical incarnations of the evil that encompassed the world. He started to run between the shadows, doing his utmost to avoid coming into contact with them; the darkness turned liquid, and became a sizzling fluid that spread out from its source of origin, growing in size and slowly engulfing the entire street. The danger was omnipresent, on the streets, in his mind, but Jack managed to escape being caught by it.

Jack runs out into the street, and, seeing an alley that appears not to have been touched by the shadows, makes his way towards it. It is as he thought; the shadows haven't reached it yet. There he stops, panting. No sign of the malevolent shadows. Suddenly, he feels something tugging at his leg, and, looking down, he sees that his own shadow has been smitten by the evil of the world-soul. He screams in fear as it starts to detach from him. It becomes separated from his body, and flows lan-

guidly into a small puddle a few feet away from him. He watches, terrified, as the shadow raises itself, takes on the shape of first a pair of feet
and then legs, rising up out of the puddle—and it keeps growing, and
soon he sees an abdomen, and then arms, and at last a head—and despite the pitch-black hue of the creature's body, he discerns clearly that
it is a replica of himself, its limbs are his, its features are his—and Jack
watches in fear as the shadow-demon raises its arm, and points at him,
and it seems to speak to him, but it has no voice; he hears, without hearing, its words resounding in his head:

"I am you and you are I."

And Jack knows that this is so; in one of those rare moments of lucid-
ity which can penetrate even the most deranged of minds, he recognizes
it; it is his guilt, his madness, and he and it are one and the same.
Gathering the remains of his courage, Jack dares ask:

"What do you want?"

To which his sane self, liberated for a moment after the murder of the
doctor, and set free from the prison of his madness because he'd realized, despite his insanity, that now he'd crossed a line, and passed the
point of no return, replies:

"There is nothing in the world except your madness. There is nothing but what you believe is there."

And a fear more profound than any he'd ever felt, greater by far than
the time he had first come to understand what he thought was the truth
about the nature of the world, seizes Jack; and a flood of understanding
drowns his for the moment sane mind.

If your pain is great enough, it eventually becomes incomprehensi-
ble. But you still need an explanation for it, because you don't want to
believe that all this pain can exist, right there in your heart, for no good
reason. And then you would prefer that God or some such entity is the
cause of your hurt, rather than believe that your suffering can exist
without any real cause being behind it. For in a world with no gods,
whether they be good or evil, nothing has any intrinsic meaning beyond
the transient here and now; and there is no hope of a requital after death
for your suffering; and nothing, including your pain, has any signifi-
cance in the long run. And at that point, you would prefer the world to
be ruled by something, even though it were a force of unmitigated evil.
Because even a universe governed by a malign world-soul is better than
one governed by nothing at all.

Jack doesn't notice the squad cars coming to a halt on the street outside the alley and the policemen opening the doors of their cars and taking cover behind them. Having received Jack's description from the

murdered doctor's secretary, they have followed him to the alley, and are now standing with raised guns, shouting at Jack to come out of the alley; but Jack does not hear them, for the world is dead to him.

The policemen, who see no reason to waste the government's time and money on a trial for this demented beast, shout at him a few more times to come out, and then empty their rounds into his still-numb body.

Jack dimly registers the shots entering his flesh. As though he were standing beside his body, his soul disconnected, he sees himself fall to the ground. He watches the blood pouring from a dozen different wounds, and as his life slowly fades away, as he drifts further and further into the darkness, he murmurs with his final breath one last question, poses it to an entity he no longer believes in—

"Why me?" he asks, not expecting an answer.

And if there really had existed an evil world-soul, a malevolent demon-god that had created the world and its inhabitants and then tormented it until it broke and was created anew in a never-ending cycle of death and rebirth, as Jack had thought there was, perhaps it would have answered:"Why not?"

MAHOUT

by Jeff VanderMeer

"MARY: THE LARGEST LIVING LAND ANIMAL ON EARTH. 3 INCHES LARGER THAN JUMBO AND WEIGHING OVER 5 TONS . . . "
— Billboard for the *Sparks Circus*, 1916.

***

You watch the bruised sky as the sun sets outside Dan's Eatery. Dan's lies off County Road Twelve, Tennessee. The farms and paint-peeled houses surrounding it form the town of Erwin.

Flocks of starlings mimic the dance of leaves on the dirt road outside. Rust-red leaves. Your hands are brown. People stare at you from other tables, someone whispering, " . . . East Indian darky . . . " 1916: you are sixty-seven years old and thousands of miles from home.

You arrived with the circus early this morning, south about a mile, where the railroad tracks crisscross a small station, amphitheater, and coal tipple: a staggering troupe of stiltmen, clowns wielding saws, and highwire women so stiff they cannot bend at the waist, at least until the next show. The trains don't even bother passing through Erwin, but this is your day off and you wanted to escape the swelter of people. Tomorrow your elephants, the ones you have trained for fifteen years, will perform for the Ringmaster. After the elephant show, you will perform again: *Come see the amazing psychic! Can read your mind! Come see the Brahmin holy man!*

You are not truly psychic. Neither are you of the Brahmin caste. You wear a Sikh turban. They expect it, even though you are Hindu and the weather hot. But at least you can be near the elephants.

***

"I have been with the shows for three years and have never known the elephant to lose her temper before."
— Mr. Heron, press agent, *Johnson City Comet*, Sept. 14, 1916, pg. 1

"'Murderous Mary', as she was termed by spectators, has been in the circus for fifteen years and this is the first time anyone has come to harm."
— *Nashville Banner*, Sept. 13, 1916, pg. 9

***

The light fades from the windows until the starlings are blurs of shadow and bar lamps reflect on the glass. You sweat despite the chill; the nervous tic under your right eye where the blood vessel has burst works in and out. Your hands become clenched claws.

The lady to the left with the matted hair and distant stare—she thinks about her next trick, the dull slap of flesh on flesh . . . the ache in her body, her heart. *Tease, you tease too much* she thinks. The man at the bar who deliberately combs his few hairs and sips his whiskey—he fears his bloodhound. It used to run for miles across his farm, but now the farm is smaller, eaten away at the edges by bankers. His wife has left him. The dog has tumors, weak back legs, and cannot hold its bladder. It lies at home by the furnace and dreams of better days. The man hates the dog. He loves the dog. If he goes home, he might find it dead, and then he will be waiting to die. Alone.

The claws bite into your palms, draw blood.

The waitress smiles as she leans over to take your plate. You smile back, her face blank to you. You can only sense the pain, enter minds through agony. Sometimes you block it by concentrating on dust motes or the pattern of raindrops on a blade of grass. You can escape it.

When you are with the solid shadows of your elephants, all the sharp edges fade away. Your clenched hands untense.

***

"Suddenly, Mary collided its trunk vice-like about his body, lifted him ten feet in the air, then dashed him with fury to the ground. Before Eldridge had a chance to reach his feet, the elephant had him pinioned to the ground, and with the full force of her beastly fury is said to have sunk her giant tusks entirely through his body. The animal then trampled the dying form of Eldridge as if seeking a murderous triumph, then with a sudden swing of her massive foot hurled his body into the crowd."

—*Johnson City Staff*, Sept. 13, 1916, pg. 3

***

You grew up in Jaipur, under the maharajah's benevolent neglect; a man who employed your parents as servants. A man who, twenty years later, would sell his elephants to the Americans to pay his debts, and your services with them.

Every day you suffered headaches or crying spells. The leper woman with her bag of shriveled flowers would ask you for coins and you saw the young woman inside her, the pretty one who would have married, laughed many days by the washing stones. If not for the decaying flesh. You ran from her, not understanding *how* or *why* you had these visions.

The merchant at the market would say, "Nice boy: have a sweet," smiling at your parents and you would hear, from deep inside his coiled thoughts: *Ugly child. Scrawny. No good for lifting sacks.* The headaches would pick away your skull. You wondered why people lied so much.

Then, when you were seven, you met the elephant and its mahout. You went with your parents on holiday—to see the Amber Palace, a tilted terrace of fortifications and tile buildings and minarets atop a mountain ridge. The snake of road circled higher and higher. Below: fields and a lake.

You gnawed your lip bloody listening to the desperation beneath beggars' prayers and your father's impatience with them as you trudged along. Your mother you could not read. Never could.

Then, sweaty, half-way up:

The elephant. Straddling the road, one front foot alone larger than you and your parents. Trunk curled, tusks capped in gold, a gilded carriage upon its back. You gasped, stumbled. And looked into its eyes.

Long-lashed, black, with no hint of reflected light. Age wrinkles spiraled down into the eye. The elephant stared at you, measured you. You shivered. *Ganesh*, you thought. The elephant-headed god of luck and wisdom.

You wanted a ride. You begged your father, clutched at your mother's sari. They, tired of walking, smiled, said yes.

That was when the mahout stepped out from behind his elephant: a shriveled man with no flesh on his bones so that his head, small on another man, seemed large. A holy man. A wise man.

You stared at your future teacher unabashedly and he bowed, pressed his palms together.

"I am Arjun, mahout of the Amber Palace."

You, solemn, bowing also: "Gautam, boy of Jaipur."

He laughed. "And someday mahout, perhaps?"

You nodded, watching the elephant.

Only after your father shoved you up onto the side ladder and you climbed into the carriage did you realize that the mendicant's pain was gone. From the dizzying height, lurching forward, touching the prickly black hairs, you could not feel the world's agonies spread out below you: the farmers on the plate-sized fields, the swimmers in the lake. Nothing. You laughed. You laughed and snuggled into your mother's arms.

You remember that moment as if it happened yesterday. You felt like a god, free of pain. Though that is impossible. The elephant was the god and the mahout its keeper.

***

"There was a big ditch at that time put there for the purpose of draining . . . and they'd sent these boys to ride the elephants. They went down to water them and on the way back each boy had a little stick-like that was a spear or hook in the end of it . . . And this big old elephant, Mary, reached over to get her a watermelon rind, about a half a watermelon somebody eat and just laid it down there; 'n she did, the boy Eldridge give her a jerk. He pulled her away from 'em and he just bowed real big; and when he did, she took him right around the waist . . . and throwed him against the side of the drink stand and just knocked the whole side out o' it. I guess it killed him, but when he hit the ground the elephant just walked over and set her foot on his head . . . and the blood and brains and stuff just squirted all over."

— W.H. Coleman, eyewitness.

***

Only one woman's face haunts you. You have been with many women, trying to block the pain. It never works; even in the throes of orgasm there is always a larger ache than before.

But you did not know this woman. Not even a name.

Four years ago—almost to the day you sit and eat at Dan's—she came to you as the shadows began to shut down your booth. Exhausted, half in trance, you had peered into the pains of a dozen men and women, lied for the contented ones who hid their disappointments deep.

The woman cleared your thoughts. She had an elegance beyond her simple cotton dress which reminded you of the leper woman as she might have been. Around her, the circus folk melted away. The Scaled Man and the Bearded Lady, the Man With Two Spears Through His Cheeks and the Lady Who Drank Blood: they enhanced her beauty all the more. She smelled of jasmine and treacle. You imagined her skin smooth beneath your touch.

You bowed to her, recited the routine the other performers had taught you, in the despised pidgin English. You speak the language with only a hint of accent.

She listened patiently, gave the drunken crowd gathered at her back a single glance, but did not wave them away. A large crowd, enlivened by an entire day of merry-making.

"Is my husband cheating on me?" A harsher voice than you imagined . . .

She had been biting back her pain and now it flooded out, embraced you. You looked into her eyes (such pretty eyes: long-lashed and black, with no reflection) and winced. The answer was wrapped around her doubts. The lies she had told herself, the imagined explanations for late night forays.

You hesitated, glanced around you at the litter of bottles and cartons, the mud and filth.

"Come on!" It was a plea.

"Yes."

The crowd roared. The circus folk chuckled, quietly mocking: the Scaled Man and the Bearded Lady and the Man With Two Spears and the Lady Who Drank Blood. A low mumble of "Fool!" and "Slut!" swept through the crowd. The wide, happy wave of amusement muffled her pain, numbed you.

You smiled. You almost laughed.

The smile left your lips when you looked up at her. You have never seen that expression before or since, the betrayal that bled from her eyes, the perfect mouth.

The woman pulled a knife from her purse. She plunged it into your chest, above the heart. Out it came, trailing red. She raised it to strike again—and on the downward stroke the Man With Two Spears caught the blade through his palm, wrenched it from her. The Scaled Man and the Bearded Lady dragged her away, she snarling and fighting them.

You stared stupidly at the wound, at the blood smeared across your costume. The crowd had broken down into its thousand parts, some screaming, some backing quietly away, a few calling for a doctor. You just stared. Time, urgency—these things were unimportant.

You daubed your finger in the bright, bright blood. *This is me?* you thought. *I am bleeding?* No pain. Like the leper in Jaipur. No pain. And, for one glorious moment, looking up into the clowns' faces, you believed you were free. But:

The clowns radiated pity. The Lady Who Drank Blood clasped your arm, aching over your wound, licking it. Your face became a mask, then crumbled. You had only become numb to your own pain. Like the old men in the Jaipur market who sucked and sucked on their opium pipes.

You are old now and the elephants have robbed you of your pain.

The cooking of crayfish brings your attention away from the window of Dan's Eatery. You know the sensation of death now (brittle, withering), have experienced it in many forms. Arjun eventually taught you to bear it, to sit still while life slipped away, though even he could never fully understand the pain.

The crayfish are lowered into the pot, their chitin turning red, dozens of eyes popping. Tiny slivers. Then: silence. Or an echo. The ghost of another, more distant pain. You cannot tell. Your hand cannot feel the heat as it clutches a cup of coffee.

You are homesick.

                    ***

"The crowd kept hollerin' and sayin', `Let's kill the elephant, let's kill 'er . . . "
     — Mr. Coleman

"Sheriff Gallahan thought he could shoot her, but he couldn't with a .45. It just knocked chips out of her hide a little."
     — Mr. Treadwell, eyewitness.

" . . . [the owner] said `People, I'd be perfectly willin' to kill her, but there's no way to kill her. There ain't gun enough in this country that she could be killed; there's no way to kill her."

— Mrs. E.H. Griffith, in a letter to Bert Vincent

***

Last night you shared the crowded freight compartment with your elephants; the *chump chump* of wheels on the track lulled you to sleep. You were so tired you slept standing up, leaning against Mary, your largest.

You dreamt.

Mary grew until her feet touched the four corners of the earth, so large that you measured less than the height of her toenails. Absurdly, the trinity—Brahma, Siva, Vishnu—whirled above her head on their appointed vehicles. She took you in her trunk, grasping you so gently that the tiniest twitch and you would have fallen to your death. She brought you up, up through the clouds until you were in the cold dark of the cosmos, looking into her eye. It seemed to question you.

You wept. In Hindi, you said, "Please, Ganesh. I am so old. Take away their pain. Give back my own pain . . . " You wept and Mary stared at you. There was no answer. It was only Mary, not Ganesh at all. The stars whispered in sanskrit, wrote messages across the dark you could not decipher.

When you woke, you brushed her and fed her cabbage heads, watermelon rinds, cooed softly in her ear when the shivering of box car metal disturbed her.

***

"Everybody was excited about it, you know—`n' come down there to watch them hang the elephant. They had a coal tipple down there; I guess the coal tipple was three hundred, four hundred feet long from the ground to the top of the tipple; and it was covered up with people just as thick as they could stand on that tipple, you know, besides what was on the ground. I'd say they `as three thousand people there . . . "

— Bud Jones, eyewitness

***

Your stomach is queasy as you walk out of Dan's Eatery into the humidity of main street Erwin. You stare up at the moon. Tonight, it is Ganesha's tusk, thin and bright through tree branches. A lucky moon.

***

"They brought those elephants down there, four or five of them together. And they had this here Mary bringing up the rear. It was just like they was havin' a parade, holdin' one another's tail . . . These other ones come up . . . and they stopped. Well, she just cut loose right there and the showmen, they went and put a chain, a small chain, around her foot, and chained her to the rail. Then they backed the wrecker up to her and throwed the big 7/8 inch chain around her neck and hoisted her, and she got up about, oh, I'll say five or six feet off the ground, and the chain around her neck broke. See, they had to pull this chain loose; it broke the smaller chain, and that weakened the other chain. And so, when they got her up about five or six feet from the ground, why it broke . . . "
 —Mont Tilly, railroad crew

" . . . And it kind o' addled her when it fell, you know. And we quick `n' got another chain and put it around her neck then and hooked it before she could get up."
 — Bud Jones, fireman on the 100-ton derrick car

***

You are running out of Erwin the moment the chain first bites into Mary's neck—down the dirt road, into the darkness of trees. The circus is a mile away. *The trains don't even bother passing through Erwin . . . How will you save her now? Your teeth bite through your lower lip, blood trickling onto your shirt. You feel nothing.*

The scene flickers across your mind, brought to you by clowns' eyes: bonfires lick across train tracks, the coal tipple engorged with people, the crowd below noisy and whiskey-slicked. Mary trumpets as she rises. The derrick strains. The other elephants, already packed onto the train, trumpet too, butt their heads against the steel doors. You choke on tears as you run, the air tightening in your throat.

Soon, you can see the fires for yourself, the tops of tipple and derrick, twin towers. Mary trumpets, *mahout!*

The derrick (in the clowns' eyes) trembles, chain breaking, and Mary falls with a soft thud onto the grass, onto her lungs. You cry out, fall with her, tumble, and lie sprawled on the ground. Blind, images super-imposed over your sight, you scramble to your feet.

The chain is brought twice around Mary's neck. You cannot breathe. A branch whips across your face, stings, but you see only Mary's shadow, lit by fires, rising again into the air. You choke on the crowd's fascination as they watch. The hooker and the man from the bar are both there, forgetting their own pain. *Tease, you tease too much.* You cannot go home to a dog which may be dead . . .

Mary against the fire sky, against the tusk of moon.

Now you sprint, sure you will die of the exertion, but not caring. You can smell the smoke, hear the crowd for yourself. So close. So close.

Mary jerks and you jerk, brought up short. Blood trickles from both your mouths. "Ere—look at the beast!" The crowd laughs. Clowns sob. The Bearded Lady rips out her hair. Mary's struggles weaken. Your legs dangle.

For a moment, a moment in which time has no meaning, you gaze out from Mary's eyes as you gently swing, look down upon the crowd, the dancing fires, across the tipple and its human cargo.

Juicy leaves; muddy waterholes; a lazy trunk across the backs of other ele-phants; hoopoo birds pecking lice from wrinkled skin; shadows of elephants at twilight, under the sanskrit sky; and then danger, danger orange and bright; fangs and tusks. Tiger.

You cry out, convulse at the moment of death, the reluctant *crack* of neck, and as Mary's eyes roll back into her head, so do yours. Your neck snaps to the side and you fall, hands clenched so tightly a knuckle pops. Your nerve ends are on fire. Everything around you shrieks with pain; every blade of grass, every tree.

The pain is an elephant eye—coronaed in amber. *Ganesh.* Then you lose yourself in the reflectionless black.

***

"She kicked a bit and that was all; see, that thing choked her to death right quick."

— Sam Harvey, train engineer.

***

1857. The smell of attar, the humid, moist taste of death, surrounded Jaipur. A bad year for you when you could not be near elephants. You had nightmares. The Sepoy Revolt, starting outside Mekut, spread until even the maharajahs seized at chances for independence.

One summer day you glanced up from the lake below the Amber Palace and saw elephants trudging across the ridge, fitted out in full battle dress. Arjun, your teacher now, rode the lead elephant, and he too was dressed for war.

Your parents had told you the plans last night, but you hadn't believed them. A show of strength, your father said. They would not fight, only bring luck to the maharajah. Your mother frowned, shook her head. Regardless, to send elephants against the British was madness. How could elephants match rifles and cannon?

You watched for a long time, while trumpets sounded and peacocks gave their mating calls. To the west: smoke and vultures. The battle. All day, after the elephants had faded from sight, you watched the trail of smoke, the circling vultures. So many vultures. So much smoke. Sometimes you imagined you heard cannon recoil, a tremor beneath your feet.

The lake waters turned a darker and darker blue, shadows long and distorted. You fell asleep. When you woke, the smoke was closer, the vultures identifiable by species. Along the ridge, the sun's rays driving like spikes into their backs: the mahouts and their elephants. Some mahouts upon litters, bodies stretched out, others slumped across their elephants. You counted. Thirty elephants had gone out. Twenty had returned. You could hear their moans, could feel their pain, even from the lake. Your heartbeat quickened. Disaster . . .

You ran up the road to the Amber Palace, breathless. Through the quiet courtyard, the gardens, to the stables, there to meet a tired, wounded Arjun, death reflected in his eyes. He reeked of smoke and gunpowder, had burns on his face and arms. All around, elephants screamed, some with shrapnel wounds, veins laid open; others on their knees, their mahouts pleading with them to get up.

Your jaw dropped and the pain twisted your joints. Not real. A nightmare. Where was Arjun's elephant?

"Lakshmi, master?" Your voice shook.

For the first time, Arjun was an old man to you, back bent, movements slow.

"Lakshmi is dead."

"Dead?"

"Yes! Please. Go away."

And you left, too shocked to cry.
Ganesh dead? How could a god be dead?

***

"We did not sit in judgment on her fate and I don't believe any of
those who witnessed the event felt it was inhumane under the circumstances. She paid for her crimes as anyone else would."
— Mrs. Griffith, eyewitness.

***

Blood drips onto the grass; the Lady Who Drank Blood laps at the
widening pool. They have hoisted Mary upside down from the derrick.
Her head hangs three feet from the ground, shadow small in the early
morning light.

You crouch beside her, the clowns behind you. Mary's eye is open
again, the wrinkles and long lashes and the reflectionless black. You
wave the flies away. You are crying. You cannot help yourself. Your
throat aches. *Ganesh* . . . You touch the bristly hair, the rough skin. Cold.
Much too cold.

You will not work the booth today. Or ever again. The clowns weep
but you feel nothing. Just your own grief. Just the chill wind blowing
through you, and you so light and heavy at the same time. Burnt out.
Now what will you do? *Take away their pain*, you said.

But, like your old mahout, you know you will never be whole again.

Quotes adapted, with permission, from the *Tennessee Folklore Society Bulletin*, Vol. XXXVII, March 1971.

FLUTE AND HARP

by James S. Dorr

There are places in the Tombs that many do not wish to wander too near to, even those of us who care for the dead. We, the crypt-keepers, the resident living, avoid these not out of apprehension—that some tomb-wraith or other night-vision beneath a blistering moon might disturb our peregrinations—but rather for respect of the stories told of those who lie within.

***

Ratcatchers know things. We ply our trade everywhere, even beyond the Tombs, for even in the glistening New City is not the rat still the poor man's supper? And there are many poor in the New City, and elsewhere across the land—even the Old City, where ghouls hold traffic with Necromancers. There some eat the rat too, or so I have been told.

It is the Universal, the rat is: Loved by all, though some feign distaste for it. Yet what I say here has not to do with rats, but of another thing loved as well, by most who will listen, both of the Old and the New and the Tomb-Cities, both north and west and south on the Great River, and that thing is music.

And of that there were two who I had met once, who each, later on, gave their all for the other.

***

It was Harp I met first. I do not know if she had any other name—she would not tell me—but only that it was an early evening during the time of the Moon of Tempests that I first saw her. There had been rain during the day just ended, a hard, caustic rain that had sizzled from a sky just begun baking with summer's portended heat, and thus I had come out, nets and ratpicks at the ready, at first hint of darkness.

I still wore my *chador*, that garment which we donned against the sun's scalding rays even at last twilight, even when black clouds still scudded across a sky that was sinking by then to its own star-pricked blackness, for, as I have said, the hour was still early. But that which I sought would be early as well this night.

Because, you see, one must think like a rat if one is to catch them. We, the two-legged dwellers, lived with the dead we protected within their tombs, sheltered ourselves by marble roof-slabs, by deep, brick-lined tunnels from the actinic day, and from the acid that rained from the clouds as well. This latter, rather, we caught in great filter-nets strung from the tomb-tops, channeling the flow of it downward through mesh-sided funnels to underground cisterns where, boiled and settled, re-filtered and made pure, we then could even bathe in it or drink it. But, as for my furry prey, their lairs were shallow.

Their tunnels, their warrens, more prone to flooding.

And thus it was, at first dark, rats would stream upward, to regain the surface. Shaking the moisture from their gray-velvet sides, swishing their naked tails. Preening and primping.

And so I, now laying my *chador* aside as to free my limbs for more vigorous action, would spring to their hole-portals, raking them outward. Would trap them in meshes of burlap or hemp, casting my nets thus filled hard onto carved stones, to granite remembrances. Then, reaching down, I would wring sinewed necks, winding a single bight about each of them of the stout catch-cord that hung from my shoulders.

And so, thump, thump, thumping against my back as I continued onward, my prey and I wandered amid the tomb-valleys, where water would run to. I always alert, my ratpick at the ready, thrusting, raking back each new small shadow.

So I nearly did not hear the sound of *thrumming*.

***

It was Harp, as I say. The moon was rising, already a waning moon—gibbous still, though, and the clouds now departed—already atop the Emperor's Pyramid, that great stone vault with its angel-formed pinnacle that crowned our tomb-land's ancient center, its compass-rose, as it were, despite the centuries of its walls' expansions, and I saw what I at first took to be, perhaps, a will-o'-the-wisp. A heat-caused vision. A vision and sounding.

I saw her seated, naked at first I thought, on the west hill-slope on the roof of a small mausoleum that had been deserted, I knew, for some decades. Ratcatchers know these things. I saw her gazing, as if at the angel now silhouetted against the moon's brightness, strumming an instrument cradled against her chest. I heard the notes she strummed, plaintive and misery-soaked. Hungered and wanting.

And I saw her beauty.

Rat-like, I skulked myself from shadowed tomb-side to mist-filled alley, keeping to darkness as not to disturb her. Drinking her music's sound. Prick-eared, I listened. And rat-eyed, beady, I gazed on her sweat-sheened skin, now turned golden in the moon's rising, sheathed, I saw now, in thin, white, silken garments, slit at the sides and stretched taut across her breasts, nearly transparent.

And I saw her harp as well, carved from the bones of an arched, human ribcage, strung with what looked like hair. Gleaming in moonlight. And her own hair, also, as white as her instrument, as white as the robes that encased her body—such parts as they *did* encase—tumbling in silver waves about her torso. Her slim waist and soft, curved hips as, her song finished, she stood abruptly.

I must have gasped then—a sudden intake of breath—because, before I could stand as well, she had whirled to face me.

"What are you?" she demanded, clutching her harp in front of her body, as if to protect herself.

"I, my lady?" I bowed as I spoke so, and turned briefly to the side so she could view my wares. "I?" I said once more. "I am but a ratcatcher, a humble purveyor of meat for men's suppers." Then hastily added, recalling the hunger I had heard within her song, "And women's also."

I saw her nose wrinkle as if to show some disgust, as if she were one who was not used to rat-meat. Except she smiled also, and this gesture showed relief.

"Then not a ghoul?" she said. "Not one who would eat *me?*"

I could not help it. I laughed when she said that. "Ghouls do not eat the *living*," I said between chortles. "It is not a thing allowed—neither here in the Tombs nor elsewhere, since time beyond memory."

"And yet I have feared it," she said. "I have dreamed it."

"You are not of us, then? Not of the Tombs?" I asked. "Not one who would know, at first hand as we do, what ghouls will do to those that are dead should we fail to build our walls ever stronger, to increase our vigilance . . . ?"

"No," she cut me off. "I am of the New City, sneaked in with the mourners when last night's corpse-train crossed over the causeway. When morning came I hid here —" She gestured downward, swinging her harp wide, at the mausoleum.

"Yet," I said, "your instrument, lady . . . ?"

She nodded. "My father bought this for me years ago, from one of your artisans." She showed it to me, the carvings of its frame, its stringing, yes, of some ancient woman's hair, braided in strands and treated with oil to counter its brittleness. "It was expensive."

"And yet he afforded it," I said. "You must then be wealthy. And yet . . . you have come here."

I left unasked that which I most wanted to know, the *why* of her being here. There were others, true, some of legends, not born of the Tombs but who had come here still living to stay. The richest of rich, a man named Gombar. Another, a woman, who had been named Trinity and who was cast out, and yet, the story went, whose bones were laid in the Pyramid itself, displacing those that were already there. But these were *just* legends—while this one who stood before me was alive now.

She nodded. "Yes. I have come to the Tombs of my own accord because, though we were wealthy—though I could have all I asked, lessons in music, jewelry, clothing—there was some *thing*, and I still know not what it is, that no one in the New City could give me."

She blushed as she went on: "I was to be married . . ."

"Yes?" I prompted.

She shook her head, shaking the white of her hair down in cascades, rippling in shining streams. "*That* was not it either," she said. She changed the subject. She gazed at my catch-cord.

"You said people eat *those*?"

I nodded myself then. I knew she was hungry, that she had not eaten since at least the last evening. "Yes," I answered. I followed her into her mausoleum-home and showed her how best to cook the rat, taking spices I had from my own pack to show how best to spice it. I took my knife showing her how to cut it, in tender filets, and how best to eat it.

Then finally she nodded, filled. "I cannot pay you. My father is wealthy, but that which is mine—save only this harp which I will never part with—is across the river."

"I know," I said—I knew also then that her *name* here would be Harp. "It is the way of the wealthy to not pay, unless they are forced to. That is how they *get* rich. And yet, my lady, you have paid already."

She looked puzzled then so I quickly added. "Your music, lady. You have performed for me and it was beautiful, just as you are yourself.

And I have friends who would wish to hear you play, if you are willing, who would bring you food in exchange for their listening, and other comforts."

And so it happened that in the weeks' waning of that Moon of Tempests, Harp played for the Tombs and once more became wealthy.

***

But it was at the new moon, the dark that presages the Moon of Lovers and summer heat's rising, that one more thing happened. It had been a time of solar flares, and strange portendings—some that even mutated the rats themselves, as I found out later, some of them anyway, making them smarter, harder to catch, cleverer, and, somehow, more *appreciative*—when a cry came from the River Gate, below the arched causeway that Harp had arrived on.

"A boat!" was the cry. "A gypsy boat coming!" And I ran with the others down the cut granite stairs, down to the river quay, such catch as I had a-thump on my back as I rushed to be first on the level landing, since rivermen, also, buy rat when it's offered them.

But this boat did not stop. Rather, it veered away, its crewmen only dropping a bundle off onto the stone pier.

A bundle that moved and groaned.

I was first reaching it, Harp just behind me—Harp, who I might have wished to be my lover, should she have accepted me, but, rather, had become somewhat my daughter, bejeweled now in cut stone and golden trinkets the color of her own skin, glinting in torchlight, the moon being new. Her gossamer-white garments swishing around her.

And so it was I who stooped, seeing the bundle still wrapped in a day *chador*, slowly unwinding it. Helping it to its feet.

Others stood back now: Revealed was a woman, her skin as white as the pearls of the river, with hair black as midnight! A twin, almost, to Harp in youth and beauty, save for their coloring—both slim and lithe-bodied, long-legged and trim-waisted, yet lushly curved of breast and hip and with soft, rounded shoulders and delicate thighs. And hair, while straight where Harp's was loosely curled, cascading, too, nearly down to the cleft of strong, supple buttocks.

She stood and she stretched, stepping over the *chador* that now lay discarded and saying not a word while Harp and I both inspected the garments she had worn beneath it, again almost Harp's twins. Sheer and diaphanous, slit for limb-movement and letting the soft summer air cool the flesh within, except, as all river-daughters did, where Harp preferred silks as pale as the moon's glow, she favored brightness. A crimson blood-color, as red as the paints of her finger- and toe-nails, the color of daylight's sun, and the bruise of her lips, just as Harp's lips were a scarlet as well, contrasting with jewelry—not earth-stone as Harp wore, of emeralds and topaz—but amber and shell beads.

And on her back—Harp saw it first, before I did! Before I realized what it was I *did* see. On her back this riverwoman had slung a hollowed bone of some great sea-creature, carved and finger-holed. Bleached and banded, as white as Harp's hair, as white as her *own* skin, and mouth-holed for playing.

Harp hated her at the sight.

But I, I questioned. A river-chieftain's daughter I knew she was from the paleness of her skin, always pampered below-decks in day's light, not even risking the sun in a *chador*, and her hair's straightness that showed it had never been braided for deck-work, even in nighttime.

But what had brought *her* here, if then a chief's daughter?

She would not answer me, I but a ratcatcher. But I heard gossip—we ratcatchers have a way of knowing such things—of what she told the head of the quay-guards when that man asked her. That she had been disowned by her father because she had refused the hand of a greater chief's son.

***

And so she was called Flute among we Tombs-people because she had given the guard no other name, even when he had asked. Perhaps she *had* no other name, her father no doubt having taken that back from her as well when she had fallen into his disfavor. Leaving her only the instrument she now played, skirling, wildly, atop the Pyramid when she would stand there, a twin to the angel that stood beside her.

While Harp would play below, down on her western slope, down below her mausoleum-home, while Flute, by contrast, always faced east. To the river she still must have loved in her heart, even if not a chief's son.

And so it happened that both became favored among the Tombs-people through the near-magicalness of their talents, Harp with the sedateness of classical measures, her right hand fingering over the ground, her left answering back in tinkling arpeggios, bold glissandi, while Flute, more untutored, played natural, wild rhythms of rivers' enchantment, of gypsy-toned rhapsodies skirling the night sky. And yet they would have nothing to do with each other, Harp during the daytime retreating, alone, to her mausoleum. Flute going to who knew where? One does not ask such things of a river-chieftain's daughter.

And suitors they had too, not mere ratcatchers such as I was, but their pick of the best of the Tombsmen, guard-chiefs, embalmers, artists and artisans, wealthy and honored. People who gave them jewels—yet they refused them.

And both seemed searching—for *something*. They knew not what. Until another month passed. Two months. A quarter and then a half of a year until it was winter, a time of thin snows, of occasional ice at night melting in day's heat, a good time for rat-catching, when the sun flared again.

This time there was scarcely any warning. It happened at night, but a night of the full moon, the Moon of Land's Starving, and death reflected off the moon itself. Neither had played that night—they did not play *all* nights—and Harp had been wandering by the River Wall, east of her normal haunts, when the cry came up.

Ghouls, was her first thought—whatever I told her, she could not shake *that* fear. The fear that had come to her once in a dream, and so had the power of a possible omen. But where could she run to?

She was far from her home, while all about her—this I heard later—people with more wisdom of the *true* danger ran scurrying, hastening to their own tunnels. Little knowing that Harp was lost. All alone. When strong, white hands grasped her, one circling around her waist, clutching its slimness. "Hurry!" a voice whispered, one seldom heard to speak—even by guard-chiefs.

And so, unyielding, Harp let the river-daughter lead her down to a chink in the stone of the boat-gate, a cleft in the granite just over the water. Just large enough to fit the two of them, but deep enough to protect them from the glare.

As each in the other's arms they huddled.

I heard these things, as I say, although much later. We ratcatchers learn things, and rats, that live in the chinks of rocks as well, have eyes to see with, and ears to hear with.

And mouths to speak with—these rats grown clever.

And so I know now how Harp must have shuddered. "I thought it was ghouls," she said.

And how Flute had laughed then, but reassuringly, her soft voice tinkling like miniature bells as she hugged Harp closer. "Then you should avoid me," she said, "because ghouls and my people have enmity. They would destroy me, if they were able. It is a superstition of theirs that in times past our boats have brought ill luck."

"But you have saved me," Harp whispered back to Flute, as their bodies rubbed one on the other, so narrow was the chink that they lay in. With room enough only to thrust their instruments farther below them, to keep them from being crushed. "While I, I admit it, I *hated* you at first—because in you I could see a rival. But later because I thought you disliked *us*, your standoffish ways, your not even speaking when you could avoid it. Not even to my ratcatcher companion when he had only asked who you were."

"It is the way," Flute said, "of we river-people, not to speak much even to one another but rather to listen to the water's flowing, the creak of boats' timbers, the flap of wind on our sails. These things we must do, lest we wreck and be drowned."

And Harp shuddered again, deliciously, rubbing against Flute's body. Her hands finding room even in the chink's narrowness to wrap around Flute's lithe thighs, as Flute's hands, in turn, found just space enough to stroke Harp's soft breasts. As scarlet lips met lips.

Both knowing now why they had been outcasts, the one self-imposed, the other unwillingly.

But both, now, *knowing*.

***

Three nights they lay there, or so it has been said, before the storm quieted enough for them to go out. And afterward, Flute moved to Harp's mausoleum, spending her days now with Harp in her arms. And Harp, in turn, loving Flute. While evenings they would emerge to play duets, taking their stand not on top of the Pyramid, nor to the west slope and their mausoleum-home, but on the Pyramid's broad, eastern plaza, surrounded by obelisks, where Flute could still see the water she craved, and Harp could feel safe with the stone spires around her, soaring above like the New City's towers.

***

And this was something new.

***

Playing together, they syncopated, their melodies weaving. Trading crescendos. Their rhythms augmenting. Once they even played back a summer storm—it was an evening of the Goldsmelters' Moon, late in the summer when rain fronts gather and lightning crackles—and thunder boomed out its own cadence behind them. But Harp answered back, strumming rhythm for rhythm, while Flute wailed and countered, screeching a melody over the lightning's flash. *And the storm held back,* until they were finished.

Then laughing, frolicking, they with the rest of us ran for shelter, just ahead of the rain's acid boiling, clapping hats to their heads, broad-brimmed hats as we all wore in summer's rain when we could not escape. Raven-haired, silver—tangling in the wind. Then gasping, laughing still, they rolled and clutched in each other's arms, sweat-sheened bodies embraced together, the tan-gold and pearl-white, in their mausoleum. One made for the other.

Playing each other like flesh-formed instruments. That night and others, when they had completed their more public concerts, and during the days too, adding their own heat to that of the sun outside. Making of *that* an even sweeter music than that which they gave us in evenings' gloom, beneath the moonlight. Their bodies still passion-sheened, still lusting, always, but fingers now dancing the holes of a bone-formed flute, gently caressing the oiled hair of harp-strings in lieu of each other's hair. In lieu of soft-formed thighs, sweet breasts, sweet clefts below. Yet dancing nonetheless, speaking their love to *us.*

Playing to us desire: That of twin-souls at last coming together, playing, each to the other, orchestrations yet *higher* than those we could listen to. We, with ears alone.

Until Flute sickened. The spring that followed, that rose to summer, again on a Lovers' Moon only just waxing, Flute, whose constitution was delicate from always breathing the river's vapors, as all river-people's were—always breathing its poisons from birth on—whose smooth, white skin, continually sheltered, had been more sensitive to the sun's deadly flare, yet who still had rushed out in its midst to lead Harp to safety, grew listless and weary. And, as the moon reached to its full, Flute's own life faded—as river-tides ebb in the heat of summer.

And Harp played no music now. Not as she realized, not just that her musician-lover had left her, but that this death came from the very sun's-poison that Flute had willingly let flood her body on that night of rescue, even though she and Harp *were* rivals.

Had hated each other.

At least had been rivals then, though now, at last, had discovered their true passion, only to have it wrenched suddenly from them—from Harp at least—before it had scarcely had time to flower.

But this much Harp could do: She called us together. She asked us for jewelry, both river-shell jewels as Flute's people cherished and earth-stones as we wore, to heap on Flute's corpse where it lay in shade outside their mausoleum for preparation for final entombment. She added to these her own, that she had earned from us, tearing her hair out as well to heap on it, and begged us for flowers, and beads, and incense, perhaps recalling the tales of another river-chief's daughter who, it was said, had had these things and more—even real coins of brass and gold!—to aid her soul's-journey. And, of that which she asked, we gave her willingly.

But there was one thing we could *not* do for Harp, as we found out later. That was to protect her.

***

A night, two nights, Flute's corpse lay, shaded, guarded in daytime by those of my trade under thick, cloth tent-tops to keep the sun from us, while Harp helped the gravediggers select a tomb-site. We kept the rats from it, the lizards and corpse-beetles, while Harp assisted in the haggling with the embalmers, the monument-cutters and inscription carvers, the epitaph-poets and remembrance-composers. And all the time we wept, too, even as Harp did, if not so deeply.

But then on the third night a cry went up: "Ghouls! Ghouls on the west wall! Ghouls to the south as well!"

And we responded. The ghouls had found out somehow, who it was who had died. Possibly some of the rats had told them, ghouls knowing how to listen as well as such as I, but, far more likely, they used the skills of the Necromancers who live among them. And that had brought them forth, risking all now to make a direct assault on our Tomb-ground, because the ghouls hate and fear gypsy-boat sailors.

It is among them, some say, an ancient superstition, some adding that it goes to a time when the world was in turmoil and the day-sun just beginning to grow large, to turn to deadliness, when the rivers themselves teemed with corpses which, so the ghouls had hoped, the river-people might drag to shore for them, to use for their own delight.

But which the boat-chiefs flatly refused them, thus starting a new war—or so some tell us.

Be that as it may, the ghouls *knew* a river-chief's daughter lay dead among us. And they would despoil her.

And we would prevent this.

So, screaming ourselves, we raced through tomb-alleys, snatching up weapons, ratpicks and sharpened spades, swords and stout, iron-ringed shafts, to west and south where blue mist congregated. The blued-gas glow of telltale ghoul-lamps! Leaving Harp, shivering and frightened as she was, to continue alone in her mourning. To finger, perhaps, the now-disused strings of her rib-curved harp, which she still continued to have with her always, or maybe to touch the hard bone of Flute's instrument, clutched as it still was in her lover's dead hands.

We cared not. We fought ghouls! It was our duty. We pressed back against their sea of blue lights, as if to fight back the river's own waters.

And yet they rolled over us, so great were they in their frenzied numbers, forcing *us* backward. Some few stopping to eat their own dead—so fiercely did *we* fight—as was the ghouls' way, but others still pushing us.

Until we heard a note. A tone sounding.

A short riff of music.

"Halt!" a voice shouted—a soft, woman's voice. A voice steeped in sorrow. And, inexplicably, *all* of us halted. Both Tombs-people *and* ghouls.

"Let me speak," Harp said, for it was Harp—we had been forced back *that* far, to the mausoleum before which Flute's body lay, Harp alone standing now between it and the ghoul-horde.

"Let me play, rather," she said to the ghouls alone, we, at her nodding, parting to let them hear. "Let me tell you of her, so as to dissuade you. Her whose flesh you would eat. Her, who in death you would dishonor, if only in that way to scorn her people."

She played another note. Another riff. Her hands at first trembling, just as her body did, in fear of those that stood, waiting, before her. In fear of dreams she had had. Yet now, as her fingers plucked the silk hair-strings, growing stronger. More sure in their music.

And now she strummed loudly, her right hand holding a firm, rhythmic bass, as strong and yet yielding as Flute's body had been once, her left now playing crescendos over it, tinkling, treble, as Flute's light fingers had once danced, tap-tapping the softness of her *own* flesh. When they had made love. And, over all, playing the love she *still* held for Flute, and Flute's for her when once they had come to know each other.

And, even before that, Flute's sacrifice for her—the courage of a river-daughter who ventured out into the sun's reflected glare, to share her cleft in the rock with a stranger. A stranger who *hated* her—just as the ghouls did. And yet found love there, also, sharing it freely until her body quit, succumbing, finally, to that light's poison.

And she played the tunes, now, that Flute had taught her: The wild, river rhythms, yet muted in Harp's own way, interwoven with New City melodies. The sad, plaintive wailings, yet coupled with New City order and hopefulness. Twined, as their love had been, one to another in souls' completeness.

A love that *transcended* death.

And so she played—and *all* of us listened—until her fingers were shattered and blood-stained, their flesh tearing off in shreds on her harp's strings. Oiling its oiled-hair with a finer substance. As, still, she played on, bone-tips now plucking hair-strings, grating on sound-board until she could play no more.

Until, at last, sighing, she placed the harp at her feet.

And, for a moment, no one made a motion.

Then one of the ghouls spoke, a leader among them: "You have, my lady, made your point well. Of your love for this corpse that lies dead before us. Yet we are what we are, every one of us here. These guards who would stop us, were we not so many. Even you, musician, who were you still able would play more to halt us—yet cannot halt *nature*."

The ghoul-chief paused, then pointed to Flute's still form:

"She is our prey, lady."

Harp shook her head. Kneeling, she shook her head, letting her long, torn hair whisk around her like river waves in a summer's sudden squall. She who, with Flute, *had* once halted a summer storm.

"No," she answered. She lay at full length on the corpse of her lover, then looked up again at the ghouls who, by now, were circling around it. Seeing us clutch at our weapons as well, but stopping us with a gesture of her hand.

She kissed Flute's corpse once, then laid her harp on it, on top of the bone flute, as she once more stood to face the ghouls alone. "If it is your nature, then, that you must have your prey, then take *my* body. In fair exchange, ghoul-chief—a song, which you have had, in exchange for a wish. Flute's corpse to lie where it is, unmolested, in exchange for a life."

This time the ghouls' leader shook his head. "For us to eat those who live is not permitted . . . "

Harp shouted then, throwing her arms wide: "*You have my permission!*"

And, nodding his acquiescence, the ghoul-chief rushed her, he with his fellows, cutting, biting, stripping her flesh from her bones as she once had dreamed—as she once had so *feared*—taking her where she stood, still alive. Screaming. The ghouls' own whistling shouts drowning her dying cries. While we stood, helpless, it having been her last wish—and, thus, a wish that must be respected.

Until they finished and let her bones clatter, as white as Flute's instrument, leaving *that* corpse untouched. As was their bargain.

***

All that was left, besides bone, of Harp's corpse was the heft of her grief-torn hair. That and her finger-tips, bleeding and shredded, which the ghouls left also, after, their grim meal done, they had departed. While we, we took these things and laid them in a box, placing the still intact harp on her ribcage, curved bone to curved bones, and carried it, with Flute's corpse, up the hillside.

We took them both, against all custom, to our Necropolis's most ancient grave-ground, specially guarded, which was reserved for our own Tombs-dead, and taboo for all others. It was against custom, but here in the Tombs, of all places, we value love.

And what Harp had done for the one *she* loved, even if neither had been born among us, demanded, at the least, this much exception: That we entomb the two together, in a stone palace that looked on the river—the river that always had been so a part of Flute—yet was itself surrounded by others, a city of tombs, where Harp whose roots had been of the New City might find comfort also.

And there we left them, the things they had valued in life around them, their jewelry, their instruments. The other death-offerings Harp had so pleaded from us for her friend's corpse—the flowers and tokens. And most important of all, with each other, the one's body shattered, the other still whole, but both lying together, arms wrapped around trim torsos. Just as they had in life.

And so they lie still, few of us going there, rather preferring to leave them to their souls'-ease, save for one night a year, that of the first of the New Lovers' Moon, when, somehow, we feel we have been invited. Some of us say, then, that they can hear music. . .

And I know this to be true.

I, a ratcatcher, catch snippets of gossip, some even from rats themselves, they with the sharpest ears of us all and grown wise in the passing years since that sun's-flaring. And so I know this well:

That these, which assemble in silence among us, come to listen also.

MADAME EULALIE'S BACK STREET BORDELLO

by Julie Anne Parks

I've always advised my friends to follow their gut instincts. Too bad I didn't follow my own advice.

It stood at the end of the block enshrouded in mist. Fogfire drifted off the waterfront and hugged the ground, obliterating the building's foundation, while evening fog hung just over the roofline. The resulting illusion was of a building suspended in cloud, hovering, disconnected from the space-time continuum. There was something unsettling about it.

But I told myself that the building was probably ordinary and it was only my mind that was fanciful—common enough in New Orleans where reality is unnecessary baggage. The haunting strains of the "second line" jazz funeral drifting on sultry delta air from Lafayette Cemetery reinforced the surrealism. Or maybe my hormonal rush sabotaged my gut instincts—my erection was enormous in anticipation, making it difficult to walk and impossible to listen to that little voice shouting alarms inside my head.

I was going to a bordello for the first time—the infamous "Madame Eulalie's Back Street Bordello." Add the fact that I was hosted by my archenemy, Robbie Packer, and you can understand why it all seemed surreal.

Two weeks before, Robbie was a co-worker who'd never so much as bought me a drink. Paying for this escapade was an attempt to make amends for pulling the proverbial rug out from under me.

"I dunno, Robbie," I said, staring at our destination. "It looks . . . creepy. Shouldn't there be more traffic? A bouncer at the door or something?"

A lazy-ass grin inched over his face like poison oak. He slung his arm across my shoulder. "Not at Madame Eulalie's. That'd be too gauche, too 'red-light district' for a place this classy."

Like a snot-nosed kid, I scuffed my toe into the pavement. He was slick and I was two steps behind, had been since he presented *my* idea to the honchos at Everson & Dunn as *his* and was rewarded with *my* promotion. As you might imagine, that thew a monkey wrench into any possible friendship, but only to a point. What Robbie knew and I ignored was that I'd stolen the same idea from Martha Kennedy so I couldn't hate him completely—only fifty percent.

Now he was trying to square things by giving me a night at a legendary place. I was twenty-seven years—what was more important than getting laid?

Listening to my gut instincts. But excitement drowned out common sense.

The building, framed by massive live oaks festooned with Spanish Moss, oozed French Quarter charm: black wrought iron balustrades and railings, black shutters, a red front door with discreet gilt letters proclaimed it "Madame Eulalie's." The effect was innocuous—the mansion of a prominent socialite lawyer, perhaps, or a small finishing school for southern belles.

Instead, it supposedly housed women who would fulfill my every fantasy—and my fantasies are base.

The structure was like me: innocuous on the outside, depraved within. Life would be simpler if things were what they seemed. Simpler, but less interesting. It made me edgy to have my fantasies fulfilled in a place that looked like a building my mother might have entered—refined and elegant. I'd be more comfortable humping my way through a place with "XXX" flashing outside, the kind of place Mama didn't even know existed. And what a stupid name! "Madame Eulalie's" . . . made me think of gents in fedoras and women with bustles and bonnets.

Warm yellow light spilled from tall windows. Muffled laughter and tinny music drifted toward us on the heavy Mississippi air.

Robbie nudged me toward our target. "You'll remember this night forever."

At least that was true.

My nerve endings tingled and everything began striking me as sinister—even the Spanish moss seemed to be whispering at me as I brushed past it to open the door. I cocked my head, trying to make out the words from a multitude of whispering voices, then felt my face flush when I realized what I was doing.

A tremble ran down my spine when we entered. The room itself was what Mama would have called "refined". Pale blue satin wallpaper and gaslights zipped me back through time to an era of strict social structure and protocol. And although laughter and music filtered out the windows when we were outside looking in, inside the silence was so palpable you could have heard a leaf quivering in the breeze. The silence stopped just short of oppressive.

A soft rustling whooshed toward us and I glanced toward the door.

An enormously tall woman—probably 6'4" or 6'5"—swept through the doorway in a whisper of black taffeta and white lace. She was drop-dead gorgeous.

"Hullo, boys," she said in a throaty alto. "Welcome to Madame Eulalie's Back Street Bordello. I'm Lucretia and I'll be your hostess tonight. I do guest orientation."

Orientation?

I didn't want to be oriented. Bring on the broads and let the party begin. But I didn't want to be crass, either. "Robbie's been here before. He's—"

Lucretia's smile widened. "You're mistaken. One visit per customer is our policy." She turned toward a small bar and slid two liqueur glasses from their rack.

While she was turned away, I whirled toward Robbie. "You said—"

He shrugged, grinning sheepishly. "I said I was treating you to a once in a lifetime night. I've heard rumors of this place for years. Even my dad used to whisper about Madame Eulalie's."

I'd heard the buzz, too, but no one I knew had actually been.

Lucretia turned and handed us glasses filled with amber liquid. I sniffed—summer fields and babbling brooks came to mind with an undertone of absinthe.

"Your friend's right, Buddy," Lucretia said. "Madame Eulalie's has been around since before the War of Northern Aggression. We're world-renowned. This very evening we have an Arabian, a Japanese and a Finnish guest amongst our own Americans. Shall we start?"

Strangely eager to find favor with this lovely woman, I said, "No business can survive without repeat clients. How does yours?"

Her black almond eyes narrowed. "You will find, *chrie*, that Madame Eulalie's does not observe your tawdry business rules. There are no other establishments like this—our 'clients' don't make reservations—they are invited. And our guest list is selective indeed. Shall we start? I must know where your pleasures lie. Male? Female? Beast? We don't offer children."

"Beasts?" I squeaked.

"Female," Robbie said.

She nodded. "Passive? Aggressive?"

"Aggressive."

"Racial or ethnic preferences?"

"What do you offer?" Robbie ventured.

Lucretia's shrugged casually. "White, Black, Asian, Eurasian, Hispanic, Native American. Plus mixtures of them all, of course."

"Of course," we both babbled simultaneously. Robbie held up his empty glass. "May I?"

Lucretia nodded, filled him up and topped mine off. "Ethnically we have every nationality except I lost my Mongolian last week and my Australian ladies are engaged for the evening. Otherwise, we can accommodate any wish, including assortments."

My knees threatened to buckle. The potential was too much to grasp on any level but hormonal. What if I couldn't last long enough to savor the . . . assortment?

"Assortment," Robbie said as nonchalantly as if he were ordering doughnuts—three glazed, two jelly, one cream filled. "Can we go together and switch off?"

She laughed heartily. "Fine," she said. "My ladies enjoy company during their amusements. Except for the southerners. They feel obligated to write 'thank-you's' after group sex and because of our business's . . . Peculiarities . . . that's not possible. It upsets them. Ambiance?"

"What about it?"

"Do you prefer outdoors? A luxury suite? A sultan's tent? An oriental garden? Tropical beach? We can provide them all."

I didn't care about "ambiance". My pick-up truck sounded good by then. I wanted to get on with it before I was too limp to enjoy myself.

Robbie was babbling something about Roman villas, chaises and hot tubs.

His voice was muffled—distorted the way a heavy fog distorts sound, making things far away sound close and things close, distant. I turned toward him. He was blurry.

So was Lucretia, almost as if I were watching them through a portrait photographer's misty lens.

Perhaps that swig of the absinthe-like stuff had been too greedy. Maybe it was sippin' whiskey.

Wouldn't it be my luck to pass out and not remember my one night of bliss?

"Okay with you, Buddy?" Lucretia asked.

I nodded, then couldn't *stop* nodding, like one of those eye-blinking, head-bobbing dogs on the back decks of rusted out Camaros.

"Fine," Lucretia said. She motioned for us to follow her through the door.

That door led into a long hallway that vanished at either end into medieval gloom. Too many doors to count—all closed—lead off the hallway. The building's façade was deceptive—what had appeared to be simply a largish structure was either enormous, or my perceptions were undependable.

Or drugged?

The acoustics were peculiar, too. Lucretia's dress rustled with each step and the sound echoed from the walls and a patterned ceiling punctuated with elaborate chandeliers. Her fishnet stockings rasped together as she walked, filling my ear drums with a murmur both tantalizing and annoying as hell, like someone tickling your belly with a feather.

At last she stopped at a door, opened it, and ushered us into small room that was sterile, blinding white, and a major letdown.

"Where's the women?" I asked.

Lucretia's forehead pleated into a frown. "They haven't selected you yet. Have a seat." She indicated two white upholstered chairs.

"*They* haven't selected *us* yet?" Robbie asked. He plunked himself down (rather unsteadily, I thought) in the closest chair, then helped himself to another glass of absinthe set on a table between the chairs. "Seems like *we* ought to choose."

She stopped pawing through a dome-lidded trunk long enough to scowl "Whichever of my ladies choose you for their pleasuring, you'll find them to your liking. Put these on." She tossed us each a length of cloth. Robbie's landed squarely on his head and plastered itself to him on his indrawn breath like Saran Wrap.

"Togas," she explained. "You wanted a Roman villa—shouldn't you dress the part?"

Ten minutes passed in fumbling confusion, while Lucretia clucked, tucked and arranged, until we stood clad in our togas. I seriously

doubted whether I was going to get laid or spend the night being humil-
iated.

She pulled one of those silent servant pull-cords you see in old black
and white movies, and a door opened.

I gasped.

A woman with waist-length chestnut hair entered. A diaphanous
pale gold toga swirled around her long legs; thin gold bracelets climbed
up her arms. She was magnificent.

Following close behind came a statuesque blonde, a lusty ol-
ive-skinned beauty, a dainty redhead, and a Nubian princess whose
hair shone blue-black. Other lovelies of every imaginable description
quickly filed in, lining up against the far wall, three and four deep.

Robbie sounded as though he were strangling when he gasped out,
"I'll take—"

Lucretia's voice sliced the air like a stiletto. "You *take* whomever
chooses you."

The girl with chestnut hair sidled over to my chair and walked
around it, appraising me. Her hand rested gently on my shoulder so
briefly I might've imagined it except that a charge shot through me at
her touch, a high-voltage slammer that took my breath away, lasting
long after she shook her head, inspected Robbie, and shook her head
again before leaving the room.

She didn't want me!

My stomach lurched. What if we didn't pass muster with anyone?
Surely at least one would . . .

A sumptuous brunette approached, a woman of Amazonian proportions. She crossed the small room with sinuous grace, draped herself
across my lap, twisted, and caressed my hair with long, gentle strokes.

It was indescribable. I nestled into the cleft between her breasts
while the shock of tickling fingers trickled down my spine and raised
gooseflesh along my bared arms. She traced her fingertips over my ears,
then moved them to my temples and rubbed tiny circles.

The tension surged when another shock zapped through me, deto-
nating a shower of colored lights in front of my eyes that rained down
my vision before dissipating, like fireworks fading into the night. All
was black for a second, then absurdly, Martha Kennedy's face appeared
in my mind's eye.

I say "absurdly" because Martha was as opposite to the woman on
my lap as satin was to burlap. Martha's a great co-worker—smart as a
whip and fun—but she's mousy, bony-chested and her nose sits
crooked on her face. What on earth brought her to mind?

"Yes," the brunette said, her voice as soft as a baby's sigh.

"Yes, what?" I asked, shoving Martha from my mind and replacing her drab image with the brunette's gloriously large breasts.

Something warm and wet enveloped my bare toes.

I never knew anything could be that erotic. What little was left of my infrastructure quickly liquefied. It was like the verge of a tickle . . . but one so incredibly sexy that the knee-jerk reaction to yank my toes out of the wet warmth was overridden by the desire for more.

I peeked around breasts to glimpse the source of this new pleasure.

My toes were encompassed by full lips the color of claret. The lips' owner—a girl of Oriental persuasion—wrapped her straight ebony hair around her hand, then gathered the ends into a sheaf which she drew back and forth across the ball of my foot.

I thought I might die from the sheer exquisiteness of living.

My eyes rolled back and only the determination not to miss one second of voyeuristic pleasure enabled them to reopen in time to see the Asian glance at Lucretia and nod her acceptance.

It couldn't get any better than that, I thought, but she promptly wedged her tongue into the crotch of my big toe and its neighbor. I thought I might faint.

The sensation—as phenomenal as it was—lasted only a second, then was overwhelmed by the memory of Carla Martin, the girl I'd promised to take to her Senior Prom.

Promised to take, but didn't.

I'd called her up on prom day, pleading flu. In reality, I couldn't face a tuxedoed evening rewarded by tepid sex with a high school woo-woo. A keg party called me instead and I watched dawn break through frothy eyes and a sour stomach.

Later, at her Memorial Service, I learned she'd been the only girl in her senior class not to make the prom.

I hadn't thought about Carla for years, not since shortly after her funeral. What in Christ's name was I doing thinking about that little twitlet at the high point of my life?

I turned to see how Robbie was faring, but my view was blocked by another toga to my left, joined quickly by another on my right. My ears were nibbled; someone lapped at my neck; silky fingers slipped beneath my toga and traced feathery strokes behind my kneecap.

I writhed in rapture. I wriggled and moaned in ecstasy marred only by memory flashes of women I'd known along the way, women so different from these lovely creatures pleasuring me.

Inferior.

Just as I thought I couldn't endure any more pleasure without going mad, it stopped.

I really feared insanity then. Being brought to the fevered pitch of erotic stimulation without release by the logical conclusion caused my whole body to arch in want, in need. Exposure of titillated nerve endings to a world suddenly and excruciatingly bereft of warm fingers, wet tongues, and teasing soft lips left me cold, weak and overwrought.

"Don't stop!" I begged.

As if in answer, hands pulled me from my chair. I could barely stand —my knees refused to lock in place, and my cock felt so hugely engorged with blood that I should've toppled forward. No fewer than eight gorgeous women latched on to me, steadying and steering me toward the door.

I glanced over my shoulder as I was propelled toward the exit—Robbie was enduring a similar fate. He must've had a dozen women maneuvering him out of his chair.

The door opened into a Roman villa of magnificent proportions. Air heavy with the exotic tang of orange blossoms and jasmine rushed over my fevered self; water splashed gaily in a marble fountain surrounded by exquisite statuary, and a nightingale sang from a gilded cage hung over a bath from which steam rose in swirling gray-white clouds.

My escorts drew me to a chaise next to the bubbling bath, where they divested me of my toga. I shut my eyes, embarrassed by my cock being the size of a Mississippi river barge, then curiosity won over embarrassment, and I peeked.

I was limp.

What the hell?

I *felt* the tumescence. It throbbed and bobbed painfully, felt harder than it ever had before.

Yet it was a lie. My own eyes couldn't deceive me and they saw a flaccid, tiny member resting passively against my leg, as pale as a slug.

My greatest fear was realized—not that I'd ever before dealt with impotence—but why here? *Why now?*

Something in the absinthe, perhaps, a drug to increase endurance so I might take maximum advantage of this glorious opportunity.

The Asian shed her toga. It puddled around her bare feet like a cloud while she extended her hand to me.

I took her hand, then followed her to the bath. I'd have followed her anywhere, limp or not. Hell, we'd paid for this—or rather, Robbie had.

She guided me into water enticingly warm and scented with something spicy. The bath was no deeper than four feet, the sides were brightly tiled and fitted with a bench around the circumference.

The oriental beauty settled me onto the bench, straddled me, and called to her sisters in a voice less rich than I would have guessed.

Did it matter?

No. What mattered was on my lap.

A glance behind me proved richly rewarding—seven other women—each incredibly beautiful—shedding their togas and striding toward me with legs as pale as moonlight, dark as night, long and muscular, or petite and silky soft.

Within seconds, breasts brushed my back, tongues traced circles on the nape of my neck, slender fingers popped a grape into my mouth, a glass of red wine appeared in front of my eyes, hands lifted my buttocks, warm lips encircled the hugeness of my cock—

For surely it was huge now, wasn't it?

—my lower body floated to the water's surface, strong fingers massaged my leg muscles. The toes of my right foot bobbed along the water's surface then disappeared into the warm mouth of the tall brunette. My left toes were delicately nibbled by the alluring black girl. A Swedish type offered me another grape, then took several and rolled them to pulp between her hands, rubbed them across her breasts, and offered them to me.

My world was a kaleidoscope of sensual pleasure, a collage of breasts, legs and smooth round asses, scents of musk and orange blossoms, and I wondered fleetingly if one could drown in one's own excitement.

Until a lightning bolt of pain shot from my toe, forcing me to look away from the moist pink lips spreading apart inches from my eyes, pain not exquisite in nature, but a flame that threatened to burst into a forest fire.

Martha Kennedy had bitten off my little toe.

Martha Kennedy?

I wrenched my foot to free it, but the hands gripping my ankles were like iron traps that had sprung shut on their quarry.

She smiled at me, not the sweet, passive smile of my co-worker, but with teeth so metallically brilliant that the Mediterranean sun glinted off them, blinding me.

When my eyes adjusted to the reflection, Martha and her dreadful stainless steel teeth bent to rip off my big toenail.

Simultaneously, a flash of pain shot through my skull from the right, while the dreadful sound of tearing flesh rasped in my ears. My stomach heaved.

I struggled with every ounce of strength left—legs thrashing, body twisting. The hands that so shortly before had soothed and caressed me to the brink of orgasm held me like vise grips.

The redhead peered at me from the right, green eyes luminescent over red lips from which hung the remnant of my ear, blood trickling down over the snowy expanse of her breast and plopping into the bubbling water now tinged pink.

I opened my mouth to scream, but the redhead's face rearranged its molecules and became Sandy Carter, a girl I'd dated in high school until the night she'd tearfully said "pregnant". I hadn't seen her since I handed her the cash for the abortion.

I'd meant to call. Meant to see if she came through it okay.

That was years ago, for Chrissakes!

Angie Robinson—whose dog I'd accidentally shot—traced lines across my belly with stainless steel fingernails, smiling sweetly when drops of blood seeped up from the seams.

Brooke what's-her-name—who teased and taunted me at a party only to say no in the backseat of her car, forcing me to force her—bobbled her breasts at me, then slid beneath the water and bit through my hamstring.

Carla Martin skinned my cock with metal teeth

Too much pain too fast is counterproductive from a torturer's point of view. The brain needs time to follow the body into shock. My brain was still processing information.

That's why the "guests" at Madame Eulalie's weren't allowed to return.

They couldn't.

They'd been eaten away by every foul deed they'd committed in life.

Shirley Kaplan stuffed a grape into my nostrils. My mouth opened reflexively for air—she poured wine down my throat.

Death by Lambrusco.

The water bubbled scarlet around me.

The light faded; unconsciousness became a goal to strive for. Let them finish me off quickly.

A prick in my arm—a flea bite relative to my other agony, noticeable only as one more assault.

A hypodermic needle prick. The edge of my pain immediately softened. Blurred.

When Kristie Callahan ripped into my belly with her teeth, then poured the wine into the mangled flesh, I knew it must hurt horribly, knew nothing could be worse than someone pulling your intestines out and guiding them over your hip to float atop the blood red water.

Knew it. Couldn't feel it.

But the sound of ripping flesh was torture enough. I was grateful for whatever drug they'd administered.

Suddenly, the bevy of beasts from my past slid from the water as if at some silent signal, blood dripping down breast and belly, pieces of flesh clinging to lips and fingers.

I slumped onto the shelf bench, wondering how long I might survive, wondering why they didn't finish me off, puzzled why they were waiting.

Mama!

Mama as she'd been in the family album, auburn-haired and twenty something ripe, walking toward me, stepping into the bloody spa, disturbing the flotsam of her son bobbing on the surface.

"Bud! I've missed you, Sweetheart."

Hands that had soothed away countless fevers and boo-boos brushed my hair off my forehead.

"Mama! Help!"

Hands that had held mine while I was being stitched up in emergency rooms, or swabbed scrapes with antiseptic ointment then patched them with Disney Band-Aids, plucked grapes from my nose so I could breathe.

"Of course, I'll help you, Buddy mine," she crooned.

My tattered body relaxed. Mama was here. Mama would fix everything.

Cool efficient hands swept over my body, analyzing, diagnosing, and prognosticating. I glanced up. She was older, hair heavily shot with gray, as it had been when I was in high school. Her tone was compassionate, but more abrupt than before.

She morphed as I watched, submitting to her ministrations, watching as she pulled the edges of the sliced belly together and held them taut until the blood stopped seeping from the wounds. Like time-lapse photography, her face aged, crow's feet and smile lines deepening.

Within moments, her face was as gray as her hair, gaunt and hollow-eyed. Her cheeks fell in heavy folds toward her jaw where the flesh beneath the skin had melted off.

Suddenly, she looked as she had the last time I saw her, her skin a waxy yellow as she lay surrounded by quilted satin and the cloying sweetness of lilies clogging my airways.

"Why weren't you with me, Bud?" she asked.

"I wanted to be, Mama. But you hung on for so long, just evaporating a little more each day. The plane tickets were non-refundable, you know. I did ask them how much time you had left. They said they thought another two weeks or so."

"But they also said it could be any time."

"I don't remember that."

"They did. You should have stayed."

"I didn't know!"

"Remember all the nights I stayed up with you?"

"I do."

"And all the times I nursed you back to health?"

I nodded, although it hurt to do so. "You always made everything better."

"I will now, too."

"I knew you would fix it," I mumbled through the grayness.

She kissed my forehead. Lips cool on fevered brow. She gazed down fondly at me, offering a glimpse of metallic teeth before she bent to my jugular.

I felt myself whooshing along with my blood, letting go of the pain and embracing the dark.

Robbie didn't fare as well. He lingered for days, thanks to their drugs. I watched his agony from the sweet bower of the orange tree.

By the time he finally died, his mind was long gone, along with most of his flesh. That they kept him going for such a long time was miraculous.

But then, Madame Eulalie's ladies are experts, well-versed in the arts of life and death.

When Robbie was disposed of, I took my incorporeal self to the live oak in front of the Back Street Bordello. There, I joined my predecessors to warn away others of our brothers invited to Madame Eulalie's. There I learned about their "plants," moles in the world whose sole purpose is to keep the lore of Madame Eulalie's alive, to keep the guest list growing. And I learned of their sister company, "Diamond Jim's Spa and Retreat," whose clients are those members of the fair sex for whom gold-digging and twitching of hips to win their way in the world is an art form. Madame Eulalie and Diamond Jim are both Equal Opportunity Employers. There is a heavy tariff for sinners; if you play, you pay.

My warnings haven't done any good. Not yet. They pass by, in sin-
gles and in pairs, beneath me and the other gray festooned souls draped
from massive branches, whispering, warning. They seldom even
glance at what they casually assume is simply Spanish Moss.

But perhaps one will someday listen hard enough to hear. Perhaps
he'll turn away.

Perhaps.

ELEPHANTS WEEP

by Jeffrey Thomas

As he pulled into the parking lot—empty except for dunes of autumn leaves like gold scales shed from the waning sun—David recalled that the Dearborn Heights Zoo had been home to Ivory, the albino elephant. He also recalled that Ivory had passed away a year or two ago.

His car nosed into a parking space close enough to the admission booth that he could see it was dark, unmanned.

He checked the time on his dashboard. It could be past closing time, he supposed, but the more likely explanation forthe desolation of the parking lot and the closed-up appearance of the booth was that the zoo had died along with its greatest draw.

Still, David let himself out from his car if only to stretch his arms and back in the open, cool air. Splayed fingers bracing the base of his spine, he wandered closer to the booth, and now he could see around its edge. A chain was slung in the air across the path that led into the zoo, and from its center hung a sign which read: NO TRESPASSING. POLICE TAKE NOTICE.

Had he been to this zoo as a boy? He couldn't recall. David was only aware of Ivory through the newspapers. He wasn't even sure whether he had ever passed through Dearborn Heights before.

Returning home from the hotel and the convention, he'd become lost. No maps in the car; he got lost reading a map more readily than he did driving.

Finally asking directions at a gas station where he'd bought a coffee, he learned he'd been going south when he should have been going north, so at least he knew he was pointed in the correct general direction now. But his back had cried out for a rest, even if the afternoon was soon to bleed away.

The sign hanging from the inadequate barricade rocked slightly in the chill breeze. David stood at the chain gazing further into the tree-enclosed zoo, which seemed to have the mood of a wooded urban park. He supposed it was as dangerous at night as an urban park, as well. Junkies, vandals, thugs and their equally tough girlfriends stealing into dark places to rut. But it wasn't dark yet, and the nocturnal creatures had probably not yet emerged. Beyond the chain, he sensed only utter silence, a forlorn emptiness.

All was cool shadow beyond the chain, the hissing of the wind through leaves sounding to him like a distant surf . . . which is always a beguiling sound. David lit a cigarette, glanced over his shoulder at the parking lot and his lonely vehicle, peered along the blocked path once again. Without even a conscious decision to do so, David walked back to his car, retrieved his suit jacket, slipped it on, locked up, and returned to the chain. He stepped over it.

Cigarette in one hand, half-drunk coffee in the other, he strolled the entrance path, which passed by trailer-like restrooms that were labeled LIONS and LIONESSES. He groaned inwardly. Why not "Cocks" and "Hens," he thought, taking a sip of his lukewarm coffee.

The path opened up into a small area with shuttered snack stands, a scattering of picnic tables, and a few miniature carnival rides whose bright colors looked almost tragically nostalgic in the gray light. There was some black graffiti sprayed on the snack stands' shutters. Indecipherable, arcane-looking symbols, jagged and ugly, which David didn't like looking at.

As a boy he had loved trips to the zoo; one of the two he best recalled was also closed down now. His mother would point to a lion or giraffe and say, "That's from our country, son. That animal lives where we come from." But David was an African-American who had never been to Africa and never would, any more than his father or even his grandfather had been there. Sometimes he felt he existed on the narrow hyphen between the words African and American. As a well-educated black man with a good job at the turn of the twenty-first century, he considered himself caught in a kind of limbo: not white, and not the street-wise, angry black man some would expect him to be.

Though divorced, he had a good relationship with his two children and was a solid part of their lives. But both children were academic, scholarly, and black classmates frequently teased them about it, labeled them white wannabes. It exasperated David, who couldn't understand why one black kid wouldn't want to see another make his mind sharp and his prospects bright. At least David, when he was the only black kid in his high school, had merely been ignored and friendless.

At the convention this weekend he had often felt just as ignored and friendless. Well, he knew he tended toward an introspective moodiness, which didn't lend itself well to convention-style banter. Or was he making excuses for those who shunned him because of his color? He hated to think he might be that defeated.

Beyond the splintering picnic tables and blistered kiddie rides the path wound through gardens gone wild—fallen leaves snagged in tall weeds—and curved around the edge of a pool which might once have contained goldfish but was now a murky soup. The gravel of the path scraped and crunched under his shoes, the rocks grinding together like teeth gnashing in sleep. Peripherally, David saw a movement close to the ground, and turned half-expecting to see a peacock waddling along, but it was only a low bush buffeted by a gust of chill wind.

The path forked in several directions now; a sign post indicated that the PETTING FARM was to the right, and SNOW LEOPARDS and WOLVES to the left. He chose the left path. He polished off his coffee and cigarette, put the butt of the latter into the cup of the former and carried it with him until he found a rusted waste bucket to drop it in. Lighting a fresh cigarette, he considered a large area enclosed by a high mesh fence, the enclosure dominated by a looming outcropping of rock like the bare crest of a mountain. There was no sign that he could see to indicate what animal might have dwelt within, but he guessed mountain goats or some such.

He watched for some time, squinting through his smoke, as if he hoped some animal would at last emerge from the crags, but of course none did.

As David stepped forward again, he heard a short deep grunt from somewhere ahead of him, and he stopped again in his tracks.

What had it been? It had sounded like an animal sound. It had been vaguely bovine, but perhaps less domestic than that. Maybe even one of the low throaty sounds a great cat makes. But it was pointless trying to imagine what sort of animal had made the sound, because it couldn't be any animal, could it? What was the likelihood that even the humblest little zoo would forget one of its animals in closing down, leave it behind? Even if they had, it would starve to death within its pen.

Unless it had escaped from its pen. Or escaped during the hectic moving/closing process. And remained in the vicinity of the zoo, afraid to venture far from it.

David smirked derisively at himself. Right, he thought.

At most, it was a dog. More likely, it was some sound beyond the zoo itself, a car or just about anything. He continued his aimless stroll, not anxious to return to his car and the road.

He'd rather lose himself on these paths than on the highway again. He realized it was foolish . . . especially where the sun was dropping steadily under its own molten weight. He didn't want to run into the police, or run into the sprayers of that cryptic graffiti he had seen. But he told himself he'd work his way back toward the parking lot any time now.

After this cigarette. Or maybe one after that, for the road.

What was there to rush home to? The kids lived with their mother and their mother had not been replaced. There was only work tomorrow. He did not want to hurtle toward that. He wanted to hear the echoes of his mother's voice, in this place, and the echoes of animal sounds, even if both were only in his imagination. Echoes of his childhood.

He peered into more penned areas and empty cages. He was reminded of news footage he had seen on TV during the Gulf War; animals in a zoo cut off due to the fighting were starving to death. He was haunted to this day by images of the cadaverous lions, crying out forlornly as they slowly died in their cage. Abandoned, all but forsaken.

There had been a magazine article about it, too; a devoted zoo worker had finally made it in to check on his charges, and an elephant had been so happy to see him that it had wept. David hadn't known that elephants could cry tears.

The story and accompanying photos had given him a physical ache in his chest.

He couldn't remember now what the final outcome had been. He supposed that the problem hadn't yet been resolved at the time of the article. Had that elephant died? Those beautiful lions? He did know, however, that Iraqi troops had been killing some of the animals for target practice. For fun.

And people thought lions were frightening.

He wondered what the fate of the animals here had been. Moved to other zoos? Or destroyed?

There was a cage that a sign indicated had once housed a vulture; now it contained only the vulture's macabre props: a grinning horse skull, a few sets of antlers, stray bones strewn about the dirt floor. David could almost imagine that the zoo he had seen on TV had resembled this at last: cages of exotic skeletons, like crumbled museum displays, carcasses picked clean by the tiny animals like mice and insects that were free to come and go between the bars.

As he contemplated the bones, there was a rustle of the bushes that hunched darkly behind him. He turned more abruptly than was logical. He saw nothing, but the shifting of leaves had seemed more than the lonely wind might produce. More focused, and more aggressive, almost as if some animal low to the ground had crashed along through the brush just beyond the path before darting off into the deeper brush and trees again.

David moved ahead at a brisker pace. He really should think about circling back to the parking lot.

The path now became long and straight, directly bordered on his right by a high fence. Beyond the fence was the street he had driven along as he turned into the zoo. Traffic on the road was sparse; only the occasional car hissed past. He hoped none would be a police car, that he wouldn't be spotted on the other side of this mesh, like one of the zoo's denizens himself.

To his left there was another enclosure dominated by heaps of rock, looming cold and shadowed. But whereas the presumed mountain goats' pen had been open at the top, this one had a high ceiling of mesh as well. A sign explained the precaution—this had been where the advertised snow leopards had dwelt.

He stopped to read a plaque which offered a few interesting facts about their habits and habitat: they lived at the highest altitude of any of the great cats.

Atop one of the thick posts of the outer barricade, someone had left and forgotten a pair of binoculars. But then David realized, as he picked them up, that the heavy rubber-sheathed instrument was attached to the post by a strong cable so as not to be stolen. It was there so that former visitors could spy on the leopards more closely.

David crushed his cigarette, lifted the glasses to his eyes and played with the focus. He imagined that the small, thick-coated leopards had been fond of perching up on the rocky ledges. He traced the lenses along those jagged shelves now, idly, the focus shifting in irritating watery waves. He was unfamiliar with binoculars and was determined to master them, to get a focus that would remain consistent.

A white figure darted through his field of vision, passed in and out in a cloud of blurred focus.

David lowered the binoculars sharply, gazed up at the gloomy cliffs with his naked eyes. Had it been there, on that ledge, that he'd seen the figure? There was nothing there now. He looked at the spot through the glasses again, fought to keep perfectly still so the image wouldn't cloud and waver. He saw nothing but some weeds rippling.

Having his eyes covered even with a viewing device made him feel suddenly vulnerable, so he set the glasses back atop the post.

What had he seen? A large dog lunging between the rocks? Something on all fours, it had looked like, and very thin. Somehow the figure had seemed both shadowy and yet pale. But it hadn't been black or white so much as simply colorless. A visible invisibility.

In other words, a figment of his imagination. He really had to get out of here; it was much too lonely, much too sad a place. Its cold wind was stirring up loose leaves inside his brain, loose memories of actual animals he had viewed in his childhood, as distant and removed as another lifetime now. He wondered if going forward would be quicker than retracing his steps. Well, he'd pick up the pace again. He went forward.

A sun-faded plaque to his right announced that the next enclosure contained a number of Mexican wolves. He didn't stop to read the facts this time, however. The wolf enclosure was very large and deeply forested. The path curved now, away from the street, circled him back toward the heart of the zoo. The path became elevated, as well, as it hugged a swelling hill. He wondered how zoo patrons had ever been able to spot the wolves in the dense vegetation of their keep.

At the crest of the hill there was another outcropping of stone, but this one he could tell was fake, plaster perhaps artfully molded into a cave. He trudged up the increasingly steep incline and at last reached the cave, cursing himself for not back-tracking after all. But how could he resist peeking into this cave, which he would have loved as a child?

He ducked inside it, and at his feet a wolf lay gazing up at him, several cubs suckling at her belly. His heart lunged in the cage of his chest.

But the nursing wolf was a statue, fused with the floor of the faux cave. Another plaque offered more fascinating wolf facts. Bastards, David thought. How many children had shrieked when stumbling upon that petrified wolf? He could imagine some poor old grandmother clutching her chest as she crumpled to the floor of the mock den, with its clever imitation cave paintings of elk or antelope and its stenciled hand prints. Amongst these symbols was more of that black, blurry spray-painted graffiti, menacingly modern and primitive at the same time.

David emerged from the cave, started down the other side of the hill.

He could be on his way home by now. He was in an unfamiliar part of the state; who could tell how much longer it would take to get home tonight? If he got home too late he'd call in sick tomorrow, whether his bosses expected his convention report in the morning or not.

But they'd think he'd had too much to drink at the convention, or shacked up with some woman he'd met in the hotel bar, as if he could ever be so lucky.

From the hill he could now see city skyscrapers, distantly looming above the tree line, deep gray against the darkening gray of sky. The city and its suburbs like Dearborn Heights would spread, flow over the wooded oasis where this zoo now hid and cowered amongst the trees, itself all bones like an abandoned lion.

Now he was on the opposite side of the wolf enclosure, and he glanced that way as he trudged down the slope.

And again his heart jolted as he saw a figure so pale it seemed to glow, ducking between the trees. He realized it was keeping pace with his descent, and even thought he heard the crackle of twigs under its feet. The separation of the mesh fence did little to alleviate his alarm. Whatever it was, it had someone got from inside the leopard enclosure to the wolf enclosure, so it could just as easily get out here to where he was.

And he no longer thought it might be a dog. Some snow leopard left behind, after all?

Or worse, perhaps—might it be a person?

But what he'd glimpsed appeared to be without clothing. And the impression he'd received was one of emaciation.

Some demented child—some homeless person, hiding out inside the derelict zoo? It wasn't beyond possibility, was it?

David broke into a trot, keeping his gaze on the wolf pen as he moved.

Did he see occasional stirrings of the undergrowth, like the swells of a dolphin cruising parallel to a ship without quite surfacing? But at last the wolf enclosure was left behind as the path veered away into another direction . . .

He slowed his trot to a brisk walk again. Still, he had the unsettling sensation of being followed. No—stalked. He should have paid heed to the graffiti, the nearness of that mountain range of city. People shot helpless zoo animals for fun. People were capable of more horrors than any alligator or panther that might once have been housed in this place.

At the base of the hill the trees receded and there was a broad clearing of cement. Its naked openness relieved David—no brush in which a person, animal or hallucination might hide. A sizable enclosure here had a large plaque wired to its mesh which featured a photo of the famous and recently deceased Ivory, the albino elephant. David had almost forgotten about her. So this was where she'd lived and been shown. A structure like a small airplane hangar adjoined the caged area; she'd obviously slept and sheltered in there.

David paused to look at the plaque, which he realized was intended as a giant card for people to pen their condolences upon. Most of the messages seemed written by children, though others were obviously from parents or teachers on school outings. "We loved you, Ivory" and "We'll miss you." But some clever soul had drawn a word balloon on the plaque, next to the photo of the white elephant, and Ivory seemed to be saying the word, "wassup?"

Most of the inscriptions were faded and washed away. This made the mysterious graffiti on the plaque seem to glow black in contrast. The word "wassup" didn't seem humorous to David; it was as alien and as ugly and beyond his comprehension in sentiment as those sprayed symbols or initials or whatever they might be.

From inside the black maw of Ivory's structure came a mournful sob. It was faint, muffled by the depth and dark of the barn-like building, and was halfway between an animal's grunt and a human moan.

David backed away from the plaque, the mesh, as if afraid something would burst suddenly from that cavern, rush the fence. He spun on his heel and resumed his brisk walk. Didn't want to seem too afraid to whatever might be stalking him. Animals could smell fear. And people relished it.

The path narrowed ahead. The pallid openness of cement was replaced by the dark closeness of vegetation. But there was no other way except through it.

The path twisted and turned, and branched off in several directions. This development did not please him; he wanted only the one clear path back to the admission booth. Was that its roof now, however, and its boards showing through the leaves and pine needles? Thank God. David tossed a glance over his shoulder. Through a break in the trees he could again see the city rearing on the horizon. The sky was so dark now, the sun below the rim of the world, that lights sparkled from those looming monuments, as icy as stars.

He reached the structure he'd spied, and it was not the admission booth but a log cabin, like something homeless people might have fashioned as a shelter against the coming winter. But yet another plaque explained that this was a mock-up of a camp that conservationists or biologists and so forth would use whilst on excursions into the wild.

It had several windows without glass or even shutters, and from a distance was as black as outer space inside.

David reached out on impulse and tugged at the door latch, but it was sealed or locked. He gingerly drew near enough to one of the windows to gaze inside.

There was a table that he could make out in the murk. And a cot, it looked like. He was certain that had been utilized for explorations of a more carnal nature. Some tattered charts and maps on the walls, but whatever other props there might have been had been destroyed or removed. David thought he saw the twinkle of glass shards on the floor. Broken beer bottles. And across one of the maps—wasn't that more spray-painted calligraphy?

Irrationally, the child in him imagined how cozy such a structure would be if he could light a fire in its metal fireplace, if he could huddle here safe against the cold autumn night as it fell around these log walls. Its simplicity touched upon some primitive, romantic side of him crouched in the underbrush of his cells.

But as his eyes adjusted more to its gloomy interior, he at last made out the vague outlines of the figure that knelt in the corner, behind the wood stove. Watching him all the while. It was an animal, hunkering, perhaps gathered for a leap. Or a person, naked and insane, sheltering here, anxious to protect its territory. Whatever it was, it turned its head just a fraction, just enough, that light somehow reached its eyes.

Maybe it was the faint, icy city light. Whatever its source, it was just enough to make the thing's eyes glisten like the shards of the broken bottles.

This time David broke into a full run. And he could swear he heard the brush crash behind him. The thing he had seen . . . he was convinced it had pounced through one of the cabin windows to pursue him.

The gravel under his shoes ground and shifted and once he nearly stumbled; he gave his ankle a wrench in redirecting his weight. Through his harsh breathing and the clatter of gravel, did he hear more gravel crunching further behind him? He didn't dare look behind him for fear of stumbling again or slacking his pace or seeing those glowing eyes more clearly. But he sensed, as a primitive hunter on a savannah or open plain might sense, the thing that loped along behind him, waiting for just the right moment to launch itself into the air.

Was that a low throaty grumble or a whispery giggle?

His instincts couldn't tell him whether it were animal or human—but really, what was the difference?—only that it ran on all fours and its eyes blazed hungry and it was nearing . . . almost on his heels . . .

and then David burst from the path onto the paved lot where the admission booth stood unmanned. He leaped the chain but snagged his ankle, tumbled hard, cracking his elbow on the pavement. He sprawled onto his back and found himself looking up with frenzied eyes at the path beyond the swinging chain.

He saw the thing for just a moment, ducking back around a bend in the path, thwarted though only the thin chain separated the two. Did it really look like some feral adolescent, nude, eyes glaring emptily in its snarling face? Was its hair kinky and close, its nose broad, lips full as though it were black? But it wasn't black, or white, so much as colorless. And skeletal, thinner than anything that could still be considered alive . . .

Clutching his elbow, David scrabbled to his feet. He limped across the lot to where his car shone dully under a street light. Autumn leaves had fallen upon its hood as if it had rested abandoned here for days or weeks.

He let himself inside. It was safe in here, safer than that meager log cabin. Steel and plastic encasing him, and the engine started without a beat of hesitation . . .

. . . but as David left the parking lot, pulled out into the desolate road which ran past the front of the zoo, he remembered that he was still just as lost.

STONE-CRUNCH, AXE-THUD, BONE-GRIND, HOME

by Robert Devereaux

The sun's hot insistent palm caressed my face with neither fuss nor invasion. The baking of fresh loaves, browned kidfists of dough, tantalized me awake. From where she stood by the stove, Momma laughed at my groans, at how I squinted against the light that splashed across our bed.

Memory, as always, stole away the previous night.

I simply couldn't recall *returning* from Granny's. It was one way only, through the woods. There, never back.

Dusk always fell upon my arrival at Granny's house. Waving to a beaming woodchopper, paused in mid-swing, I would knock. Granny would welcome me in, her peculiar warmth and hearthlight embracing me, her "Come to Granny" growly with need.

Without fail, I forgot what came next. The following morning, there by the stove stood Momma, laughing at me as I groaned in protest.

"Morning, princess," she said. "Good morning, sweet Red. Did you sleep well?"

Again I groaned, louder and more exaggerated, making a game of it. Momma, in mock commiseration, said, "Oh you poor darling." Bacon sizzled. Her silver fork poked and prodded the thick banded strips.

"I'm tired," I said.

"Breakfast is almost on the table, dear."

I knew what that meant. "Oh Momma, do I have to go again?" I couldn't remember a single day spent idly or otherwise at home, feeding the pigs or watching chicks tirelessly peep in the wake of their mother's meander.

Every morning, it seemed, I voiced the same protest. And every morning, as she did this one, Momma sat beside me, leaned in to plant a light peck on my cheek, and said, "Granny's not well. She's suffered the bite of a wolf, an attack that happened so long ago, she can't remember it. Her wound never heals. Her pain is unbearable. But your visits bring her joy. Please. Red. Don't be selfish. Don't disappoint your granny."

Momma had a way with words. She persuaded me, yet I didn't feel persuaded. It seemed instead (she and I were so in tune) as if the desire welled up in me, and I could only obey. "I'll go," I would say. So I said now on this lovely spring morning, a morning as fresh and breezy as any morning I could recall.

I rose and stretched and made my ablutions. My body felt vaguely bruised, yet my skin was smooth and white and unsullied. As Momma set out the breakfast (none for her, *never* any for her) and checked the bread, I ran my comb through a skull-clutch of auburn hair, no snarls to speak of, scarcely any need to comb at all. When I dressed, my undergarments, skirt, blouse, and boots were always clean-smelling and spotless. Likewise my body, which, save for the merest touch of water, had, to my recollection, never been thoroughly bathed.

Despite my woolen skirt, the oak chair that had once been my father's felt cold and hard against my bottom. I hunched over eggs and bacon, Momma humming cheerily as she packed the basket and tucked a checkered cloth over it to keep the loaves fresh and warm. She seemed so large and kind and delightful, it was always hard (like staring at the sun) to look at her directly. My fork scraped up the last of the yolk. "Have a lovely walk through the woods, Red," she urged. "Stay on the path, let no distractions divert you, be kind and obedient to your ailing relative, and above all, no matter how great the temptation, do not taste Granny's blood."

"I won't, Momma." Yet I vowed, in my heart, that I *would*. Everything I did and said and everything Momma did and said felt rehearsed, redundant, as polished as a tale told and honed over countless recountings. Many times out of mind—*far* out of mind—she had let shadows of warning steal over her sunny voice, and as many times, though none I could quite recall, I had vowed in just this way.

I lifted the checkered flap and sniffed the loaves, bothered by an uneasy feeling that they were really dead rats. But I couldn't quite see them, nor could I detect a hint of decay beneath the aroma of newly risen dough. "No nibbling along the way," cautioned Momma with a mock slap to my hand. Then she cloaked me in red, tied the ties at my breast, hugged me long and hard, and placed the basket handles over my left arm. Her kiss lapped at my face, her embrace was a bear hug. My cheek, snail-tracked under her lips, emerged wet and slimy.

"Be a good girl," she admonished.

"I will," I said.

"Don't be beguiled by smooth talkers."

"I'll pass them by."

"Above all, don't taste Granny's blood."

"I won't." But I *will*, I told myself fiercely. This time, I *will* taste Granny's blood.

The cottage door closed behind me and I stood in the warmth of the sun. Strange, I thought, all I could recall from the cottage were the bed, the sunlight, the table and chair and breakfast, and the basket. And Momma of course, but not quite all of her. Surely there ought to have been more: a chest of drawers, a grandfather clock, a pantry, tossed heaps of . . . of something brown and dimly lit, scattered helter-skelter in a corner. But what it was, I hadn't a clue.

I went my way.

The air smelled fresh and sweet, a slight chill lending it a crust. The silence of the forest startled me. Yet I sensed that that silence was shaped like sharp wedges of pain, that my ears deliberately shut out a harsh volley of chops and the cries of a white-barked tree which rustled with shelled nuts. But the only sound that came to me was the soft crunch of tiny white stones beneath my boots. For the path from our cottage to Granny's was precisely delineated with spills of stone spread where fertile earth and patches of moss might otherwise have tempted me to stray.

As I walked, I mused at how uncanny the resemblance was, down to the last detail, between Granny's cottage and Momma's. At times, I half suspected that a single dwelling existed only, that Momma and Granny, for reasons unknown, indulged in some elaborate trickery at my expense.

But Momma insisted the two places were distinct.

The way she told it, she had been so completely devoted to Granny that my father, one of many suitors, discovered (ages before he was wolfed down) a spot in the woods that, tree for tree, branch for branch, twig for twig, exactly matched Granny's. There arose under the skill of his hands a cottage that, straw for straw, stick for stick, stone for stone, found its precise twin in Granny's cottage. Thus he won my mother's love, and thus came the fruits of that love, red and hooded and obedient to her mother's wishes, into the world.

I encountered no one along the way. I might have walked for days, hours, minutes. Time lost itself in a dazzle of tiny white stones underfoot, in the hypnotic fall of my boots and the deadmarch of trees passing by at either side. As always, the daylight drained away. The stones' dazzle dwindled to a mere sparkle. Then even the sparkle faded, the white dulled to dim gray beneath the waning sun.

Chop! went the axe. *Chop!* There, before me, stood Granny's cottage. Off to the right, the woodchopper swung his great axe, punishing the base of the pure white tree with hefts of *Chop!*

The tree cried.

My ears, if no one else's, heard its cries. As the woodchopper's left hand gripped the butt of the axehandle, his right hand slid along its worn haft, hoisting the silver head up, bringing it thudding down. *Chop!* He caught me in his eye, paused, set the axe down, gave me a hearty wave and a broad smile. I returned them. He was my friend. I wished he didn't have to hurt the tree, its lofty shells shaking with each blow he delivered. Always this tree. I knew how it would whoosh through the air as it fell, how the ground would shudder under its deathcry. White gashes angled from its base. Again the woodchopper drove the silver blade into the wound. *Chop!*

Reaching Granny's front door was like coming home. Identical pocks and scores lay upon the wood; so precisely had my late father matched them that now it was as if they existed in sympathy, gouges and scrapes and the effects of weathering perfectly mirrored there.

I knocked.

"Who is it?" a graveled voice called out.

I piped my reply.

Chop! went the woodchopper.

The door swung open. The sun sank behind me.

But I wasn't frightened because a hearthfire blazed and there were candles and lanterns aplenty wherever my eyes fell. "Come to Granny," she said, looking like Momma but larger and darker and older and rheumier. She smelled like a granny, mildewed and muffiny. She fussed over me, oohing and aahing over the basket, folding back checkered corners, tearing a crust from a loaf—a rat's head, blood, a stench that shuddered me but in a trice was replaced by an enticing whiff of warm rye—and setting it aside. More fussing. I was in thrall, mewling as she unlaced my cape, fielding her barrage of questions with sufficient force to keep her kisses and pawings from engulfing me. But time passed confusedly in all that smother, and before I knew it, a squat candle or two had slumped down, lazing up waxy smoke, and Granny had undressed me and tucked me beneath the covers.

Puttering on unsteady feet, she removed her shawl, unwrapped her spectacles and placed them on the mantle, lifted like restless cottontails her dress over her head, then too her slip, until she stood unclothed. The crease between her buttocks was as thin and straight as a dagger blade. She turned and advanced, her shadow preceding her to the bed. Below her left breast, I glimpsed the wound Momma had mentioned. It pulsed and wept, wet, pink, open, where the wolf had bitten her.

Through the dark door came the steady thuds of the woodchopper's axe, the cry of the nut tree, the rustle of its shells.

Granny raised the bedclothes and in came the cold. Then the covers dropped. Granny lay hot and engulfing beside me. Her hands were huge on my back, tracing my spine, curving to sculpt buttocks and thighs. Whispering madness in my ear, she lifted my leg and pushed part of herself—moist, protuberant, a nub—into me. I begged for her to stop, but she shushed me and sank deeper. I hurt there. Then something tore, and the hurt liquefied with gooshiness. Granny's great nose was sniffing, catching the lure of my blood. Her bulky hot hairy limbs writhed and shifted as she sniffed at me beneath the peach-lit canopy. Four squat bedposts cowered around us.

I was sticky. I dripped. My blood, came the absurd thought, would ruin Granny's sheets. She would hate me, horsewhip me, look petulant at me. Never again would I see that toothsome smile stretch her old-lady lips. In a moment of inspiration, I said, "I have to go poo-poo." I would cup the blood in, I thought, ease out of bed, make my way without dripping somehow toward a bucket of water and then to the outhouse.

But saying so *made* it so.

I *did* have to go poo-poo. Badly.

Granny's hands, unspeakably eager, were all over me. "Do it," she said harshly. "Do it now. Here, quickly, in my hand." As she spoke, her index finger found my blood, dolloped a thick drop and brought it to her lips. That same hand she now cupped between my buttocks, tense and waiting.

"Oh, but Granny, I couldn't," I whined.

"Better here than inside me," she shot back. What she said made no sense, but I was too cowed to question her. "Do it," she insisted. "Push it out."

So frightened was I by her words and her roughness that I had little trouble complying. I felt them emerge, hard dry things, three of them, the sort that require no wiping. "Ah, that's my good girl," husked Granny, her words watery with spittle. "That's my obedient little Red."

She hurled them away, her swift hand tenting the blankets. Like tiny cannonballs they flew, sure their trajectory, through the hearthlight to add to a brown mound of dung in one corner, waist-high. I had no time to wonder at this, for no sooner had she finished, than she gaped open her jaws and stuffed me headlong into them, her foul drool lubricating my passage downward, her huge hands seizing and shoving me by the nether parts until I slid straight down her throat and landed in a heap inside her stomach. This, to my good fortune, was such an expansive place that breathing, though difficult, was manageable, and moving freely was not out of the question.

I sat there stunned, adjusting to the dark. So swift had been Granny's attack that only now could I remember my final scream, a piercing cry muffled by her rough tongue moving against my mouth. The moment my cries stopped, I heard the nut tree shriek as the woodchopper's final axe-blow brought it whistling and thundering to the earth. Had he heard me? I could only hope so.

I began to discern shapes, the odd curve of fibrous walls, a knothole of not-quite-light diastoling several yards in front of me. I rose, the underfloor squishy and sucky, a fenlike membrane that palmed my feet and released them reluctantly with each step. Halfway there, I passed what had seemed at a distance to be unchewed carcasses waiting to be digested. These resolved into the sleeping forms of an aging servant and three horses, saddlebags empty. Though I shook them and shouted, they could not be roused.

The knothole, in truth a whorl of flesh that pulsed to Granny's breathing, proved to be her bellybutton. Standing on my tippytoes, I spied a headboard and pillows through it. A sharp rap sounded at the door. The pillows blurred left, an obscuring blackness of bedpost, then the pitted surface of the door, rocking and growing as Granny approached it and flung it open. I saw his checked shirt and a gleam of silver from his axe-head. "What have you done with Red?" he demanded. His outrage thrilled me. The woodchopper was my deliverer, I thought. He would rescue me. "Just what I'll do to *you*, old nosy bones!" rasped Granny. At the right and left edges of my view, fingers grown brown and hairy flexed with savagery. Then the world rocked and heaved. Riots of pigment streaked past my peephole, the agitation so jarring as to make standing upright—even with my feet firmly apart and my fingers clawed into Granny's stomach lining—well nigh impossible. The horses and the servant jounced behind me, toys upon a mattress.

From above, yet another growl, greater than before, gaped open. The woodchopper gave a sustained protest, an "Oh my God please no!" that made my heart sink. Above me, a dim gray pudding-surface swirled open, the valve through which I must have fallen. Out of it tumbled my deliverer, clothed, whole, clutching his axe to his chest.

He was shivering. I bounded over, raised him to his feet, and held him. "It's all right," I said. "You're okay. That's Granny's bellybutton. Those are a few of her victims. I think you'll be all right. I don't see any teeth marks on you." It was so. She had swallowed him whole, just as she had swallowed me. At our feet lay his great axe, a grimly pillowed scepter.

He grew calm in my arms, then concerned. He began to feel me, as I had felt him. Only then did I notice how odd his right hand had become. I brought it up to inspect it. "Why are you stopping me?" The woodchopper had to have been in shock. He had lost all but his middle finger to two clean Granny bites. And that finger, its nail torn off, had swollen to twice its normal size, wide and long.

"You poor man," I sobbed.

"No matter," he assured. "I can stand the pain. I'll get by."

"But you . . . " He resumed his inspection. The hurt finger I had sorrowed over went now to my lips and inside my mouth, probing my palate, my tongue, threatening to gag me as it sought for damage. His blood tasted bitter on my tongue. At last he withdrew the finger. "You might have a hurt inside. In your secret places." These also he probed, though I wished he wouldn't. My hurt touched his hurt, where Granny's nub had been thrust. Then the other place, the place she had eagerly cupped, he poked and filled. Shame filled me too, as his rough-shaven jowls filled my vision, his wolfish breath halting and erratic.

He stifled his pain. At last, relief spread across his features. "You're all right." I was worried about his wounds, glad his inspection was complete, but angered at his well-intended violation. But I didn't dare show it. The woodchopper was my deliverer, my friend. Friends, thought I, should overlook much, forgive much, for the sake of their friendship.

I thanked him, then wished I hadn't. I felt no gratitude. Sometimes, through a lazy sort of uncaring, little lies escape unbidden. But there would be time enough to sort out my feelings once our ordeal was over.

"Okay, Red," said the woodchopper, gathering resolve. "It's time to find out how thick-skinned your granny really is!" Releasing me, he swooped up the axe, his hands steady as a knight's, pressed into service for a cause right and just. Then he ran, or bounded rather, a spring to his step lent by the very flesh he was about to hack his way through. In the lint-hazed light of Granny's bellybutton whorl, the woodchopper's upraised axe-head glinted, solid and silver. Down it slashed, painting a scythe-blade in the air, slicing through the confining walls, aslant the peephole, down and left. Stroke after stroke, he beribboned her, reddening the ragged strips of flesh, letting in light from outside, jags of rain and lightning betwixt whips of dead gray blood-bathed fiber. I clapped my hands and saw, like cuts of sun, hearthfire rippling and playing upon the slumbering bodies behind us. Dead to the world, those dusty sleepers dozed.

"Come!" he shouted, grasping me with his good hand and yanking me through the gap in Granny's belly. The hearthfire blazed. Though I stood there unclothed and both of us were coated in slime, sheer joy and the warmth of the flames made me oblivious to my nakedness. Granny bled on the floor beside us. Dead rats reeked unbearably from the basket. My hero swept me into his arms.

Don't taste Granny's blood, sounded my mother's voice and right on top of it my own *I* will *taste Granny's blood*. But as soon as the thought welled up, a great fear seized me.

"Are you all right?" he asked.

In reply, fighting the terror that had found me, I raised up on my tippytoes and kissed my deliverer smack on the lips. Instantly, I began to shrink and he to alter, his beard drawing up into his chin, his black hair streaking with gold and then being *choked* with gold as it lengthened past his shoulders. But I was shrinking into myself. Or so it felt, my eyes tumbling down along the woodchopper's torso, my limbs constricting with each passing moment. I was falling, yet not falling, plumping down, my legs bowing out, my face at once shrinking and swelling up, my arms withering to the half-arms of a deformed infant. My rescuer's clothing rustled, creamed, grew gauze and glitter, length and body. A gown. His thick mud-caked boots had become prissy white slippers on the white-stockinged feet of a . . .

He was a princess!

And I?

My size, my shape. I guessed at once. Had I never been anything more than a frog? Tears would have come, had I not been so deep in shock.

She bent to lift me. I felt as clumsy as a beanbag in her hands, my left leg extending awkwardly into air. Granny's dungheap had turned to rubies, gleaming like blood-colored glass. On the table, the basket overflowed with squares of cornbread. The princess took one, bit into it, steam rising from it and a warm white maize aroma, enticing despite my lack of olfactory equipment.

"Mmm," she said, "try one."

"No thanks," I croaked, the words like a wad of slime in my throat. I burrapped mournfully.

The princess giggled. "You cute thing!" she said, lifting me up and pressing her luscious red lips to my wee wide slit of a mouth. The instant we touched, my body and hers and the cornbread in her hand roiled once more in liquid confusion. She shrank and greened, dropping my burgeoning body, which thrust out legs and arms and grew pendulous at the crotch, silk and sash and boots and finery rustling to cover my manly frame. As firewood hissed in the fireplace, my head spun. *Taste Granny's blood*, the voice again urged; but fear warred with courage in me. It was too soon. I'd *never* taste it. *Coward!* Or was I merely being prudent? Fear swept so quickly through me, it was impossible to sort things out.

The deep red of the dung-rubies had collapsed into silver. A high wave of polished coins gathered where, a moment before, gemstones had beaded in a dark bloodclot of gleams and facets. At my boots, the frog, for so he had become, tasted cornbread-turned-to-cake, pink, obscenely icinged, studded with tight tiny gumdrops. "This tastes ten times better than the cornbread." He grinned inside a faceful of crumbs. "You must try some!"

Was it the sudden flood of testosterone? Or was it the tone he used, my hero-turned-amphibian? Whatever it was, as he goggled up at me, my body felt alien and wrong. Alarms began to clang in my head. I snatched froggy up and kissed once more where no crumbs befouled his foul mouth. Like a sail taking wind, he billowed. I brought my other hand, girlish again, to the one that held him, then let him slip through them to the floor. My body felt as if it were finally coming home, my breasts swelling, my hair spilling along my back. From shoulders to mid-calf, a rag-dress fell about me.

Fire swept the heap of silver coins, plumped them, turned them gold. They were honey, combed and hardened, a hillock of wealth waiting to be claimed. But their tantalizing gleam was trumped by the aromas that wafted from the basket on the table and the near-irresistible sight of the loaves, so inviting, glowing as if new-baked. My prince, for such he

surely had to be, took one, tore into it, his lips an overwhelming temptation to me even before a soulful *Mmm!* issued from them. I melted toward him. "My love," he said, manna in his outstretched hand, "taste
this, please."

I reached for it, the hunger strong in me.

But when my hand moved toward the loaves, I knew it was a sight I
had registered countless times before. It maddened me, my inability to
grasp the consequence of my tasting. It lay, hinting sidelong at violence
and vileness, beyond my best efforts to recall. My arm was etched in
hearthlight. Whatever its cause might be, I felt revulsion.

Taste Granny's blood, the voice within me shouted, *do it now!* At once,
without intervening thought, I turned away from hurt and hunger and
fear, swooped down to plunge my fingers into Granny's steaming
belly, and brought the bitter liquid to my lips.

"What are you doing?" shouted my deliverer, knocked off-balance
by my first-ever free actions. But the taste swept confusion from my
mind's eye. For the first time, I saw things as they really were. It amazed
me then, it amazes me now, how clear life's choices become when decision chops through obscurity, when, despite waves of terror, truth is
given its head. I heard at once the woodchopper's true intent, skittering
beneath his every breath. *Gotta get her back on track*, came the rush of his
blind pink long-tailed thoughts. *Gotta feed her, so all the piss and vinegar
drains; gotta unchop Granny, my sweet bitch, my dear hairy co-devourer;
gotta sail into little miss pure perfect princess here and . . .*

I had heard enough. "Wait! What're you doing?" he said. But beneath that, his litany of *gotta's* spewed on, detailing act after act I had endured, and forgotten, and had come close to enduring again. The
woodchopper's truth shone through the gaps in his princely facade . . .
ugly, grumbling, stewed in meanness. The more clearly I saw, the more
flustered he became. By the time he thought to protect himself, I had
snatched up his axe, raised the flashing blade above my head, and
brought it down ka-thunk upon his forehead. His arms flew up like a
wooden jointed soldier on a stick . . . too late to halt the quick axe's
downward hurtle, too late to avoid sacrificing a finger or two to its
edge. I stove in his forehead. His skull warped about the wound, a V
shallowed in bone and blood. Out sprang too, as he collapsed into
death, a rust-flurry of hair, thick, coarse, random, a glimpse of the true
face that hid beneath his false one.

The axe radiated power. Unchopping, he had said. *I can do that*, said
the axe. *Is that what you want?* "No," said I. "Not yet." I told it to keep up
the good work. It assured me it would.

When I struck off the woodchopper's head, the heap of gold coins turned to doves and flew, white and breezy, their wingtips flecked with red, out the window. As they went, they beaked back the curtain of night, so that sunlight washed the cottage clean.

And when I brought the same axe blows to bear upon Granny—whose body spasmed so vehemently, it seemed it might unchop *itself* if I hadn't been quick enough—out of her belly bounced the servant in mid-snore and his three sleeping steeds. They struck the floor, spinning and skidding like ice upon ice before lying still. A fetlock moved. Another. A halfhearted whinny fell before me. A second lifted into the air. The servant raised a hand to his face, fingered his eyelids, blinked, and sat up.

"Who am I?" he asked.

"That remains to be seen," I replied.

He nodded in confusion. White-haired and thin, he seemed, despite an imperfect memory, a man very much in control, a servant willing to give fully from the heart, asking nothing in return. Behind him, the horses hobbled up, manes of shiny auburn curving from head to neck. At a stirring in the forest, they turned as one to the window. There came a cry, an outpouring of sobs hitherto thralled from all hearing. Sap wept, falling upon moss.

"It's my master," exclaimed the servant. He put a finger to his lips, trying to taste memory.

My heart ached. Someone dear to me in some way had been ensorceled as I had. It was time to free him. "This way," I said, and the door to the cottage swung open. There lay the path of white stones I had trod upon day after day, suffering torments best not contemplated until I was ready to heal them. I was about to set foot on the path, when I noticed a stirring. I knelt on the doorstep and peered at the stones. They struggled. Or rather, each held captive some struggling thing.

"Be free," I whispered. And on the instant, a smooth hard clear casing melted from each of them. There rose up like a carpet of ivory blossoms a dispersing exhilaration of butterflies. So numerous they were that I could hear their massed wings beating, feel the caress of the breeze they made. The path lifted and ribboned upward behind a copse of trees, so that I could no longer see the under-earth restored. But I caught glimpses of white uprising and fancied I heard the stretch and flutter of innumerable wings long after that were possible.

Treading new ground, I and my waked entourage entered the forest. The axe, though weighty, hung at ease in my hands. It sang to me. *Unchop?* it asked. Soon, I said. Soon. The sharp silver head, despite its grim cleavings, remained clean and shiny. So too the handle, white as an almond's heart and free of knots.

The nut tree lay there, weeping and in pain. It had fallen thunderously. But not a nut had been unbranched in its fall. The sounds of crying issued from the cruel cut. White jags of peeled wood bent this way and that in the mayhem the nut tree had suffered. *Now?* asked the axe. Yes, said I, lifting it high and bringing it down.

It had chopped. It knew precisely how to unchop. I supplied the desire and it the wisdom to replace what had been displaced, to make flinders fly inward, homing and reattaching. At the first blow, the tree swept upward, raised by air that had whooshed aside on its way down, and seated itself once again upon its stump. Subsequent blows brought healing and an end to its crying. The woodchopper had achieved this reversal, I thought, day after day, only to attack the tree once more at sundown as a hooded little girl passed by.

When the tree stood whole and unharmed, I thanked the axe. *My pleasure*, it said. I gave it to the servant and asked him to affix it to the saddle of the most regally caparisoned mount. Barefoot in my rag dress, I approached the tree, brought my body flush against it, embraced it, and pressed my lips to its snowy bark. At the purity of its scent, I shut my eyes. I felt its transformation all about me, fancying for a moment that I had begun to shoot upward. But *it* was shrinking down into humanity, growing arms, a back, hips and thighs, the smoothness of raiments. Bark became lips, warm and vital, perfectly blending with mine.

When I opened my eyes, there, gazing back at me stood a living mirror. Words passed between us. I can't remember what they were except that they were the right ones, the ones that brought us together in health and harmony. His skin smelt of bark. The sole remnants of his enthralled state were the three shells that hung in his hair and tapped upon his forehead. In relating his travels and how he had fallen under the spell of a wicked witch . . . she I had known as Granny . . . he confessed a fear that his father might turn against me. Although he, the prince, loved me with all his heart, the crotchety king was adamant that he wed only a princess.

"Don't worry," I assured him between hugs. "It's bound to work out for the best."

I have no idea how I knew that. My origins were lost to me, no doubt a temporary lacuna. But confidence flowed abundantly in my veins. Once, while he slept, I peeked inside the nutshells on his brow. The first shell held a gown as sparkling and blue as a moonlit sea; the second, of silver spun so delicately that relenting had found its way into the weave. The third, woven from gold and love, made me cry just to look upon, a gown that would restore completely my memory of pains past and of joys forgotten, that would melt the heart of a monarch I had yet to meet, that would bring my life and that of my slumbering prince into perfect harmony at last.

I closed the shells then, kissed him gently upon the brow, and settled down to sleep.

The next day, we broke free of the forest, not once looking back as we began to cross the verdant plain, bent toward misty mountains and the promise of a new life.

MATTERS OF FAMILY

by Gary A. Braunbeck

"Man has places in his heart which do not yet exist, and into them enters suffering, in order that they may have existence."
—Leon Bloy

Albert stared out the window and watched the world melt under the weight of rain. Small sections of tree bark slid off a stump and sank into the mud, all of it flowing toward the fence where it picked up a few thin branches of shrubbery that looked like twisted arms reaching, a form too much like the misshapen thing on the bed behind him; silent, unmoving, his responsibility now.

"Did she give you any . . . trouble?" he asked.

"None," replied Fran. He turned toward her voice, searching through the gloom for some echo he expected to take form over his head. Beyond the bed, down near the corner of the door, a small blue nightlight glowed. It was shaped like an annoying cartoon character from Saturday morning television. He almost thought the voice had come from its mouth.

"Will you . . . um, is there anything you need?" said Fran.

"Not that I can think of. Has she been . . . did she go to the bathroom?" He blinked, cursing himself for phrasing it that way. *Of course she didn't go to the bathroom, you idiot. In order to do that she'd have to be able to stand, know where it was, and walk there on her own power. What you really want to know is did she pee or shit herself, and did Fran change the diaper?*

"Yes," replied Fran. "She's all taken care of for the night."

Albert lit a cigarette, took a deep drag, watched as the blue-tinted smoke curled toward the ceiling. He remembered the way his mother had always gotten angry at having to change the diaper twice, sometimes three times an hour; she always rolled her eyes toward the ceiling, as if. expecting something to drift down and spare her the task. Of course, that was always the way around the house, at least when he lived here there was really nothing wrong with Suzanne, she was just a VERY ILL little girl a girl who would someday GET BETTER, a SICKLY child who, with time, patience, and caring, would be UP an AT 'EM in no time, just you watch.

"I hope you don't mind my asking," said Fran, "but, well . . . how was . . . ?"

"The turnout? A lot of people came. I hadn't realized that Mom and Dad had so many friends." Something shifted within the blue cartoon glow, blocking the tall of his smoke snake. He took another drag as the rain drummed impatient fingers along the metal gutter. Small strands of smoke twisted before his face: he'd just walked into a spider's web, and Fran, with a wave of her hand, swept the web up toward the ceiling before he became entangled.

"May I fix you some coffee?" she said. "Maybe something to eat?"

"Some hot tea might be nice." His eyes were fixed on the bed and the thing lying upon it. He remembered that he'd known it. It was his sister. It had a name. Suzanne wasn't it?

Her eyes were glossy, blank, open.

Staring toward the ceiling like Mother so often did. Had.

Somewhere heavy streams of water and mud were pulsing toward the open graves, pouring over the edges, slipping down, pools slowly rising drowning the caskets. But then Mom and Dad were used to that; they'd drowned once already. Dad and his little boat. Mom hadn't wanted to go out with him that day, the weather looked too unstable, but Dad was never one to let something like that stop him from enjoying the open sea and—

"Come on," said Fran, taking his hand. Before he left he turned once more toward his sister. She also, was tinted in cartoon blue. Had he not known better he would have thought she was suffocating. And what if she were? Would she even realize it? What could he do?

He could close the door, pretending not to notice.

Which is what he did.

***

The brightness of the kitchen's overhead light was too much for him; he flipped the switch and dropped the room into a greyness like the brief flashes one might see behind closed eyes.

Fran prepared the tea, then sat across from him as he sipped. She'd made it too hot.

"What are you going to do with her?" she said.

"Hell if I know. Maybe put her in some kind of home. I don't know the first thing about how to take care of a . . . of her." He set his cup down and looked at Fran. "She always scared me, even when I was a kid."

"You mean she's . . . older than you?"

"She's thirty-one. She stopped growing by the time I was eleven. All the doctors expected her to die before she turned eighteen. Mom never wanted to put her away; she thought it was cruel."

"And your father?"

"He never talked about it much. I never saw him go into her room, ever, except for this one night. I got up, it was about, oh, three in the morning and I saw him at the foot of the stairs. He was standing at her door, staring in. Then he looked around took this real deep breath, and went in so . . . quickly. Like he'd been doing it for a long time and hadn't gotten caught. I remember I tiptoed down and stood by the door, listening.

"He *read* to her, as if he couldn't believe that she couldn't . . .

"It was pretty strange. I tried, I really tried to love her. I knew that I should've because she was my sister; she came from the same part of Mom and Dad that I did, so we were both kind of . . . *the same* in that way, you know? No one ever mentioned putting her away when there were other people around. It was one of our private things, one of those matters of family that never left the house under any circumstances." He sipped his tea again; the temperature was just right.

"I even tried reading to her one night, but it got to the point where my voice sounded like it was being sucked into the walls. She never so much as blinked. All I ever wanted from her was just some kind of *reaction*, something that would tell me I was getting through. And I remember that night when I listened to Dad reading to her, I *swear* she giggled. I dunno, though; maybe it was just wishful thinking."

"Would you like me to hang around for a while? I can, you know. Jim's with the kids and he's not expecting me home at any certain time."

He looked through the greyness at Fran's eyes. Kind eyes. He wondered why he hadn't snatched her up when he had the chance.

"Probably wouldn't be the best idea," he said. "I make no guarantees that I'd behave myself." There was a brief glint of something that might have been mischief in her eyes, and he wondered if she really loved her husband and children or if—like him—she'd awakened one morning and found her body wrapped so tightly in family matters that backing out was impossible. As he reached over and took her hand he wondered if love within a family—or between a man and a woman, for that matter—took a back seat to necessity, a nagging feeling that you didn't love so much because you wanted to, but because you felt obligated to. And what then? Easy: the happiness and welfare of those you loved, things you once vowed to hold sacred became less a loving task and more a burden you no longer wished to bear, draping its arms around your neck like a child wanting to ride piggy-back, pulling in, slowly cutting off your breath. But you couldn't just cast it away, this burdensome child, because you were all it had, like it or not. Everything became secondary to the burden of that obligation. Even love.

"Little Miss Muffet," he said.

"*What?*" said Fran, the word a half-laugh.

"Little Miss Muffet. Dad was reading that to her. I remember I heard her giggle at the part about the spider." He watched the thin streams of steam rise from the tea a vanish into the greyness, taking on no certain shape before it dissolved.

A sound came from the back of the house. A child-sound. Fran didn't seem to notice.

"I don't know what made me think of that," he said, lighting another cigarette, wondering if Fran would wave her hand before the strings of smoke entangled his neck and choked him to death. He wondered how blue his face would get before he lost consciousness—or did suffocation victims die that way, their features twisted and discolored forever?

He glanced at Fran through the sputtering flame of his lighter.

She was looking at the ceiling.

***

Fran kissed him when she left, a kiss that was a little too friendly and went on a little too long. She promised to call him in the morning and come over to help him with Suzanne if he wanted. He held her hand for a moment, gently brushing his fingertips over her palm once so soft and now showing signs of hardness, dryness brought on from washing too many dishes, mending too many socks, changing too many diapers. As he watched her dash out toward her car, he saw—through the droplets of rain that seemed to shimmer from within like a candle flame—what would become of her, what became of all women he'd known who chose the life of wife and mother; a young woman so vibrant and trim and lovely, going happily away promising to return home one day a woman of the world, waving with hands that always became calloused, running on legs that always grew too heavy, smiling a smile that always grew tired, uncertain and finally false—all this he saw ignite around her in brief shimmerings of rain. She'd kissed him as a young woman, smiled at him from the steps middle-aged, and climbed into her car an overweight, dreamless matron, driving off toward a marriage that would one day seem futile, trap-like, if not outright parasitic.

He closed the door on this image and shook his head.

Get a drink. Something stronger than tea.

Four drinks and six cigarettes later, he opened the door to his sister's room and stared at her. She was still breathing, Cartoon Blue hadn't done her in yet. He walked in, closed the door, and pulled up a chair. He downed what was left in the glass, sat next to her.

"Why didn't you ever giggle for me?" he said, watching the ash of his cigarette grow long. "Why couldn't you have given me just one lousy little response?" He watched as the ash fell off, just missing the covers.

An idea came to him.

"I could do it, you know? Just blow on the cherry until it's real hot, lay it next to your pillow and leave, drink a little more. I might go to court but I'd never do any time. A young man—well, not old anyway—his parents not ten hours in their graves, saddled with the responsibility of caring for a . . . his sister, drinks a bit too much to ease the day, falls asleep with the cigarette, and—"

The holes in that story began presenting themselves to him with loud and annoying fanfare.

It wasn't in him

But Suzanne frightened him; worse than anything he'd ever known.

He winced, knowing how ashamed his father would be were he still alive and knew the horrid thoughts his son had been having.

"Do you miss them?" he whispered to the still form. "Were you ever even aware they were here?"

The smoke danced about the ceiling, jumping around like water on a hot griddle. Then it once again began to take form.

"Little Miss Muffet sat on her tuffet," he said.

—wagon wheel the smoke looks like a wagon wheel don't it Sis?

" . . . eating her curds and whey . . . "

—what the hell is whey I never ate that crap and goddamn boy no son of mine would ever think something like that you ought to be ashamed she knows that you're around she d your sister and she loves you just like your mother and me—

" . . . along came a spider . . . "

A sound from within the pillow. No. On the pillow.

He leaned in close.

Her breathing, soft, smooth, constant, broken by a slight sound like a plump bug being squashed—

A tiny, almost imperceptible giggle.

He crushed the cigarette out in his hand, grinding in the hot ash.

"I feel so much better," he said, then leaned in and kissed her on the forehead. Her face felt funny to him, wider than he remembered. Although Cartoon Blue gave off some light, it was not enough to make out her features. He cupped both his hands on the sides of her face, gently pushing back her hair. His fingers felt where her left ear *should have* been, only there was something *hard* there, something sticking out. He took a breath, slowly turning her head so as not to put a strain on her throat—*God knows we don't want anything to happen to her breathing*—and bent down, blinking his eyes until he was sure his vision was clear. He ran his fingers down her cheek to where the side of her neck *should have* been, but there were pink wet lips there. He stood back to look. It seemed so natural to him that the two of them should be together like this, and which, *you might ask yourself*, is the real face and which is the Halloween mask that has slid to one side?

A small laugh escaped him.

Suzanne's face lay toward Cartoon Blue.

His mother's face lay staring up at him.

"I wondered how long it would take," he said to her.

"You have to be good," said his mother from the side of Suzanne's head. "You have to help us, Albert. Take care of us."

"I always did, Mom."

"Yes, honey, that you did." Her eyes darted up to a string of Suzanne's hair. "Please cover me back up. I don't want to frighten Fran when she comes back."

"I will. It's good to see you again, Mom."

"Goodnight, Albert."

He brushed the hair down, taking one last look into his mother's eyes, now only the briefest of glimmering stars behind the nightclouds of Suzanne's hair. "Goodnight, Mom."

He then turned his sister's face back around and again kissed her on the forehead. "They never could let go of you," he said. He rose, went to the kitchen, poured another drink, stared at the clock.

It was almost ten p.m.

He checked her again at midnight, his chest burning from booze and cigarettes.

Dad was back now, a second mask on the other side of Suzanne's head, but he was sleeping; Albert new that one did not disturb his father's sleep for any reason. They'd talk in the morning, like they always had. *Did.*

Back to the kitchen now where his parents sat waiting for him, their faces gone and in their place a smooth sheet of sallow flesh. They reminded him of those "Any Face You Want" dolls he'd had as a child, dolls that were dressed like soldiers or policemen and had nothing for a face, but that was all right because they came with a pen that could draw in four erasable colors so you could draw whatever face you wanted with whatever expression you chose.

He looked at how they sat.

Dad-doll sat at the kitchen table, hands folded together as if in prayer, a cup of cold coffee before him. Albert remembered many nights of seeing his father this way alone, sitting in the dark, lost in deep concern over his family, finances, or where his younger dreams had gone once the marriage vows had been taken.

That's how I remember you Dad. So quiet, so serious. You never once smiled, not that I saw. I always meant to ask you why.

Mom-doll was over in the living room, sitting in her favorite chair with a cup of tea and a sandwich on her lap, waiting for a late night re-run of a once popular hospital drama that had a cute young doctor. It was always the high point of her day. Albert waited for her to turn toward him and ask if he'd like to join her, she had no company at night and watching the show was so much better if you—

But she had no mouth to speak with. Or eyes to see. Still she waited for the show to start.

And Albert had no four-color pen with erasable ink.

Why these? he thought.

Why, of all the memories you could have left me, did you choose these? I remember these so well, Mom and Dad, because, to me, they *were* you. If all images and memories of you were to be sucked out of my brain, these would be the ones too powerful ever to leave me.

And they were also the worst. Because he'd know at these times his parents gave everything second place to obligation. And were alone and lonely because of it. Helpless and entangled and choking and nailed down to a life and family, neither of which had turned out as they'd hoped.

He turned away, grabbed the bottle of scotch and a fresh pack of cigarettes, and went to his old bedroom in the back. It was just as he'd left it—sparse. A bed, a dresser, a chair, a desk, and nothing more. He kept a makeshift work space here, just in case his own apartment grew too quiet some night. He could always come back here.

Back to the family.

And matters of.

The burning in his chest grew worse over the next four hours but he kept smoking one cigarette after another, at one point discovering that he had five going at the same time.

Around four-thirty in the morning he heard another child-sound from Suzanne's room. He crept slowly toward the door, pressed his ear against it.

She was giggling.

" . . . and frightened Miss Muffet away," came the dull echo of his father's voice, speaking in rhythm with the drumming fingers of rain on the roof. A silent flash of lightning, raindrops into candle flames and Dad began reciting another, different verse.

"You never read stories to me," whispered Albert to the door. "I always wanted you to, but you never did."

He turned and went back to his drink, to his cigarettes. He tried to fall asleep, but the constant murmuring of their voices kept him around. At five he picked up the phone. Dialed. Listened as the phone buzzed, buzzed, buzzed into a click and then a hiss and then—

" . . . lo?" The voice was soft, thick with sleep.

"Fran?"

The voice coughed, cleared its throat. "Albert? That you?"

"Yeah, Jim. Sorry to wake you." There was the sound of sheets rustling. Whispering. He closed his eyes, imagining what Jim had been doing to Fran before sleep took them away to a false safety and security. The things. Warm and moist.

Fran, at last.

"Albert? Is everything all right?"

I should've snatched you up when I had the chance. "I didn't mean to wake you, Fran. I'm sorry."

"Don't apologize. What is it? You okay?"

You'd never have let me come back here. "Could you . . . come back?"

"Is there something wrong with Suzanne?"

"Sort of. She won't stop giggling."

" . . . what?"

I never would have felt so goddamn responsible. "It's not so much . . . so much her, though." The smoke of his new cigarette blew up, scattered, pulled back, webbing, webbing, coming toward him— "It's Mom and Dad, they're keeping her awake."

Silence from the other end; the web kept coming and Fran wasn't here to wave it away . . .

" . . . drunk?"

"Maybe a little," said Albert.

"I knew I should've stayed."

Would you have let me be warm and moist with you like Jim? "I think they're mad at me. They didn't give me any pen to draw . . . their faces with."

"I'll be over in a few minutes. You just stay put and don't drink any more, all right?"

" . . . sucked it all out, all of them but those two . . . don't know why . . . "

He felt weak, as if his limbs were wrapped in rope.

The smoke-web widened.

The giggling grew louder.

He didn't even hear Fran hang up. He kept talking into the receiver.

" . . . always wanted to help them out, you know . . . but I never counted on having to run their whole lives . . . poor little thing, I should've been more . . . love her, really I did because maybe she understands love, maybe, and . . . "

Click. Squeak.

Suzanne's door opened.

Giggling.

He kept talking.

"Was never really a part of things . . . wanted to be, though. The thing is that I never really tried. I just worried about it too much . . . " He didn't realize that he'd begun weeping. He took another drag, another drink. The burning grew worse, snaking through him. He looked up at the ceiling. Something dangled there, thin, vein-like, rough-looking . . . Maybe . . . Hairy . . . ?

" . . . never read to me. I always wondered why. He always worried so much about things . . . "

Giggling. A brushing of something against his leg.

He leaned back closed his eyes, let the receiver drop.

Weight shifted around him; he felt arms, legs, lips touching against his cheek, words, whispered embraces, warm, so many hands, long, thin, weak, bumpy, strong, twisted . . .

. . . he opened his eyes and saw the web descend toward him.

Pounding, pounding . . . he thought maybe in his head.

No, the door.

Fran. She'd wave it away, save him from being strangled by Cartoon Blue.

He started to move from the chair, found that he was already standing.

Looking back where he sat the Albert-doll, no face, no tears, only the cigarette ash on his pant leg, the cherry growing brighter, falling off, flames licking at his clothes like the tongue of a lover . . .

He moved toward the door as his father spoke.

"Your sister wants you to read to her, Albert. Would you like that? I'll read to you, too, if you'd like. Seems the least I can do."

"Let's all read to her," said Mom.

"Yeah," said Albert. "That would be nice."

Suzanne giggled.

It was good for them to be together like this.

Behind film, the Albert-doll was sitting there, holding hands with Mom-doll and Dad-doll, all of them seeming so happy, burning away as the smoke-web wrapped around them, arms twisting together, legs sticking out like—

Mother's voice: "*Little Miss Muffet sat on her tuffet . . .* "

Flash of lightning and Albert saw their reflection in the mirror, so clear, turning full circle so each could get a good look at the face—

Father now: " *. . . eating her curds and whey . . .* "

The flames spit up higher and Albert knew he'd let the cigarette drop for a reason, because they needed the web, yes they did, there was no other way for them to entangle, and entanglement was the only action left them . . .

. . . *Poundpoundpoundpound* . . .

"Albert!" Fran's voice. She sounded so worried. *No need to worry now, Fran, everything's fine, we've settled our private family matters.*

" *. . . along came a spider . . .* " said Albert, reaching for the door, turning the knob.

. . . *and sat down beside her . . .* said all of them.

Freed, the door swung open.

Pleased, Suzanne giggled.

Completed, the web offered shelter.

Scuttling around on the arms and legs, twisting and smiling, Albert and his family looked up.

Given a clear look by the pouring firedrops, Fran began screaming.

—for Charles L. Grant

THE WILL

by Brian Stableford

He had always been able to make her do whatever he wanted.

If it had not been for that, Helen would not have returned—not even for his funeral; not even to hear the reading of his will. But he would have wanted her there, and she knew it. She hadn't needed the solicitor's letter, or the plea which Aunt Judith had sobbed down the phone; all that it took was the knowledge that he wanted her there. He hadn't wanted her there in some time—not for ten years—and while he hadn't wanted her, she hadn't gone, even though the house was still in some abstract sense her home; even though he was her father.

She didn't go to the house first, but to the funeral parlour where his body was laid in its coffin. They could be together there, just the two of them, both of them in their best suits.

He looked thinner, his skin discoloured despite the best efforts of the embalmer. His mottled hands were shrivelled, less hairy. She didn't touch him, and even though there was no one to observe she remained impassive and expressionless. She didn't shed a tear.

She shed no tears at the graveside, either, and there was no doubt that it didn't go unnoticed there.

Judith cried, of course, for the departed brother whose housekeeper and nurse she had become; but Judith was one of life's criers. The cousins wept a little too, but not for their uncle—their tears were sympathy tears for their mother, exhibitionist tears. Colin and Clare were paragons of a kind of showy sympathy which might easily pass for virtue.

Helen's brother, Michael, could not hold out in the face of their example; like the dutiful son he was he managed a dampened eye to set off his miserable face. But Helen was immune to all moral pressure; she simply stood, and listened.

She could imagine, all too readily, what the others thought of her performance.

Why did she even come . . . frigid bitch . . . is that dark grey the nearest thing to black she could find? . . . not a hair out of place . . . face like a plastic doll . . . always his favourite, though . . . where was she when he was ill? . . . never came near the place . . . always his favourite . . . doesn't look a day over twenty-one . . . not one day older than the day she left . . . but it's all make-up, all fake . . . so thin . . . wouldn't surprise me if she were anorexic . . . frigid bitch . . .

Afterwards, though, they tried after their fashion to be kind.

Judith did, anyhow. The cousins only put on a show of trying to be kind. The show, of course, was far more extravagant than the real attempt:

"Mother did everything for him, you know....worked her fingers to the bone . . . wasn't easy . . . not his fault, of course, but he wasn't the most reasonable man in the world, once he fell ill . . . terrible thing, cancer . . . eating him up from the inside . . . not very nice for mother . . . "

Undoubtedly, they were right. Not very nice for mother. Not very nice for Saint Judith. Not as if the old man understood the meaning of gratitude.

"Of course we understand . . . your career . . . not very easy for you . . . half a day's drive from London . . . so busy . . . but you'll be too old for it soon, won't you . . . can't last forever . . . "

A sarcastic little thing, Clare, loud in her airing of unspoken questions. Where had Helen been? Where had Helen been, through all those years? Why wasn't it Helen who looked after the filthy old man, cleaning up after the thing which was eating him away inside?

Michael hardly had a word to say to her. He had always been a master of inarticulacy; he had learned to wear his silence well. People liked him for it. Judith fluttered round him when they all got back to the house—not like a moth around a flame, more like a mother hen working out some excess of maternal feeling in compulsive clucking. She fluttered round the vicar, too, as though trying to draw strength from whatever authority he had to deal with the aftermath of death. But such authority as he had was the authority of habit; he did this all too often, it was part of his way of life.

"I'm sorry," said a neighbour, conscientiously intruding upon Helen's isolation. "We were all very sorry. But he didn't suffer much.

Morphine, you know. It must be ages since we saw you . . . are you famous now?"

"Ten years," said Helen, baldly. "It's been ten years."

"Such a long way from London," said the neighbour. "In the sticks."

That was the longest conversation she had. She froze them all out, one by one.

Frigid bitch.

Once, she could almost have sworn that she had heard the words spoken, but when she turned to stare at Colin and Clare, they weren't even looking in her direction.

The reading of the will seemed to Helen a complete absurdity. She had never thought of the reading of a will as something that was actually done in real life; the idea seemed to her so essentially theatrical that it ought surely to be confined to the screenplays of old films, where it could be used to determine who might be murdered. There had been no reading of a will when her mother had died, shortly before Helen had left home. Presumably her mother had left no will; she hadn't, after all, left a note.

When the family actually gathered around the dining table, with the owl-eyed solicitor at its head, the day's events seemed to Helen to have strayed into the realm of the surreal. She found it hard to focus her attention on what the little man was reading; his slow, punctilious manner of delivery was not conducive to concentration.

" . . . To Michael, the bulk of the stocks and shares . . . to Judith, the sum of five thousand pounds . . . "

Colin and Clare, seated one on either side of their saintly mother, seemed rigid with outrage when that was read out. Not that they had expected anything for themselves, of course, but for their mother . . . five thousand pounds, after all those years . . . only right, no doubt, that Michael should inherit the old man's investments, but the house . . . surely Judith deserved the house.. . .

" . . . And to my daughter Helen," the solicitor read, in a voice like the creaking of old attic timbers, "the remainder of my estate, and all my love."

He coughed, then, in a disapproving manner, to show that the final phrase had been none of his doing, and did not really belong where the old man must stubbornly have insisted that it should be put.

The remainder of my estate.. . .

. . . and all my love.. . .

Colin and Clare were staring at her, wishing that she might be struck down, begrudging her the love as much as the house, because they were both unearned income, both undeserved reward. Clare's eyes were light blue, capable of an iciness that was barely imaginable.

There was more for the solicitor to say . . . about probate, about death duties . . . estimated time-scales, estimated amounts. The figures drifted by her, almost unheard. The house . . . worth a hundred and fifty thousand . . . twenty or thirty thousand on top of that . . . would she want to keep the house, or sell? . . . not rich, by today's standards, but well off . . . comfortable . . .

"Of course," St. Judith was saying to Michael, "I didn't expect him to think of me at all. You're his children, after all, and he was very kind to me after the divorce . . . he gave me a home . . . I don't think of it as payment for looking after him . . . I didn't expect any payment . . . it's just a small gesture of kindness . . . five thousand pounds . . . "

Michael murmured something in reply, retreating from her fluttering presence, looking at the floor, finding himself frustratingly cornered.

"You won't live here, of course," said Clare to Helen, in a challenging tone. "You live in London, now . . . when you're not travelling."

"I don't know," she replied, distantly. "Too early to make plans."

"But it's mother's home," said Clare, with an edge of aggression in her voice. "She's lived here for ten years. Ten years."

"Excuse me," said Helen, turning away from the icy eyes. She crossed the room to the corner where Michael was trapped, and touched Judith's arm. "Where am I to sleep?" she asked. "My things are still in the car."

"Oh, I'm sorry," said Judith, dabbing her bosom with her fingers as though performing some peculiar ritual of penance. "In your old room, of course. The attic room . . . I thought . . . will it be . . . ?"

"That's fine," said Helen, "that's fine."

But when she had taken her case up to the room she came away again, immediately. She wasn't ready for it yet; even a long-drawn-out confrontation with the family, with the cousins she loathed and the brother she couldn't love, was something that could be endured . . . passed through . . . by way of delay.

It wasn't too difficult, even in the quiet hours after dinner, when Judith sought the comfort of the television . . . all the programmes she didn't like to miss. Helen remained quite calm—impassive, inviolable. Nothing that was said got through to her, all enquiries were turned away, all conversational gambits squashed. What they thought of it, she didn't care. If it made them all uncomfortable to think that this was her house now, all the better. If envy were eating them up inside, the way cancer had eaten up the old man's flesh, then let it eat away. It was no concern of hers, nor any part of her purpose to soothe their anxieties, to try to make things right.

He wouldn't have wanted that.

He didn't want it.

That wasn't what he wanted at all.

When she finally went up to bed, and switched on the light, it all slipped out of her mind, and was gone. Instead, there was the room, just as it had been ten years ago: the red patterned carpet; the flowered wallpaper; the slanting ceiling; the neat bed with its polished wooden headboard; the posters blu-tacked to the wall; the dressing-table. Even the counterpane was the same. Why not? No one had slept here for ten years; there had never been any occasion to change anything, to buy anything new. Judith had come in to clean, week by week, but had moved nothing, had disturbed nothing, had wanted nothing from this part of the house.

Helen opened one of the drawers in the dressing-table, unable to remember what she would see, but knowing that when she looked, the memory would come back, and she would know that nothing had been disturbed.

She was right.

She sighed, and flipped open the case which she had abandoned on the bed, removing her clothes, her make-up . . . everything.

She had to go downstairs to the bathroom, but it was a stair that led nowhere except to the attic room: her own private passage, to her own private life. She saw no one in the corridor below.

It was not until she had undressed for bed, and turned the covers back, that she looked into the far corner of the room—the most shadowed corner, where there was a green chair with very short legs: a nursing chair. She stared at the chair for more than a minute, then went over, and moved it to one side, to expose the corner of the carpet. She lifted back the corner to reveal the varnished floorboards beneath. There was no dust; Judith's vacuum-cleaner had seen to that.

Helen lifted the loose floorboard, and put her hand within, groping in the shadowed pit between two beams. She lifted out an old magazine, folded vertically to fit it to its hiding-place. Its pages, once smooth and glossy, were brittle now; it had grown old and desiccated, and the colours were mottled, like the skin on the back of the old man's withered hands. It was very old; though the cover bore no date it was at least twenty-five years out of date. It had lived in its hiding-place for twenty-three . . . undisturbed for more than ten. It was old, and dead, fit only to return to some former state.

Ashes to ashes . . . dust to dust. Had they said that at the graveside?

She turned the pages gingerly, looking at the pictures. Little girls looked back at her. Seven-year-olds with their bums to te camera, peeping over their shoulders; nine-year-olds dressed in bizarre parody of French cabaret dancers; twelve-year-olds with careless fingers toying with their crotches. Thirteen-year-olds, sucking.

She looked mostly at their eyes, discoloured by the years, sometimes hollowed by darkening of the pages, sometimes softened and shadowed . . . but the faces were still doll-like, the poses carefully maintained. Little models . . . future professionals . . . the apples of their fathers' eyes.

She folded the magazine, wrapped it inside the blouse which she had worn to the funeral, and put it in her case.

Then she lay down, wondering what to think about in order to avoid the shabby memories of the day. She tried to empty her mind, to drift off into unconsciousness.

She was on the brink of falling asleep when the rain began, drumming upon the roof. It was a sound she had not heard for ten years, but she had known it so well that she recognised it instantly, and was quick to perceive its subtleties: the lighter tapping of the drops which struck the window-pane, the rattling of the spring-green leaves of the wych-elm which grew to the height of the eaves.

She listened to the rain for some little while.

Although she was awake, the sound of the rain seemed to carry her into a kind of dream, in which she seemed to be in the kitchen, standing beside the ironing-board, smoothing the creases from a white sheet. Her mother—or was it Aunt Judith?—was in the armchair beside the Aga, speaking about something in a matter-of-fact drone, though the words made no impression on her mind. Her own face was flushed, and she knew that someone was behind her, although she was staring at the iron and could not turn to look him in the face. She felt his hands, moving over her buttocks, moving into the cleft between her legs, the hairs on the back of the hands tickling the tops of her thighs. She tried to remain perfectly still, to give no sign to the woman in the armchair that anything was happening; but the woman in the armchair noticed nothing—she just went on talking, murmurously, meaninglessly . . .

The dream dissolved as she forced herself wide awake.

She thought for a moment that there was someone in the room.

She was sweating. She was very conscious of the sweat standing on her skin, wetting her night-dress, and could not understand why. It was an experience she had had before, when overheated by too many blankets, and she remembered now that she had sometimes woken up to a fleeting moment's alarm lest the house should be on fire, and she trapped beneath the eaves, with that private stair blocked by sheets of flame.

Often, when she was a child, she had extended a hand from the bed, leaning down to touch the floor, reassuring herself that the heat was only in her and not in the room. This time, though, she remained quite still. She knew that there was no fire consuming the floorboards from below.

The dream was no longer sharp in her mind, though it had not faded beyond recall. The feelings associated with the dream persisted; she was wettest of all between her legs. She could feel the sweat on her face forming into tiny droplets, and knew that her cheeks must be very red—though that was wrong, because she always used a pale foundation, and never blushed.

She had opened her eyes to stare into the darkness, and the room was briefly illuminated by a distant flicker of lightning. The storm was over the hills to the west, and the thunder which followed long after was a mere groaning in the wind, though some kind of echo of it seemed to ripple inside her, ascending into her viscera like a warm wave.

I'm ill, she thought. These are symptoms of disease.

Images of an ambulance-ride flickered through her mind, followed by images of herself lying awake upon an operating-table while a green-masked surgeon cut into her belly with a scalpel, and slipped a rubber-gloved hand into her abdomen, searching for something inflamed, something which was radiating heat.

The telephone's downstairs, she thought. I can't reach it. Am I going to die here?

She lay perfectly still, trying not to tempt the disturbance within her, thinking about appendicitis, wondering what it felt like when a cancer in the body first announced its presence in theatrical flourishes of mocking pain.

She hoped that the lightning would not cut the night in two again; she did not think that she could bear the thunder.

Her throat felt dry, and she swallowed, uncertain now whether she really felt pain, or whether it was only a dream that had bathed her in heat, in imaginary fire. She had always had such dreams, but had never burned . . . But she did not normally sweat like this, had never sweated like this before . . . had she?

It was very dark outside, but the window was not curtained, and enough light came in to crowd the room with misshapen shadows, which seemed as her eyes struggled to make sense of them to be moving.

Something seemed to be moving inside her, too, more insistent than a ripple or a wave . . . not sharp, like the surgeon's knife, but solid.

I'm possessed, she thought. There's something taking possession of me . . . a demon made of darkness.

Then the lightning lit up the room again, a little more brightly this time, and she saw all at once that the attic was quite empty of any other human presence. There was no one in the room. She was still puzzling over this when the thunder came, rumbling over the far-off hills.

Her legs, which had been closed tightly together, were prised apart. The sweat-sodden material of her night-dress clung briefly to the flesh of her thighs, and then rode up, exposing her crotch to the touch of cool, clean cotton. For a moment, the coolness was a welcome relief, but then the cold began to move up inside her, as the heat formerly had, like a shaft of ice sliding into her belly.

She opened her mouth to cry out, but no sound came because her throat was suddenly gripped by an insistent constriction that was neither cold nor hot, but terribly tight. A weight seemed to be upon her, pressing her back into the soft mattress, and she felt that something foul and dangerous was inside her, drawing her deeper into herself, as though there were a vacuum in her heart, and she collapsing about it, imploding.

What does it feel like, she asked herself, when your appendix bursts? How long does it take you to die?

She was surprised that she was still so completely conscious. She seemed to be too keenly aware of everything that was around her, everything that was inside her. She was thinking too quickly. The coldness was gone now, but there was still something inside her, stirring her as if it were a liquid tide, ebbing and flowing, much slower than her heartbeat. She felt that she had to get away from it if she could, and suddenly squeezed her eyes tightly shut, thinking that if only she could close herself off the demon might be expelled, forced out, exorcised. If only she could rescind her faith in demons, she thought, she would be safe from their assaults . . . if only she could cease to believe.. . .

But when the lightning flashed again, she realised that her eyes were not shut at all, that she had opened them again even though she had fought so hard to shut them.

The wych-elm in the garden shook its emerging leaves in response to the cruel wind, yammering and chuckling, as though some idiotic night-hag had perched herself beneath the lintel of the window, to delight in her predicament.

Helen suddenly arched her back as the thunder seized her, consuming her senses with its throaty roar, and instead of imploding about her vacuous heart she was suddenly taut inside her skin, straining at the boundaries of her flesh.

She managed to cry out at last, but it was only a tiny whimper—as meagre a sound of protest or pain as anyone could ever have imagined.

The rain laughed as it pelted the window-pane; but then the wind veered, or died, and the wych-elm slowed in the paces of its madcap dance, released by the force which had driven it.

Minutes passed, languorously, painlessly.

The sweat began to feel cool upon her skin. It began to go away . . . soaked up, perhaps, by the cotton sheet. She was able to turn upon her side, and knew now that she was not ill, was not dying. She knew that the visitor had gone, and left her to wait until the day she went to hell, before she burned in earnest.

She drew her thin knees up towards her tiny breasts, assuming a quasi-foetal huddle, comfortable in her self-enclosure.

When she was completely calm again, she drifted back into that state between sleep and wakefulness where daydreams could turn into real dreams, and at last she began to go over in her mind the events of the day.

She remembered the graveside, and began to weep, very quietly, and very gently. She remembered the grotesqueries of the funeral party, the bizarre reading of the will.

To my daughter Helen, the remainder of my estate . . .

. . . and all my love . . .

It was her heritage, and it really did not matter in the least whether she lived in the house, or in London . . . or whether she sold the house, or simply abandoned it to the dutiful care of St. Judith. None of that mattered . . . not any more.

Her father had worked it all out.

He had always been able to make her do whatever he wanted.

Always.

Printed in the United States
26374LVS00001B/39